THE AUGUST

5

THE AUGUST

JENNA HELLAND

FARRAR STRAUS GIROUX · NEW YORK

Farrar Straus Giroux Books for Young Readers
175 Fifth Avenue, New York 10010

Copyright © 2015 by Jenna Helland
Printed in the United States of America
Designed by Elizabeth H. Clark
First edition, 2015
1   3   5   7   9   10   8   6   4   2

macteenbooks.com

Library of Congress Cataloging-in-Publication Data
Helland, Jenna.
    The August 5 / Jenna Helland. — First edition.
        pages cm
    Summary: Tommy Shore, one of the twin sons of the chief administrator of
Seahaven, learns to his dismay that the government has been keeping secrets, and
when he joins up with some rebels at the Seminary, he must go against everything
his father stands for.
    ISBN 978-0-374-38264-3 (hardcover)
    ISBN 978-0-374-30286-3 (e-book)
    [1. Totalitarianism—Fiction.   2. Social classes—Fiction.   3. Twins—Fiction.
4. Brothers—Fiction.   5. Fathers and sons—Fiction.   6. Fantasy.]   I. Title.
II. Title: August Five.

PZ7.H37414Au 2015
[Fic]—dc23

                                                              2014040407

Farrar Straus Giroux Books for Young Readers may be purchased for business or
promotional use. For information on bulk purchases please contact Macmillan
Corporate and Premium Sales Department at (800) 221-7945 x5442
or by email at specialmarkets@macmillan.com.

To Owen and Rebecca

THE AUGUST

I

TAMSIN HENRY CLUTCHED A WOODEN matchbox that fit neatly into the palm of her hand. The initials *M.H.* were carved on the bottom, and inside was a single match. The box had rested on the shelf near the woodstove in her family's cottage for as long as Tamsin could remember. In a few hours, her mother would reach for it to light the fire for the morning meal and her fingers would find nothing but dust.

Tamsin shivered inside her tattered coat, her breath visible in the air of the unheated warehouse. Inside her pocket was a scrap of paper with the word *candlelight*. A tiny cat face had been doodled inside the *a* so she would know it was truly written by her father, Michael Henry. There was a reddish smear on the back of the paper that looked like a partial bloody fingerprint. Maybe her father had been injured when he wrote it. Or maybe the blood belonged to the messenger who had carried it across the Midmark Sea to Tamsin. By now, the plan had been set in motion and there was no way to find out.

"Please be all right, Papa. Please be safe." She mouthed the words over and over. Perhaps if she said it enough times, her father would be protected from harm. It was the morning of August fifth, and she knew that nothing was going to be the same again.

"When will I die?" Tamsin whispered to the deserted warehouse. She stared at the rough wooden planks and imagined her father's face materializing out of the grainy pattern. "Not today," he assured her. "Today is not the day."

Tamsin gently shook the matchbox, listening to the rattle of the lone match. She was so nervous that she felt ill, but not because she was worried she'd be caught. The soldiers who normally guarded the warehouse had gone back to their barracks up the coast. The day before, a huge shipment of grain had been loaded onto four side-wheel steamers that had set sail for the main island. All that was left of Aeren's harvest was the chaff littered on the warehouse floor. Although the grain had been grown by cottagers such as herself, it was now in the hands of the Zunft government, who had done nothing to earn it.

"I'm scared of fire," Tamsin whispered to the wooden wall. Talking aloud calmed her nerves, but the only response was the scurry of rat feet behind the planks. "And I'm not sure if I can run fast enough."

She reminded herself that it was her father who had sent her to this darkened corner, and she trusted him. Michael Henry had chosen August fifth for a reason, and he was the greatest man she knew. A hero to the cottagers, Michael Henry was a famous journalist who gave fiery speeches on the streets of Sevenna City. Since cottagers weren't allowed to publish newspapers, Tamsin wasn't able to read her father's articles very often. Sometimes the illegal newspapers arrived clandestinely as packing material in shipping crates. Tamsin and her sisters would search through the crumbled pages for their father's byline. Above it would be headlines such as "Zunft Arrest Innocent Man!" "Zunft Factory Fire Kills Fifteen Workers!" "Chamber Votes Down Freedom of the Press!"

It had been five years since Michael Henry had left to work in the capital while his wife and their daughters had remained on Aeren Island. When Tamsin was younger, it felt like her father had deserted his family, but now she understood that he had done it to protect them from the Zunft. She missed him terribly, but he was working for justice in Sevenna City. Her mother, Anna, tried to shield her from politics, but Tamsin refused to be passive and weak. As a cottager, she was destined to a life of blisters from doing someone else's chores. Where there should have been open doors there were really dead ends. The Zunft believed that cottagers were *born* to obey.

Her father was going to change all of that—today, with her help. Tamsin rattled the match one last time. Then she gently opened the lid, but instead of looking into the box, she lifted her eyes to the stars that she could see through the greasy pane of the window. It was not yet dawn. Somewhere in the darkness— on Aeren and elsewhere—she imagined other cottagers hidden in dark corners, waiting for the first ray of morning light. Their tasks would be much harder than hers. Tamsin took a deep breath and began humming a tune, an old Aeren lullaby that mothers sang to their sleepy children: *Alas, the emerald land of our fathers gone / Forlorn the empty hallowed home.*

The match was poised to strike, ready to set the world on fire.

2

IT WAS STILL DARK WHEN TOMMY SHORE
awoke in his bedroom at his family's manor house on the west
coast of Aeren. He climbed out of bed and crossed into his
sitting room where the fire was already blazing, courtesy of
Mrs. Trueblood, the cottager woman who kept house for his
family. Shore Manor was a gray stone palatial estate with three
wings and substantial gardens and grounds. It was built on a
high, rocky peninsula that stretched into the ocean. The rear of
the mansion—including Tommy's room—faced the crashing
waves and the endless horizon.

Standing in the warmth of the fire, Tommy checked his silver chronometer. It was nearly six a.m., later than he had thought.
The sun would rise soon, but outside his bay windows it was
still too dark to see any distinction between the dark waves and
the black sky. Tommy quickly pulled on his old trousers and a
gray sweater that Mrs. Trueblood had knitted for him the year
before. He was going to hike all the way to the top of Giant's
Ridge, the highest peak on Aeren Island. The summit offered the

best view of the world that Tommy had ever found. He could see the ocean to the west, the patchwork of croplands to the east, and beyond to the rich vineyards and orchards of Middle Valley.

When Tommy was seven years old, he'd hiked to the top of Giant's Ridge with his father, Colston Shore. His mother, Rose, had died when he was a small child, and he couldn't remember why his twin brother, Bern, hadn't hiked with them. It was one of his few memories of time spent alone with his father. To Tommy, it had been a perfect day. Together they scrambled up the steep slope that seemed insurmountable, but he hadn't complained once. When they had reached the top, Colston was like a king surveying his domain. He gave his son a rare smile as he pointed out the boundaries of the family's land far in the distance. Tommy felt as though he would explode with happiness—until they reached home. They were in the boot room, pulling off their muddy shoes, when Colston sighed. "A wasted day," he said to himself. "What a wasted day."

Colston Shore was a high-ranking member of the Zunft government, which controlled Seahaven, an island chain in the vast Cobalt Sea. He served in the Zunft Chamber, so he lived in Sevenna City most of the year. Located on Sevenna Island, the city was the capital of Seahaven and the seat of the Zunft government. Colston had arrived back at Shore Manor a few days earlier. The Chamber was not in session, and he planned to stay for several weeks. Tommy hated it when Colston was home. His father was demanding and easily angered, and he had been particularly testy lately. Something had happened in the Chamber right before the session closed, and it had made Colston even more temperamental than usual. A hike to Giant's Ridge was the perfect opportunity for Tommy to avoid his judgmental father.

Now Tommy opened his door and headed into the unlit corridor, but someone was waiting for him. Hands reached out and clamped down on his throat. Tommy yelped in surprise and reeled backward, slamming his shoulder into the door frame. His brother materialized out of the darkness and howled with self-satisfied laughter.

"Bern!" Tommy cried when he saw his twin.

"Hey, T," Bern said. "Where are you going?"

"Out," Tommy muttered. He hated being startled, and Bern knew it. "Giant's Ridge."

"It's one of our last days of summer. These are our last moments of . . . dare I say it . . . childhood. Why bother with Giant's Ridge?"

"What are you doing up so early?" Tommy hadn't expected to run into Bern. His brother usually slept until noon.

"I haven't been to bed yet," Bern said. Bern knew a group of lads who liked to meet at the Golden Standard pub in Port Kenney to play cards. Tommy had a standing invitation, but never really enjoyed himself when he went. Besides, when the lads played Emperor's Stand, they liked to put actual money on the line. Bern always had spare cash but Tommy didn't. He assumed their father gave extra money to Bern, but left out Tommy, as usual.

"How much did you lose?" Tommy asked as Bern fell in step with him.

"I won, actually," Bern said. He wasn't very good at card games, particularly Emperor's Stand because it required a lot of math.

"Were you playing with yourself?" Tommy asked.

"Hey, watch it," Bern said, shoving his shorter brother with enough force that Tommy slammed into the stone wall.

"Jeez, relax," Tommy mumbled. Now he had two sore shoulders and, apparently, Bern's company. When they were children, the brothers had been inseparable, with little supervision save Mrs. Trueblood. Their father was gone most of the time, in Sevenna, while Tommy and Bern lived at Shore Manor studying with private tutors. But as the brothers entered their teenage years, Bern's bravado and seemingly limitless good fortune began to irritate Tommy, who tried to find ways to avoid his twin. At the end of this summer, the boys would enroll for the first time in Seminary, in Sevenna City, and Tommy wondered if the change would bring them closer once again. Seminary was the institute of higher learning for the sons of the Zunft. At age fourteen, young men enrolled to study either engineering or jurisprudence before being officially accepted into the Zunft Party, which made all the laws and ruled the Islands. Tommy was nervous about starting a new school in Sevenna, but it was the only option. If your father was a Zunftman, you were expected to follow in his footsteps.

As they headed down the wide staircase to the lowest level of the manor, Bern kept prattling on about his adventures the night before. "You know Roger? Well, he was there last night. He was telling me about this club near the waterfront . . ."

"There's a club in Port Kenney?" The village consisted of two streets and a handful of businesses clustered around a major Zunft warehouse.

"Are you listening to me?" Bern asked with annoyance. "I'm talking about when we get to Sevenna City."

Tommy hated the idea of living in the capital city of all the islands of Seahaven. Sevenna was crowded and grimy with nothing green except tiny kitchen gardens and a few untouchable Zunft parks. As with many things, the twins had opposite opinions on the matter. Bern viewed the city as his own personal playground.

"Are you going to hike with me?" Tommy asked.

"I don't have anything better to do," Bern said, and sighed. "Maybe next year we can stay in Sevenna over summer holiday."

"I only asked Mrs. Trueblood to pack one lunch," Tommy said.

"So? One of her lunches could feed six of us." Bern snorted.

"Have you seen Mrs. Trueblood?" Tommy asked.

"She's in the kitchen, probably. Isn't that where she always is at this hour?"

After the boys had put on their leather gaiters and heavy walking boots, Tommy picked up his knapsack, which Mrs. Trueblood had laid near the door. Bern was right. She had packed enough lunch for both of them. There were several chicken sandwiches wrapped in brown paper and small jugs of apple cider. Mrs. Trueblood was the only mother Tommy had known since his own mother had died. When he left Aeren for Seminary, Tommy knew he would miss the kind cottager woman most of all.

In the kitchen, Mrs. Trueblood was kneading dough at a long wooden table in the middle of the room. Bunches of dried flowers and herbs hung from the ceiling, and the room smelled like cinnamon and vanilla. A huge fire blazed in the iron woodstove on the west wall.

10

"Last chance to stay nice and warm," Bern said. "It's almost breakfast time."

"Good morning," Mrs. Trueblood said.

Greta Trueblood was a slender woman in her fifties with graying hair that she kept in a tidy bun at the nape of her neck. She smiled at Tommy, who grinned back. Bern didn't acknowledge her. He didn't like Mrs. Trueblood, which had never made sense to Tommy. Maybe it was because Colston was disdainful toward her, so Bern acted that way, too.

"Good morning, Mrs. Trueblood," Tommy said. "Thank you for the food."

"Where are you hiking today?" she asked.

"Giant's Ridge," Tommy said.

"Well, be safe," said Mrs. Trueblood. "Your father will expect you at dinner."

"Yes, ma'am," Tommy said, already dreading an evening with his father.

"What are we having?" Bern asked.

"Corned beef and cabbage," Mrs. Trueblood said.

"Are there guests?" Tommy asked, ignoring Bern's exaggerated grimace about the menu choice. Bern always acted like he hated Mrs. Trueblood's cooking, but that never stopped him from eating it.

"No, it's only the family," Mrs. Trueblood said.

Tommy said goodbye, and he and Bern left the warmth of the kitchen and took the flagstone path through Mrs. Trueblood's extensive vegetable garden.

"What's wrong with Father anyway?" Tommy asked.

"I don't know, but I could hear him yelling for half the day yesterday," Bern said.

"Maybe his Honor Index is low," Tommy joked.

Bern shrugged. "Father's honor is impeccable—he's reminded us of that a million times."

Tommy glanced at his brother, trying to gauge his emotions. The twins had a running joke about something they called the Honor Index. Colston seemed to measure everything on a cosmic scale that only he could decipher. When they were young, their father's disciplinary talks revolved around which direction they were heading in life. Were they headed up the scale toward being an honorable Zunftman? Or were they sliding down the scale toward ruin and degradation?

The twins had turned it into a secret game. Steal a cookie: lose fifteen points on the Honor Index. Break a vase: lose thirty points. Then Bern made the rule that as long as you didn't get caught, it didn't affect your Honor Index at all. Bern had always enjoyed the game in the past, but it didn't seem to be amusing him now.

"I've been reading the *Chronicle*," Bern said. "At the end of July, Father's faction tried to oust Chief Administrator Hywel, but their plan failed. The editor-in-chief called Father misguided for challenging Hywel."

"Oh, no wonder he's in a bad mood," Tommy said. The *Zunft Chronicle* was the official newspaper of the state, and Colston would hate being the object of public criticism. "But I thought that Hywel's power was waning because of his cottager sympathies?"

"Apparently not," Bern scoffed. "Maybe you should pick up a newspaper now and then, Tommy."

Tommy wasn't really interested in reading about politics, but he wasn't going to admit that to Bern. Besides, it was his father who had told him that Hywel was unpopular because he was giving in to the cottagers' demands. Colston was the leader of the Carvers, the most traditional and conservative faction in the Chamber. The small but vocal faction would align with almost anybody to get a majority vote, but they always demanded favors in return. Tommy knew that his father hated the current chief administrator, Toulson Hywel, who had recently passed a substantial subsidy on bread, which made it cheaper for cottagers living in Sevenna to buy their daily allotment.

"Did the *Chronicle* reopen?" Tommy asked. He'd heard Mrs. Trueblood talking about a protest at the newspaper offices, and how their headquarters had closed down.

"When did it shut down?" Bern said. "I heard that the cottagers attacked the building and damaged it, but the presses were running by the next day."

They left the garden through the little gate and followed the gravel walkway to the front of the manor where a high-wheeled carriage was parked in the circular driveway. Ever since the Zunft had released its new model of rovers, Colston had stopped using horse-drawn carriages, so this must belong to one of his allies from the Zunft Chamber. It was common for members of the Carver faction to spend part of their vacation at Shore Manor. They were usually locked away with Colston in the library as if they were planning a war. As the boys passed the carriage, Tommy noticed the dull outline of a missing Zunft emblem on the polished exterior of the carriage door. High-ranking Zunftmen were required to display the Zunft emblem when they traveled, but this one had been removed. Someone had unhitched the horses and taken them to the stables, meaning Colston and whoever this guest was had probably been in a meeting all night.

"I thought Mrs. Trueblood said that it would be the three of us at dinner," Tommy asked. "Is someone visiting?"

"I think that's Father's old carriage," Bern replied, staring at the eastern sky, where the horizon was streaked with a red sunrise. "Maybe he's selling it."

The road angled north and as the boys walked, Tommy had to turn to look back at the house. A light burned in Colston's third-floor library and Tommy could see the silhouettes of two men standing near the window.

"But someone is visiting," Tommy insisted. "There's a man with Father in the library."

"What of it?" Bern asked. "Maybe if you minded your own business you wouldn't make Father mad all the time."

Tommy shrugged and paid attention to the sound of his boots crunching through the gravel. This summer, Bern had been particularly touchy, and Tommy decided to walk in silence rather than risk getting his head bitten off by his irritable brother.

"Which way?" Bern asked when they reached the crossroads.

There were two routes they could take to Giant's Ridge. They could follow the well-traveled road known as the Strand, which hugged the rugged coastline, or they could climb up the steep ridge until they reached Miller's Road, which was a rutted dirt road that meandered through the forest. Both routes eventually led past the ridge to Port Kenney on the coast, but Miller's Road was less traveled.

"Miller's Road," Tommy decided, surprised that Bern had actually let him choose. The best apple orchard in the world was on the ridge, but that was the only detour Tommy intended on taking until he reached the summit.

"Okay, but no moping about leaving for Sevenna," Bern said. "Getting off this backwater isle will be the best thing that's happened in your short miserable life."

The sun still hadn't crested the ridgeline as the brothers walked in companionable silence through the stubble of the west field, which had recently been harvested. The wind carried the scent of peat smoke as they headed up the steep slope toward Miller's Road. The trees had changed early, and the twins crossed through a stand of oak with brilliant red and orange leaves that seemed to glow in the first rays of the dawn. When Bern paused for breath, Tommy watched the sky. Black clouds roiled on the horizon. A storm was moving in, but Tommy didn't mention it. He was sure they could make it up to the summit and back before it got too bad.

When Bern recovered, they trudged on through the old-growth forest. Tommy glimpsed a cottage through the trees. It was one of a handful scattered in this area. Mrs. Trueblood's family lived on the ridge, as did many of her relations. All of the cottages in the area technically belonged to the Shore Estate, and cottagers living in them were supposed to work for Colston Shore. According to the old laws of the Zunft, bond families were required to serve the same family generation after generation. But the old laws were breaking down. Many cottagers emigrated to Sevenna rather than work at the estates that they had been born to serve. Mrs. Trueblood was the only member of the Shores' bond families who actually worked at the estate. Colston's estate manager hired nomadic workers out of Middle Valley instead.

Tommy never liked walking near the cottagers' homes. He felt like he was trespassing even though it was his father's land. Bern didn't care, though. He would march straight through a cottager's front yard as if he were daring someone to stop him.

"Let's cut north," Bern huffed. He seemed exhausted from staying up all night. "It's faster that way."

"Nah, there's too many homes in that direction," Tommy said.

"I'll go wherever I want on my own land," Bern said, and headed north anyway.

Colston Shore owned everything for miles around their manor house—Giant's Ridge, the dense forest along its slopes, even the ancient rings of standing stones that dotted the countryside. Much of the western coast of Aeren was their family's domain. The Shores were one of the founding families of the Zunft, and their property went inland for at least a hundred miles. Many of the great estates throughout the Islands had been broken down into smaller holdings throughout the years, but their land remained untouched.

As they crested the ridge, they passed a cottage nestled between two towering elms. The cottagers tended to have stonework houses with colorful doors and painted woodwork beneath the eaves. According to Mrs. Trueblood, many homes were built near giant trees because the cottagers believed that families drew strength from living above the roots. Firelight glowed in the cracks between the shutters of this cottage, and intricate braids of dried flowers and herbs hung over every window and door.

In view of the cottage, Bern stopped and motioned for Tommy to hand him a jug of cider. Bern had stopped intentionally to embarrass Tommy. Annoyed at both the sound of Bern's gulping and the need to take another break so early into the journey, Tommy glared at his brother.

"If you're tired, you could head home," Tommy said.

"And let you win?" Bern said. He belched loudly, and the curtains in the front window moved. A man peered out at the twins. Bern noticed him and belched even louder. The face disappeared and the curtains didn't move again.

"I didn't know this was a competition," Tommy said, but of course it was. Everything was a competition with Bern. The twins had always been different, but as they grew older, the differences seemed to be intensifying. Of the two brothers, Bern had been born first. According to Mrs. Trueblood, he'd been a placid towheaded baby who loved being the center of attention. That much hadn't changed, at least. The second twin, Tommy, had been a squalling, hard-to-please surprise. Whereas Bern had grown into a handsome, broad-shouldered youth, Tommy was dark haired and slender. He always felt like an afterthought and shadow to his gregarious, athletic brother. He wondered if his father would have been happier with only one son, particularly after his wife died so unexpectedly when the boys were young.

"Let's go down to Port Kenney and grab some breakfast at the Golden Standard," Bern said. "Forget hiking. It's boring."

"You just got home from the Golden Standard," Tommy said. "You seriously want to spend another day at the pub?"

"One of the girls is going to be working this morning," Bern said sheepishly. "Kate? Black hair and green eyes?"

"You like a cottager girl?" Tommy asked incredulously. Most

Zunft lads wouldn't be caught dead admitting they liked a cottager girl. Especially Bern.

"That's not funny, Tommy." Bern scowled. "Kate is the owner's daughter. She's the hostess."

"So she doesn't have to do much," Tommy said.

"That's right," Bern agreed with a grin. "She has plenty of time to chat. So, breakfast?"

The food at the Golden Standard was delicious, but the pub was owned by a retired Zunftman and rumor had it he raised his prices on days the cottager workers received their wages. You could end up paying triple the price for a simple meal. The last time it happened, Bern started talking loudly about who their father was, and their bill was replaced by a much cheaper one, but the situation had embarrassed Tommy.

"You go on—" Tommy began, but he was interrupted by a commotion in the woods behind them. They whirled around, but it was only a raccoon darting out of the trees, sprinting like mad as if it were being chased. It must have startled a flock of blackbirds resting in the bushes because dozens of birds flapped into the air, cawing noisily at the disturbance.

"Aren't raccoons nocturnal?" But Tommy's words were drowned out by an explosion that jolted the ground under their feet. Another short blast, followed by a long, low rumble and then billows of black smoke rose from the valley.

"What was that?" Tommy gasped. The blast reverberated off the mountains in the distance and the rumbling continued even after the earth stopped shaking.

"Port Kenney," Bern said. "Come on! Let's see what's going on."

But Tommy hesitated. Last year, they'd stumbled across a wounded dog in the forest. Bern insisted on approaching it and almost got his hand bit off. When it came to danger, his brother was like a moth to a flame.

"Let's go tell Father," Tommy said.

"No way, I want to see if Kate is all right!" Bern insisted. It was a short distance down Miller's Road to Port Kenney. Worried that people might need their help, Tommy sprinted after his brother.

The sky above Port Kenney was smudged with black smoke. In the final descent into the village, Tommy had a clear view of the massive fire raging near the edge of the sea. The Zunft warehouse was over a hundred yards long, easily the largest structure in the handful of buildings along the coast. The inky outline of the timbers made Tommy think of the bones of a dying animal, and the smoke from the fire made his eyes itch, even though he was still several blocks away. There were half a dozen businesses along the pier, including the Golden Standard, and they were all threatened by the inferno.

When they reached the waterfront, the boys paused in the shadow of a shuttered fish shop. A sign hanging on the door told them *Come Back Monday!* Everything was eerily quiet except for the crackle and roar of the raging fire that had completely engulfed the Zunft warehouse.

"Where is everybody?" Tommy asked.

"Maybe they cleared out?" Bern said.

"And left their homes to burn?" Tommy asked. There should

have been frantic people running around the streets. In most villages, soldiers doubled as firefighters, and they should have dragged the carriage pumps into the street by now.

"Maybe they were all in the warehouse," Bern said.

"The entire *village* wouldn't have been in the warehouse," Tommy said. He imagined bodies inside the warehouse and his stomach turned over.

"Do you think a rover exploded?" Bern wondered. Rovers were mechanized wagons powered by the volt-cell, a new energy source invented by the Zunft. Leather seats were mounted on the chassis in front of the earthenware vat where the cell was suspended in a chemical bath. The rovers tended to explode if they ran into anything, even at slow speeds. Tommy had overheard cottagers refer to them as boomers, which he found amusing. But cottagers had to be careful because any language that disparaged the Zunft could earn them a fine or even jail time.

"Does anyone have rovers here?" Tommy asked. As far as he knew, Colston Shore was the only man on Aeren Island who owned a rover. The army probably had a few rovers in the larger port town of Black Rock, but there were not likely to be any in this oceanside village.

"A rover wouldn't have made such a big fire anyway," Bern said. There was a harsh chemical smell on the wind that made Tommy's eyes water.

"What if someone did it on purpose?" Tommy said, suddenly afraid. Colston Shore had raised his sons to believe that the cottagers could rebel at any moment and the Zunftmen would be slaughtered in their beds and their property stolen. For most of his childhood, Tommy's nightmares featured the thud of cottager boots invading the corridor outside his bedroom door. But then he had realized that the Zunft had the gunpowder, the technological innovations, and control of the Islands. The Zunft had the power. Why should they be scared of the cottagers? Recently, Tommy had stopped believing his father's warnings. None of the cottagers he knew seemed very angry.

"Let's go in the customs house," Bern said, pointing down the road at the two-story brick building with a black-and-silver Zunft flag flying from the roof. "The soldiers must be there."

"Wait, something's wrong," Tommy warned. He tried to grab Bern's arm, but his brother shrugged him off. A gust of warm wind blew down the street, sending a shower of embers in their direction.

"Don't be such a girl, Tommy," Bern said.

Tommy reluctantly followed Bern along the muddy road toward the customs house. Every port had an official Zunft office, which monitored shipping between the four main islands of Seahaven. In small villages like this, it was the locus of Zunft control. Soldiers were often stationed at customs houses, where they acted as the constabulary as much as the military.

"Do you know where Kate lives?" Tommy asked. "Maybe we should—"

They had reached the corner of High Street and Bern stopped abruptly, so that Tommy bumped into him, forgetting the rest of his sentence. They could see the steps of the customs house where two men waited, staring aggressively as the boys approached.

In Sevenna City, Zunftmen always wore tailcoats and bowlers, so it was obvious who belonged to the elite and who didn't. But here on Aeren, it wasn't always easy to tell Zunft from cottager as both groups often wore plain wool jackets and trousers. Then Tommy noticed that the two men wore flat caps and wool vests without coats. A Zunftman wouldn't deign to wear a vest without a coat, and flat caps were a badge of pride for cottagers.

"Cottagers?" Tommy whispered.

"Yep, bloody thieving bastards," Bern whispered back.

The taller man said something to his companion, who unsheathed a knife. The taller one reached for a metal bludgeon attached to his belt.

"Bern!" Tommy warned. The men looked like fighters—mean and angry. Bern liked to tussle with the lads, maybe bloody a friend's nose, but he'd never been in a real fight. And Tommy had never thrown a punch in his life.

"Come on!" Bern said, and the boys whirled around and ran back up Miller's Road. With a rush of adrenaline, Bern easily outpaced his shorter brother. Frightened and disoriented, Tommy couldn't make his wobbly legs move very fast. His breath was ragged in his chest as he scrambled toward the top of the ridge.

"Wait!" Tommy shouted, stumbling over a rock, but Bern disappeared from sight. After a moment's panic that Bern had left him alone, Tommy realized it would be easier to lose his pursuers in the forest, so he ducked into the trees along the side of the road. In his haste to get out of sight from the road, he barreled straight through the middle of a blackberry thicket. Thorns tore at his clothes and scratched his face and when he stumbled out the other side, he found himself under old-growth trees that offered little cover. Spinning wildly, he expected to see the two cottagers, but there was no sight of them.

Tommy tried to collect his thoughts. He couldn't take Miller's Road because the cottagers might be waiting for him, but he could head down the forested slope to the flatlands. No matter where he ended up, he'd be able to see Shore Manor, which was built on a tablet of rock jutting above the flatlands, the beach, and the ocean. It seemed like a good plan, but Tommy struggled to traverse the steep, rocky slope as the undergrowth grew thicker. He could hear something thrashing behind him and kept expecting cottagers to come barreling at him with knives.

He scrambled over a mossy boulder and dropped onto the other side. Unexpectedly, he found himself in a sheltered grove surrounded by a dense ring of towering oak trees. At first, he thought he saw a black rock in the shadows on the far edge of the grove, but with an unpleasant jolt, Tommy realized that it was someone was kneeling on the jade-green grass. The person was gasping for breath, and Tommy wondered if they'd been chased from Port Kenney into the forest like he had.

Stepping closer, he saw that it was a young woman, probably about his age, with long copper hair and green eyes. The skin on her throat was red and angry, as if it had been scorched. She clutched at her side, where blood stained her lavender dress. Their eyes met, and she snarled at him like a frightened animal. The girl was a cottager. He could tell by the embroidered yoke on her dress, a style that was common among cottager girls. Mrs. Trueblood sewed dresses in that style for her nieces.

"Get away from me," she said, even though he hadn't moved any closer in her direction. She tried to crawl into the woods, but instead she crumpled and passed out on the forest floor.

Tommy wanted to help her, but she'd told him to stay away, so he remained as still as a statue. The wind rustled the leaves, but he couldn't hear anything that sounded like the cottagers who had been chasing him—no shouts, no crashing in the undergrowth—only the croaking of frogs announcing the approaching storm. After a few hesitant steps, he crouched down and studied the girl. She was breathing rapidly, which worried him. He'd seen wounded animals take short shallow breaths that didn't seem to fill the lungs at all. He couldn't leave her here, breathing like a dying animal. But what if she'd been in Port Kenney? What if she'd been involved somehow?

His father's words rang in his ears. *The cottagers are thieves and liars. They don't believe in decency or honor.* In the distance, a rover rumbled along Miller's Road. The Zunft soldiers might have acquired a rover to search the forest for the rebels. If he helped the girl in the lavender dress, he might get caught. Tommy gazed at the sky, as if the darkening storm clouds would tell him what to do. *Lose a hundred honor points for leaving an injured girl in the woods?* He could turn the girl over to the soldiers, but then she'd get in trouble even if she hadn't been involved in anything illegal. *Gain a hundred honor points for reporting a possible rebel?*

A cold rain began to fall. The girl was hurt and Aeren storms could be unexpectedly vicious. Father would punish Tommy severely if he were caught helping a cottager, especially if the rebellion he'd always warned about was finally at hand. But Mrs. Trueblood would say that all life was precious, no matter if you were born in a molehill or a mansion. As the sound of the rover engine grew louder, Tommy crossed the grove to the girl. He could take the girl to one of the nearby cottages and his father would never have to know.

Tommy lifted the girl in his arms. He wasn't much taller than she was, but she weighed less than he expected her to. She didn't wake up, not even when he jostled her as he tried to navigate through the trees and around the blackberry thickets. Through a gap in the canopy of leaves, he could see wisps of chimney smoke rising into the air. Finally, he reached a white-stone cottage nestled in a glen of oak trees. His arms were aching, but he stayed in the shadows and watched the cottage. Someone was definitely inside—he could see the flicker of firelight dancing through the shutters. In the distance, he heard the rover engine roar to life again, rumbling down the road. With a sudden burst of speed, Tommy crossed the open ground in front of the cottage and laid the girl on the wooden bench under the porch roof where she would be dry. He knocked loudly on the door and ran toward Miller's Road. Terrified of being caught, he never looked back.

3

TO AVOID SUSPICION, TOMMY MADE
himself stop running when he reached Miller's Road. He reminded himself that he had every right to be here if he wanted
to—it was his father's land. He rehearsed what he would say if
the soldiers stopped him. *I'm going for a hike. I was heading up to
Giant's Ridge, but the storm set in.* He wondered where Bern was,
and if he'd already made it home. Tommy walked quickly, splash-
ing through the puddles that formed in the deep ruts made by
wagon wheels. As he approached the bend near Harrow Trailhead, Tommy raised his arm to wipe his eyes and was horrified
to see blood on his sleeve. He realized his clothes were covered
with the cottager girl's blood. He imagined what the soldiers
would say: *Going for a hike, huh? Then who bled all over you?*

His gray sweater was completely ruined, but the stain wasn't
too noticeable on his dark jacket. With numb fingers, he was
trying to close the brass buttons when he heard the engine of a
fast-moving rover approaching from behind. Tommy dove into
the undergrowth just as the vehicle came into view. It was a newer

model with the clay vats holding the volt-cells mounted in a padded box at the rear. The driver's platform was on the same level as the spoke-wheels, but unlike the standard model, there was a boxy passenger compartment fastened in the middle of the extended chassis. It looked exactly like the rover that Colston had had shipped to Aeren at the beginning of the summer holiday.

The rover stopped a few feet away from where Tommy was hiding in the bushes. The engine sputtered off, which was a surprise. Rovers were notoriously hard to start, and it was often a two-person job to crank the wheel and flip the appropriate levers. Usually, the driver would keep the machine running unless he was certain that it was done being driven for the day. When the door to the passenger compartment opened, Tommy could see the golden Shore crest that his father had affixed to all his machines. It *was* his father's rover. But why was it up here, in the middle of nowhere? The rover had been driving up and down this stretch of Miller's Road as if the occupants were searching for something, but what? Rebels? Him and Bern? The girl? What if they'd seen him with her?

Frozen with fear, Tommy huddled in the bushes, expecting to see his father. Instead, a Zunft soldier emerged from the rover. The driver hopped down and waited while two more men climbed out. With a sigh of relief, Tommy saw that *none* of these men was Colston Shore. The three men crossed behind the rover, then headed for the entrance to the Harrow Trail. From his hiding place, he watched the men closely as they passed by him. The two soldiers were dressed in silver-and-black uniforms with green patches on their lapels. He'd seen one of the men, the one with the curly blond hair, with Colston at the manor. He hadn't seen the other soldier before. The third man was tall and wearing clothes that were more appropriate for a Zunftman in Sevenna City than in the wilds of Aeren. Tommy didn't see his face clearly, but he wore a long black coat over a bright purple silk vest and he had a bowler pulled low over his forehead.

The men were obviously heading somewhere specific—not searching for the wayward son of Colston Shore. Tommy felt the knot inside his stomach relax a little. The Zunft were already searching for the rebels. Maybe they even had information on who was responsible for the Port Kenney fire. Still, he wouldn't risk the road anymore because there was no good explanation for his bloody clothes. He tripped down the ridge to the flatlands and didn't stop running until he reached the garden gate.

"Tommy!" Bern was standing in the open kitchen door. His clothes were dry and his face flushed, probably from sitting in front of a comfortable fire. While Tommy had been running scared in the rain, Bern had been cozy as a cat. Trying to hide his irritation with his brother, Tommy slipped off his jacket and held it in front of his ruined sweater.

"You made it back," Tommy said, stumbling into the warm kitchen. He expected to see Mrs. Trueblood, but she was nowhere in sight. Bowls of flour, diced vegetables, and uncooked meat sat on the table. It was almost dinnertime, and it wasn't like Mrs. Trueblood to be late with anything.

"Where is everyone?" Tommy asked.

"Father's waiting for you in his library. He said to get changed and then report to him."

"I meant Mrs. Trueblood," Tommy said.

"Oh, all the cottagers are to report to the barracks in Black Rock," Bern said.

"They're arresting them?" Tommy asked.

"Not the ones who report to the barracks," Bern said with an odd smile on his face. "Come on, get changed. Father wants to talk to you before he goes."

"Goes where?"

"The cottagers attacked more than Port Kenney," Bern said. "Something is happening in Sevenna, too. There could be a massacre."

"He's going back anyway?" Tommy asked.

"Father isn't afraid of the rebels," Bern said. "Some of the Zunftmen might cower in their estates, but not him."

"Why didn't you wait for me?" Tommy asked. *Lose fifty honor points for deserting your brother.*

"I thought you were right behind me," Bern said. "Wait here. I'll grab you some dry clothes."

Tommy added logs to the woodstove. He waited until Bern was gone to toss his sweater and jacket into the flames. He shut the iron door of the stove and hoped they would burn to ashes eventually even though they were soaked from the rain. Then he turned his attention to the uncooked food on the table. He wrapped up the meat and vegetables. In Sevenna, they had iceboxes that could keep things cool for a few hours, but his father hadn't purchased one for the manor yet. Tommy wasn't sure how long Mrs. Trueblood would be gone and he didn't want the meat to spoil.

"Father's getting impatient," Bern said, coming back with fresh clothes for Tommy. "Quit fussing with the food. I'll find you something to eat afterward, okay?"

Under normal circumstances, Bern would never have volunteered to get Tommy food or dry clothes. Tommy wondered if he actually felt bad for leaving his brother behind.

Colston Shore's third-floor library had high ceilings and a large bay window with a view of the sprawling lawn and the wooded ridge in the distance. Standing on the threshold of the library, Tommy knocked lightly and waited for his father to acknowledge him. Colston was a tall, lean man who always wore an impeccable Zunft uniform. He hated things around him to be disorderly or imperfect. Tommy always felt like an unwelcome speck of lint in his father's otherwise tidy life.

Colston finished the sentence that he was writing, jabbed his pen into the inkwell, and impatiently waved his sons into the room. "Bernard. Thomas. Sit down. I only have a few minutes before I leave for Sevenna."

The twins sat in the two straight-back chairs in front of Colston's desk. As they waited for their father to speak, Tommy tried to remember the last time he'd visited Colston in Sevenna. It had been years. He vaguely remembered the quiet street lined with plum trees that blossomed in the spring. The house reminded him of his mother, and the awful night she died. He was too young to remember it himself, but his imagination filled in the details if he let his mind dwell on it. Instead, he made himself focus on his father.

"Unless they are stopped, the cottagers will slaughter every one of us," Colston said. "After Port Kenney, the violence will escalate. The news of the rebellion here stirred up the rabble in

Sevenna. There are riots going on now, and cottagers have taken the Grand Customs House."

Colston pointed out the window at a group of soldiers patrolling the grounds.

"You will be safe while I'm gone," Colston said. "Unfortunately, not every Zunft family is so well guarded. Hywel must be held personally responsible for every life lost during this travesty."

"This is going to be bad for Hywel, isn't it?" Bern asked. He sounded almost gleeful.

"Hywel deserves everything that's coming to him," Colston said. "He didn't have the moral fortitude to make the correct decisions and now he's ruined Seahaven."

Tommy knew what his father considered to be moral and correct: The Zunft were the rightful leaders of Seahaven and the estate system was the foundation of their rule. The Zunft were expected to provide dwellings for the cottagers, who, in turn, must provide labor for the estate owners. Women should know their place, and that was in the home. For the peace and prosperity of all, certain rules must be obeyed.

"You witnessed a sad chapter in the history of the Zunft," Colston said. "I've warned that the cottagers were capable of this sort of violence for years, and the Zunftmen in the Chamber didn't listen."

"Yes, sir," the boys agreed.

"And instead of listening," Colston continued, "Hywel gave them cheap bread and inflated wages. No one learns how to take care of themselves when everything is handed to them by the government. Waves of emigrants leave Aeren and overcrowd

Sevenna. Our income has suffered with the loss of our bond families, and the life of the cottagers is far worse in the city than when they worked the land as intended."

Outside the window, Tommy could hear a horse and carriage approaching the manor along the gravel drive. He resisted the urge to turn and see who was arriving. Tommy knew that Colston expected absolute attention when speaking to his sons. As children, Bern had been better at sitting still and listening to lectures. Tommy had spent hours standing in corners as punishment for fidgeting in front of his father.

"The rebels are trying to tear down what I've worked so hard to build," Colston said. "To destroy my legacy. Hywel made them feel like they were *entitled* to rights. And how did that turn out?"

Colston paused, and Bern piped up: "Disastrous!"

"I am the only man who can save Seahaven from slipping into degradation and economic chaos," Colston said. "Now the Zunft Chamber will listen to me. Now they will join the Carvers. Otherwise they will be massacred by cottagers, and I will personally remind each and every one of them of that fact."

The carriage rolled into the front circle and stopped out of sight under the window. A horse nickered. The door slammed. Faint voices could be heard below.

"Thomas, tell me exactly what happened in Port Kenney."

"We came down Miller's Road and turned onto the Strand," Tommy said. He tried to keep his voice from shaking. He couldn't betray anything about the girl in the lavender dress or he'd be in trouble. "We decided to see if there were soldiers in the customs house, but two men chased us."

"When did you and Bern get separated?" Colston asked.

"After we left Port Kenney," Tommy said. "I headed into the woods near the top of the ridge and that's where I lost them."

"I stayed on Miller's Road," Bern said. "I thought Tommy was right behind me."

"Did you see anyone else in the forest?" Colston asked.

"No, sir," Tommy said without missing a beat. He was relieved that he had been able to lie to his father so easily. Usually, it was Bern who was good at deception, not Tommy.

"Good," Colston said. "You boys are not to leave the manor until further notice. I'm headed to Sevenna tonight for an emergency session of the Chamber. I'm going to demand that Hywel take appropriate actions. Let him try to defend the cottagers now."

"Yes, sir," the twins said together.

"My driver has arrived to take me to the port at Black Rock," Colston said. "Seminary begins in a few weeks, and you will relocate to Sevenna as scheduled. I will not let thugs disrupt my sons' education."

"Thank you, sir," Bern said.

"You can thank me when there is justice," Colston replied.

4

COTTAGER REBELLION!

Sevenna City is in a state of siege as the cottager rebellion that gripped the Islands spread to the capital city. In Norde, the Long Barracks was destroyed in a fire and the cottagers took control of the port. In Catille, the governor's mansion was ransacked and the governor's children were terrorized by cottager thugs. But the worst is in Aeren, home to the largest population of cottagers on the Islands. The rebellion began in Port Kenney. The entire village was razed to the ground and three brave soldiers died in the ensuing battle for the port.

—*Zunft Chronicle*, August 5, Evening Edition

Tamsin cried out and felt a hand clamp down over her mouth. Her eyes flew open and she expected to see fire. But instead she saw the dazzling stars in the night sky above her.

"Shhh, Tamsin, it's all right," said a voice in her ear. It was her younger sister Eliza. One of her braids had come loose and her face was smudged with dirt. It was Tamsin's job to keep her sisters tidy, but she hadn't been there this morning to help them get dressed or bring in water for washing. Eliza patted her arm and it was such a motherly gesture that it made Tamsin feel guilty. Maybe she would wake up and find that Port Kenney was a dream. She could fix Eliza's hair and everything would be normal again.

"Eliza?" Tamsin muttered. "Where are we?"

"Heading to the coast," Eliza said. "We're almost there."

The girls were tucked under wool blankets in the back of a wagon, bumping down a rough road. They were surrounded by hay bales, so Tamsin couldn't see much of the countryside. But the scratchy wool against her skin and the sickening lurch of the wagon were too real for Tamsin to pretend otherwise, even in her groggy state.

"I'm not asleep, am I?" Tamsin asked.

"How did you get to Mr. Fields's house?" Eliza asked. "You were lying on his porch, half dead."

"Am I half dead?" Tamsin asked stupidly. Her limbs felt heavy and her mind sluggish, like the time when, as a child, she'd broken her arm and her mother had given her root tea to take away the pain. But when had someone given her tea? She tried to remember what had happened since the warehouse, but her mind was almost blank. She had a few blurry images of searing flames, jade-green grass, and a young man's face.

"Port Kenney is in ruins," Eliza said. "Everyone had to report to the barracks at Black Rock. The soldiers are everywhere. You've got burns. We're afraid that if you're seen, they'll know you were involved."

"Mama registered us?" Tamsin asked.

"Not on Miller's Road," Eliza said. "Don't worry. The Zunft don't know where we really are."

All Aeren cottagers were required to register their address and employment status with the customs house in Black Rock. When Michael Henry had become famous in Sevenna, he had feared reprisals to his family. So he faked a registration for them in Black Rock, but in actuality they only moved up Miller's Road to a different cottage. As far as the Zunft knew, none of the Henry family lived on the Shore Estate anymore.

"What happened to Papa?" Tamsin asked.

"Oh, Tamsin," Eliza said. "No one knows. When the fighting started in Port Kenney, it spread to Sevenna. That's what people keep saying, but I don't really know what they mean."

It meant that Tamsin had been the catalyst for rebellion. What was happening in Sevenna was the result of her and her match.

"Is Mother all right?" Tamsin mumbled. "Is she mad at me?"

Instead of answering, Eliza patted Tamsin's arm again. Tamsin and her mother, Anna, had been quarreling a lot lately, especially over politics. It infuriated Tamsin that her mother wanted to hide her head and hope the Zunft wouldn't give her a second thought. She secretly believed that her mother didn't love her father anymore, and she'd started to blame Anna for chasing him away from the family.

"So she's sending me away," Tamsin tried to say, but her words came out slurred. Eliza didn't seem to hear her.

"Why did you go to Port Kenney?" Eliza asked.

Candlelight. Flames like a giant flower had bloomed in that empty space and demanded access to the open sky.

"Papa told me to," Tamsin said.

"Who blew up the warehouse?" Eliza whispered, but Tamsin shook her head. She didn't know who was driving the wagon and whether they could overhear what the sisters were saying.

"What's going to happen to me?" Tamsin asked.

"Mama found friends who can take you to Sevenna," Eliza said. "You've got to get lost in the city for a while."

"What will the little ones think?" Tamsin asked.

"Hush, it won't be for long. Besides, Papa needs somebody to help him."

That wasn't true—Papa didn't need anybody. But when she tried to protest, burning stabs of pain shot through her injured side, so she kept quiet. She was getting sleepy despite the pain, the jolting ride, and the sadness about leaving her home.

"Do you remember Mr. and Mrs. Leahy?" Eliza asked. "They brought their son, Navid, to Aeren a few summers back. The father, Brian, is going to meet you at the docks and give you a room."

Tamsin conjured up an image of a curly-headed boy that might be Navid, but she had no memory of the rest of the family. Before Michael Henry moved to Sevenna, scores of people used to come visit from all over the Islands every summer. It was like a weeklong party where families slept in canvas tents on the ridge and played music until the sun rose. Her father always had a lot of friends even before he left Aeren and became the hero of the people.

Tamsin lost track of time then. In her weary and confused mind, the night sky became like the waves of the ocean, rolling across the heavens. It was past midnight when a rustic fishing boat left from the secluded bay several miles outside of Black

Rock. This bay had no Zunft presence. This was a smuggler's bay, and it was not the captain's first time carrying human cargo. He laid the semiconscious Tamsin into the small compartment under the deck. It had a glass porthole, but Tamsin never saw it. She slept soundly, courtesy of her mother's root tea, and dreamed of fire spreading along the cobblestone streets of Sevenna.

5

GRAND CUSTOMS HOUSE UNDER SIEGE BY COTTAGER REBELS!

The last of the cottager rebels are holed up in the Grand Customs House at the mouth of the Lyone River. A group of fifty extremists cowardly invaded the Grand Customs House, terrorized the workers inside, took them hostage, and then blockaded the entrances. Steamer travel between the Islands has been disrupted by the cottager violence, and Chief Administrator Toulson Hywel has not returned to the capital city from his home in Norde. The Chamber is holding an emergency session today to plan a response to these villains.

—*Zunft Chronicle*, August 7, Evening Edition

Dozens of noisy rovers skidded to a halt on the pier beside the Grand Customs House. Navid Leahy had never seen so many rovers at once and never ones with cannons bolted to their frames.

He lay on his stomach on the roof across from the ornate customs house, which had weathered many storms as it kept watch over the port of Sevenna City. It was the focal point of the deepwater harbor, where modern schooners shared the water with old-fashioned mast ships. Michael Henry had told him that before the War for Aeren, the customs house had been the manor of a powerful local estate, but when the Zunft had won the war, they had transformed it into the headquarters for all Zunft shipping operations. For nearly fifty years, the city had expanded around the Grand Customs House as the Zunft monitored everything that came in and went out of the harbor.

The customs house was the heart of the Zunft, or so Michael Henry had said in a speech a few weeks ago. He'd stood on a stone wall on the corner of Ash Street, and the people kept coming until the streets were jammed with listeners. Navid had been perched on the wall near Michael Henry's feet, where he could hear every word from the great man's mouth. It was from the Grand Customs House that they collected the taxes that kept his family poor. It was from there that they regulated travel among the Islands. Cottagers faced harsh fines and prison terms unless they submitted to the customs house the proper paperwork for everything from birth to death. But the rules were so complex that no one could ever do it right—and that was the point, said Michael Henry. The Grand Customs House, with its gilded windows and authoritarian air, was a symbol of everything that cottagers hated about the Zunft.

And now the customs house was about to be destroyed. Not by the small band of cottager rebels who were holed up inside of it, the last vestige of the cottager rebellion that had been easily suppressed on every island but here. It was about to be destroyed by the Zunft and their cannons mounted on rovers. Eleven-year-old Navid monitored the situation from the roof of one of the many unassuming warehouses that shared the waterfront. He didn't think he was close enough to be hit by an explosion from the volley cannons, but if the wind picked up and sparks shot across the sky, he would run. Running was his job. Running and watching. Born and raised in Sevenna City, Navid knew the avenues and alleys of the city better than anyone. He knew which roofs were close enough to jump between and he could make it for miles across the urban landscape without ever touching the muddy streets.

Another group of rovers sputtered to a stop along the pier. These were vehicles designed for transporting troops. Zunft soldiers, in their distinctive silver-and-black uniforms, jumped out and began preparing the volley cannons. Navid inched away from the edge of the roof until he was out of sight of the street. Then he hopped up, ran to the far side of the roof, and leaped across the gap. On the neighboring roof, two teenage boys were crouched near the heating pipe, arguing over a map printed on ragged paper. Navid skidded to a stop beside them.

"They brought cannons," he gasped.

At this news, one of the older boys jumped up and ran to carry the message to his superiors. Navid knew the boy who remained by the heating pipe. Tilo Locke was seventeen and worked in the mill although he was really a musician. Navid's parents ran a pub, and when Tilo and his band played, *everybody* danced. Tilo was usually a carefree boy who liked to make people laugh, but there was not a trace of happiness on his face now.

"How many rovers?" Tilo asked Navid.

"Eight, at last count," Navid told him. "One had loads of chatter-guns."

"Okay, back to your post," Tilo said.

"Who's still inside?" Navid asked.

"It's down to fifteen men," Tilo told him. "They sent ten of the younger fellows out last night."

"The *Chronicle* says they have hostages," Navid said.

"Yeah, right," Tilo scoffed. "Since when do you believe the *Chronicle*?"

"Is Mr. Henry still in there?" Navid asked. Michael Henry was close friends with Navid's father, Brian Leahy. He ate every Sunday dinner at the Leahys' house and Navid always enjoyed his visits.

"Of course," Tilo answered. "You know he'd be the last to leave."

"They're gonna die," Navid said.

Tilo squinted at Navid. "Return to your post." But when Navid turned to go, Tilo called out: "Does Brian know you're here?"

Navid nodded, which was enough to convince the distracted Tilo. In truth, Brian Leahy thought Navid was helping at Ash Street Garden. He had forbidden his son from going near the waterfront and the Grand Customs House, but Navid wanted to help Michael Henry. While he was glad his father wasn't down there facing the cannons, Navid didn't understand why his father hadn't joined the fight with his friend.

Navid had just leaped across the gulf to the warehouse when the cannon fire began. He could see Tilo waving his arms and yelling at him to come back, but the noise was deafening. He flopped down on his belly and inched like a snake toward the roof's edge as the blast reverberated across the rooftops. He wanted to witness this. He had to see. He had to know what was happening to Michael Henry.

As he reached the edge, the façade of the Grand Customs House crumbled to the ground in a heap of smoking rubble. As the volley cannons continued to pound the building, a group of cottagers charged out the side door. Bullets whizzed from the soldiers' chatter-guns and smoke blurred Navid's vision. A man was hit, blood bloomed across the back of his jacket, and he fell to the ground. Navid leaned over the edge to see who it was, but rough hands grabbed him from behind. He turned his head and saw a grim-faced Tilo. The older boy caught him by the back of his jacket and dragged him across the roof away from the violence. Below, Navid could hear the familiar voice of Michael Henry shouting: "For Aeren! For freedom!"

But the thud of cannons was the only answering call.

6

COTTAGER REBELLION OVER!

The last rebels were arrested outside the Grand Customs House, which was destroyed by the cottagers during the recent violence. The five cottager leaders are now in custody in the Zunft Compound. Those charged with treason are:

Brandon Cook of Sevenna City

Hector Linn of Port Catille, Catille

Michael Henry of Sevenna City

Kevin Smythe of Black Rock, Aeren Island

Jack Stevens of Sevenna City

They will be given a fair trial. If convicted of their crimes, they face execution by firing squad.

—*Zunft Chronicle*, August 8, Evening Edition

Even from the loft high above the floor, Gavin Baine could catch snippets of the urgent conversation among the men of the

Chamber. The well-dressed lawmakers who sat below him ruled Seahaven not because of merit or even popularity, but because of birthright. They were all landed gentry and men of Zunft. People like Gavin, a cottager who had been born to a mason in South Sevenna, wouldn't be able to speak their mind inside these walls—washing the tiled floors would be as close as a cottager could get to the Chamber floor.

"Where is Mr. Hywel?" the men kept asking one another. "Why hasn't he returned?"

The Chamber was a long, narrow room with shiny mahogany pillars and a high ceiling, which had been painted with a scene from the War for Aeren. But the paint was chipped and faded, and even from his position high in the viewing loft, Gavin could barely make out the image. Below him, two tiers of wooden chairs faced each other over an empty expanse. The East Tier, which traditionally represented the more moderate wing of the Zunft, was mostly empty. This was Hywel's faction, and when the Chamber had last been in session in July, almost every seat had been filled.

The West Tier, which represented the more conservative sector of the Zunft, was Colston Shore's kingdom. In sharp contrast to the July session, every seat in the West Tier was filled, and there were junior members standing in the back and along the railings. After the cottager rebellion, many of Hywel's supporters had opted to join Colston Shore. Even some of Hywel's closest compatriots, such as Karl Anderson, had made the "short walk," which meant they had switched allegiances in the wake of the cottager violence.

Gavin was a cottager journalist who paid close attention to

Zunft politics. Of course, being a cottager journalist was as illegal as the newspaper that Gavin had started with Michael Henry, an enterprise he intended to continue in Michael Henry's absence. After months of attending sessions of the Chamber, the fickleness of Hywel's supporters did not surprise him. Colston Shore was a fearmonger and skilled manipulator. The so-called August Rising had ended only a few days earlier and Shore had already run an opinion piece in the *Chronicle* warning that there would be mass killings of Zunft unless the cottager rebels were dealt with swiftly.

From the cottagers' perspective, Hywel had been the most generous chief administrator in generations—and Colston Shore was now twisting that to his advantage. Especially since Chief Administrator Hywel was conspicuously absent. Gavin was disappointed. Hywel was a talented speaker and a charismatic man. Gavin hoped that if Hywel stood up in the Chamber and defended himself against Colston Shore, many of the men would return to his side.

Adjudicator Kaplan rapped the gavel against the wooden table. The adjudicator sat at a table between the two tiers and was supposed to be an impartial moderator between factions. A massive tome of Zunft statutes sat on the table in front of him. If there was disagreement in the Chamber, the adjudicator had the final word. Kaplan pounded the gavel harder and the din in the Chamber finally died away.

Colston Shore rose and waited to be acknowledged. Kaplan pointed at him with his gavel.

"The cottager violence has been stopped," Shore said, and both sides erupted in applause. "But lives were lost. The cottagers destroyed the Grand Customs House, a great symbol of our

Zunft heritage. Despite these tragedies, we must do our duty as Zunftmen. We must repair these Islands for the sake of our children and their legacy. But I ask you, where is Mr. Hywel? Why is our chief administrator not here to do *his* duty?"

Richard Shieldman jumped to his feet. He was the highest-ranking member of Hywel's supporters who had not defected to the Carvers, and his chair clattered backward in his haste to interrupt. Gavin felt sympathy for Shieldman, who was only in his late twenties and now thrust into a leadership role far beyond his experience.

"He was regrettably delayed on Norde," Shieldman called. "Your insinuations are insulting to our chief administrator."

"You must wait to be acknowledged!" Kaplan reprimanded Shieldman.

"Is that so, Mr. Shieldman?" Shore replied. "Karl Anderson arrived yesterday and I believe his estate is farther north than Mr. Hywel's. Is that true, Mr. Anderson?"

Mr. Anderson rose from his seat on the West Tier and waited until Kaplan jabbed the gavel in his direction.

"Yes, it's true," Anderson said. "I came from Norde and I had no difficulty with overland travel or sea travel. Perhaps cottager violence isn't *important* enough to bring Mr. Hywel back from his holiday."

Anderson looked pleased by the laughter of the men behind him in the West Tier. Shieldman flushed red and shook his head in disgust. Two months ago, Anderson had sat by Shieldman's side, voting in support of Hywel's policies.

"You know that's a falsehood," Shieldman retorted, and the men in the East Tier shouted in agreement.

"I know that he isn't present today," Anderson said. He

47

studied the men around him with exaggerated deliberation. "These gentlemen have arrived with haste from the far corners of Seahaven. Everyone acknowledges the gravity of the situation—except for the man who should be here to answer for his actions."

"What are you implying?" Shieldman asked.

"It was his misguided policies that caused the violence," Anderson bellowed. "It was his lack of control that brought us here. His pro-cottager measures are to blame. And that is why I have switched sides. That is why you see us standing together with Colston Shore!"

Loud voices filled the air as the two sides shouted accusations across the floor. All except Colston Shore, who sat back and let the others squabble. Gavin's attention zeroed in on the lean, arrogant Shore. His cool detachment in the midst of the heated arguing made Gavin nervous. Kaplan stood up and slammed his gavel against the table. In the stillness that followed, Karl Anderson raised his hand and was acknowledged by the adjudicator.

"I move for a vote of no-confidence for Mr. Hywel," Anderson said. "Given his absence in a time of national crisis, we need a leader who can act decisively."

"I second the motion," Shore said. His supporters stamped their feet in approval while the members in the East Tier hissed their disapproval.

"I nominate Colston Shore as his immediate successor," Anderson said.

"I move that the vote of no-confidence be postponed," Shieldman called. "There are extenuating circumstances that must be taken into account. Mr. Hywel must be given a chance to justify his actions."

The disapproving utterances of the Carvers in the West Tier were louder than the shouts of approval from the East Tier. By law, the chief administrator was the only one who had the right to postpone a vote in the Chamber, but because of Hywel's absence, the decision fell to the adjudicator. All eyes turned to Adjudicator Kaplan, an elderly Zunftman who had declared himself a Carver at the beginning of the summer. It had barely registered to anyone at the time, but now his allegiance to Colston Shore took on exaggerated importance. Adjudicator Kaplan made a show of consulting the ledger and then proclaimed:

"The vote of no-confidence will proceed."

The Carvers stamped their feet in approval. Hywel's supporters glanced at one another uneasily. If the vote was held today, Colston Shore would be the next chief administrator, which had been inconceivable only a few months before. Shore had tried to force a vote during the last session on a sweltering day in July, but he'd failed to oust Hywel. Now Colston Shore was poised to ascend to the highest position in the Zunft.

Gavin shifted uncomfortably on the wooden bench of the viewing loft. Despite the gravity of the proceedings, there were only two spectators in the cramped balcony above the Chamber floor: Gavin, and the official journalist from the *Zunft Chronicle*—Gavin recognized his face from the portrait that ran with his articles in the newspaper. At the moment, the man was polishing his pocket watch and seemed to be paying little attention to the proceedings below him.

One of Hywel's reforms had been to open the proceedings of the Chamber to the public, which, for the first time, allowed cottagers to witness how the laws of the country were made. But Michael Henry had discouraged cottagers from attending the

Chamber sessions, saying the system was rotten from the inside out. Gavin and Michael Henry were close friends and Gavin didn't disagree with that assessment. But he went anyway, in defiance of his friend, saying that there was much to learn from watching the Zunftmen in the Chamber. After the Rising, he had expected the viewing loft to be packed with curious onlookers, but it was as empty as it had been during the previous session.

The adjudicator raised his hands for quiet, but it took several minutes before the ruckus died down.

"All in favor of continuing the term of Mr. Hywel?" Adjudicator Kaplan asked. The East Tier did its best to vocalize support for their absent leader, but the diminished ranks of Hywel's men sounded small in the echoing Chamber.

"All in favor of electing Mr. Shore to be chief administrator of the Islands?" Kaplan asked. Even before the old adjudicator finished his sentence, the Chamber erupted into deafening support for the leader of the Carvers.

"The Zunft has spoken!" Kaplan shouted above the noise. "Colston Shore of Shore Manor, near Port Kenney, Aeren Island, is the new leader of these Islands, our great Seahaven!"

With a sinking feeling, Gavin stopped writing and shoved his spectacles higher on his nose. How had that happened with just one vote? Because Seminary was not an option for a cottager, Gavin had studied jurisprudence on his own and he knew that the proceedings hadn't followed the letter of the law. Shouldn't it have been a vote of no-confidence and then a separate vote for the next chief administrator?

Shore strode to the center of the Chamber. With gray hair, sunken eyes, and a thin, prominent nose, he reminded Gavin of a bird of prey. Gavin wrote in his notepad: *Very much a predator despite his unassuming appearance.* Shore laid his hand on his heart in thanks and bowed slightly toward his supporters.

"My fellow Zunftmen," he began. "My greatest fears have been realized. The cottagers have shown their true brutish nature. Mr. Hywel insolently accommodated them, which was a grave error indeed. Still, they resorted to violence. Now there is no end to what they'll demand. They would see us all dead in the ground!"

The West Tier erupted in stomping and hissing, while the remainder of the Hywel supporters gaped at the blatant disrespect directed toward the former chief administrator. Shieldman raised his hand and waited to be acknowledged, but Kaplan's gavel remained on the table. *So much for being a partial observer,* Gavin thought as Shore continued.

"As reported in the *Zunft Chronicle,* we have arrested the ring-leaders and charged them with treason. I move that the trial be held immediately. Let's deal with this situation en masse and hold swift executions for the guilty. We must demonstrate our ability to render swift justice before the situation worsens."

All of Hywel's supporters were on their feet, shouting out in protest. Gavin sat in stunned silence. A mass trial and execution meant the August 5 could be dead in less than a week.

"Under Statute 389 of the penal code, you may not hold a mass trial for treason," Shieldman shouted. "The accused are entitled to separate trials."

"An absurd law that simply slows the wheels of justice," Anderson called, leaping to his feet. "I see that Mr. Shieldman is continuing Mr. Hywel's soft-fingered approach to the cottagers."

Shieldman flushed, and even some of Shore's supporters

seemed embarrassed by Anderson's language. *Soft-fingered* had a number of meanings, ranging from insulting to derogatory.

"Quite the contrary, Mr. Anderson," Shieldman replied, his voice shaking with anger. "I'm protesting a *soft-fingered* approach to our code of laws."

There was an uneasy silence as Kaplan consulted his ledger, flipping slowly through the pages and running his finger down the page. With a slight nod, he acknowledged the existence of the statute. The new chief administrator's first act had not succeeded, but he seemed surprisingly undeterred.

"Due to the precariousness of our state, I'm presenting the Ancestral Homes Act." Shore motioned to Kaplan, who held out his right hand with his palm facing up. Gavin knew that this motion indicated that proper procedure had been followed. Colston Shore must have submitted the Ancestral Homes Act before the Chamber had convened that day. Shore probably knew that his attempt for a mass trial would fail and had devised a backup plan. Gavin considered the extent of Shore's manipulations with a growing sense of unease. In July, after Shore had failed to oust Hywel, Gavin had assumed that Shore was no longer a player to be feared. But that assessment had been painfully wrong.

"You may read the language yourselves before the vote, which will be held tomorrow. But here are the fundamentals: All cottagers must present official identification cards when questioned. If they cannot, they may be detained immediately and deported to their ancestral bond estates as determined by Zunft Records. Anyone without proper paperwork can be detained for an undefined amount of time until such an investigation is concluded."

With that, Kaplan slammed the gavel and ended the session.

Gavin felt as if the floor had dropped out beneath him. In Sevenna City, most cottagers were required to register their addresses with the Zunft, but they simply ignored the rule. This legislation meant that people would have to carry the proper paperwork or they could face arrest for no reason at all. Colston Shore had come to power and his first act was against the cottagers' rights. Gavin had a sudden urge to go back to his newspaper offices, write an article, and tell the world what he'd witnessed in the Chamber. He pulled off his flat cap, tucked it under his arm, and ducked out the door. He didn't care how many more times the Zunft destroyed his printing press. He wouldn't let himself be silenced by a man like Colston Shore.

7

SHORE REPLACES HYWEL
AS CHIEF ADMINISTRATOR

Toulson Hywel failed to attend the emergency session of the Zunft Chamber. At least thirty of his supporters succumbed to Colston Shore's manipulation and switched their allegiance to his faction, which is known as the Carvers. Using unlawful tactics, Colston Shore ascended to the highest office of Seahaven. In his first act as chief administrator, Shore tried to avoid the Zunft's own statutes and hold a mass trial of the August 5. By law, those accused of treason are entitled to separate trials and competent legal representation. The motion was suppressed, but will the August 5 be given a fair trial under a chief administrator who is willing to break the laws of the land?

The *Zunft Chronicle* reports that maritime traffic delays forced Hywel to miss the session, but this reporter found no delays in the ferry schedule. Where is Toulson Hywel?

—*JFA Bulletin*, August 12

"The vote was staged. Without Hywel, there was no one to stop it!"

"Can they truly enforce the Ancestral Homes Act? Some of those bond records are a hundred years old! It will be economic chaos."

"Forget economics. It's slavery!"

Tamsin could hear the urgent conversation through a grate in the floor, but it didn't make much sense to her. Her head still felt like it was stuffed with cotton from drinking root tea to take away the pain of her injuries. The only voice she recognized was that of Brian Leahy, the patriarch of the Leahy family and her father's close friend. Tamsin was staying at the Leahys' home, a narrow row house near the Lyone River. Heat from the wood-stove rose through the grate into the little sleeping room that had once been a closet and could barely accommodate the cot where Tamsin rested. But instead of being dark and oppressive, the tiny room felt cozy and safe. The walls were painted a bright yellow with a vibrant mural of a sunflower above her cot. In Sevenna, several cottager families would often share one row house, and space was at such a premium that even the unlikeliest of spaces were inhabited. The Leahys had made a special effort to make this windowless room a pleasant place for their guests.

A white candle flickered on the nightstand beside her. Tucked under a colorful quilt, Tamsin lay on her uninjured side. She felt lonely and wished she had the strength to get up out of bed and join the people downstairs, but whenever she sat up, she felt too nauseated to stand. She listened as the voices grew more agitated:

"Where were the people during the Rising? Too scared to take to the streets!"

"What about the pub, Brian? What's going to happen now?"

Brian and Katherine Leahy ran a popular establishment known as the Plough and Sun. Cottagers couldn't own property, so a Zunft family name must have been on the title to the pub, but everyone referred to the pub as the Leahys' place. The urgent conversation continued as Tamsin dozed off. She dreamed that she was walking with her mother, Anna, on a rugged beach back on Aeren. She tried to hold on to Anna's hand, but her mother kept disappearing into the mist. In her dream, the waves crashed loudly and the mist encircled her like a funeral shroud. Finally, she saw her mother's blond hair gleaming through the fog, but when she reached out to touch her, Anna shattered like glass.

When Tamsin awoke later, the candle had burned down to a stub. The many voices she'd heard beneath her were now gone, replaced by silence. In her drowsy state, she had the impression that the front door had clattered opened and slammed shut. Maybe that had jarred her awake. She wondered what time it was. It seemed like it must be the middle of the night.

"Hello, Gavin," she heard Mr. Leahy say through the grate in the floor. "Take your coat off. Have a seat."

The rocking chairs creaked as the men sat down in front of the fire. When they began to talk, their words were so clear it felt like she was in the room with them.

"Are you all set up?" Mr. Leahy asked.

"Everything is operational," Gavin answered. "We assembled the presses last night. I printed the first newspaper today with the news about Shore and the Chamber. He's obviously bought Kaplan off. Having the adjudicator on Shore's payroll is going to be a serious problem for us."

"Everything will be harder from now on," Mr. Leahy said. "Colston Shore is a dangerous man. He's a bigot and an extremist in a way that goes beyond most Zunftmen."

There was a long silence. Tamsin tried to imagine what was happening. Were they staring into the fire? Was someone getting a cup of coffee?

"Any news about Hywel?" Mr. Leahy finally asked.

"No," Gavin said. "Shore and his cronies have tried hard to destroy his reputation. But if he arrives tomorrow, I still think he could put his faction back together."

"What was the vote on the Ancestral Homes Act?" Mr. Leahy asked.

"Seventy-five to twenty-five," Gavin said. "I'll list the names in the newspaper for the public record."

"What about the trial?" Mr. Leahy said. "Has anyone been to the prison to see the fellows?"

"No one can get in to see them," Gavin replied. "Jack's wife, Meg, is at the jail every day, petitioning for a visit. She needs to be careful or she's going to get arrested herself."

"I'll do what I can," Mr. Leahy said. "Michael's daughter arrived a couple of days ago."

"Does she know what Michael did?" Gavin asked.

There was an awkward pause, and Tamsin imagined Mr. Leahy pointing at the ceiling. It may have occurred to him that she could hear the two men talking through the grate. It sounded like a chair scraped along the floor, and their voices grew quieter as they moved toward the kitchen but she could still hear them. She wondered if she should feel bad for eavesdropping, but there wasn't really any way to avoid it.

"Can you make her fake identification?" Mr. Leahy asked. "She'll have to find work eventually."

"Now that the presses are running, we can start forging cards," Gavin said. He stopped when someone knocked at the front door, which opened and closed loudly. Their voices were muffled as they talked to the newcomer in the kitchen. After a while, Tamsin heard someone climbing the squeaky stairs and then a timid knocking on her already open door. Navid, the Leahys' only child, was standing on the threshold, holding a tray with soup and a slice of bread. Tamsin pushed herself to a sitting position.

"What time is it?" Tamsin asked the boy. She felt disoriented. Maybe it wasn't even the night of the gathering she'd overheard earlier.

"It's only half past eight at night," he said, giving her a wide smile. "How's your head?"

Navid was an endearing combination of little boy and young adult. He was tall and lean with wiry arms and legs, but his face was still round with baby fat.

"Healing up, thanks," she said, smiling back. The wound in her side had gotten infected, and she'd been fighting a fever ever since she arrived at the row house.

"Good," Navid said. "You haven't seen any of Sevenna yet. Have you been to the city before?"

Tamsin nodded. "I visited Papa here once. Maybe when I'm better I can work in the garden with you?"

"Well, if Mama says it's all right," Navid said. He set the tray on her lap and plopped down at the foot of the bed. "You don't look so good."

Tamsin pretended to be offended and swatted his shoulder,

but she actually loved the honesty of children. There was no guile, no hidden agendas. The burns on her neck felt scabby and raw and she'd been cooped up inside for a week. She could only imagine how sickly and pale she must appear.

"I just need to brush my hair," Tamsin joked. "Then I'll be ready for the formal dance."

Navid looked doubtful. Apparently her humor was lost on him.

"You were at the customs house?" she asked. "Your father told me that Papa was arrested, but I'd had so much root tea, I can't remember everything he said."

"Are you sure you want to talk about this?" he asked. "When a bad thing happens to me, Mama tells me to think happy thoughts."

"That's good advice," Tamsin agreed. "But I need to know what happened to Papa. What happened on the last day of the Rising?"

"They brought cannons on rovers," Navid told her. "They hit the building over and over, even after the fires started. The Zunft had the building surrounded, and when the first man tried to flee the smoke and flames, they shot him."

"Who was that?" Tamsin asked. Mr. Leahy hadn't told her that part of the story.

"Christopher Stevens. Jack's son."

"Did he die?" Tamsin asked.

"Right there on the street," Navid said.

Tamsin felt sick. Jack was one of her father's friends and another journalist. His son, Christopher, had been a childhood playmate and her first crush—although she'd never told anyone but Eliza. She hadn't seen Christopher in four years, but she remembered how they'd dodged fireflies on summer evenings and raced with the other children along Miller's Road. She and Christopher had been the same age, but she was faster and would leave him gasping in the dust, yelling at her to slow down and wait.

"What happened then?" Tamsin asked.

"The fire engulfed the roof. It was about to cave in. They must have split up because they came out in two groups, one group out the east door and another through the north door. They tried to take cover but the soldiers had them surrounded on all sides. There were sparks flying everywhere, so I had to run while they were still shooting."

"Did you see my father?"

"Yes, he came out the east side."

"Did he have a gun?"

"No, none of our side had guns," Navid said.

"What happened then?"

"Your father led his group away from the customs house while the soldiers shot at them," Navid said. "They couldn't get down the alley because they were blocked by the flames."

Mr. Leahy had told her this part. Nine were killed on the spot. Five escaped death, including her father. The soldiers had arrested the survivors. Her father was in the hands of the Zunft. His trial would be a farce to humiliate the rebels and condemn the cottagers. Michael Henry would be found guilty and executed. There would be no justice for the cottagers—the August Rising had failed. Fighting off a sense of hopelessness, Tamsin reached out and gently squeezed the boy's hand.

"I'm sorry," Navid said. "I like your papa. And your mama, too. She made me a toy rabbit the last time we were on Aeren."

"I remember," Tamsin said. "Do you still have him? Can I see him?"

Navid's face brightened. "Sure, but don't tell the fellows. I'm too old for toys."

"Run and get him for me. I could use a bit of home."

As Navid ran to his tiny room at the other end of the corridor, Tamsin wiped the tears from her eyes. Navid returned, clutching the fuzzy rabbit whose soft ears had been well loved.

"You can sleep with him until you're better," Navid said. When he handed the toy to her, Tamsin saw that his palms were a mass of angry red scars.

"What happened to you?" Tamsin asked.

Navid shrugged. "I got caught by a soldier on top of a warehouse. He glued my hands to the roof and left me there. When I tore free, it took all the skin. I can't feel as much with them anymore."

"That's horrible, Navid," Tamsin said.

"Yeah, it was," Navid agreed. "I wish I could take all the Zunft and put them on a faraway island so they can't hurt anyone anymore."

"Me, too," Tamsin said, hugging the rabbit tight. She wondered if her mother already knew the fate of her husband. Her mother was the realist. She would make sure that their family soldiered on, no matter what. Her father was the dreamer, but now his dream had died in the ashes of the Grand Customs House.

CHAMBER PASSES
ANCESTRAL HOMES ACT

With the passage of the Ancestral Homes Act, all cottagers must carry official identification cards that list their current registered addresses. Those without cards may be arrested and deported by the Zunft.

—*Zunft Chronicle*, August 15

The ocean waves lashed at the pier while Tommy kept watching the dusky horizon. As soon as the ferry arrived, the twins were leaving for Sevenna and their new life as Seminary students. The capital city was peaceful again, or so their father said in his most recent letter, which had arrived with the official seal of the chief administrator's office. Tommy still couldn't believe that his father was now the most important man in the Zunft. From the day of the August Rising to this moment on the pier, everything felt unreal to Tommy. It was like a strange dream that occupied his mind even after he woke up. He could try to guess its meaning, but he'd probably be wrong in the end.

While leaving Aeren felt like a momentous occasion to Tommy, the sleepy port of Blackwater was unimpressed by his presence. Blackwater was the largest city on Aeren Island, but it was still small compared to Sevenna or even Stokkur Town on Norde. The port's population was about ten thousand during the winter months. Now, in late summer when many cottagers were working in Middle Valley, the town felt as sleepy as a provincial village. Soon the fishmongers would set out their wares, and the town bells would ring the start of the workday. But for now, it was only Tommy and Bern, waiting for the ferry to arrive. Tommy paced up and down the dock anxiously while Bern dozed on the wooden bench, oblivious to the crashing waves and crimson sunrise.

Normally, the twins would have boarded a ferry in Port Kenney, but most of the village had been razed by the fire. So they had endured a bumpy carriage ride north to Blackwater, with Bern pouting the entire way because Colston's new rover had been co-opted by the Zunft for the hunt for the rebels. Their driver was a Zunft soldier, and Tommy had expected that the soldier would wait with them until the ferry arrived, but he unceremoniously dropped them off and left.

The longer Tommy waited for the ferry, the more nervous he became. He wandered down the pier and kicked at a heavy coil of rope. He couldn't shake the feeling that something was missing. It wasn't like he expected a brass band and people throwing confetti to commemorate this next stage in his life, but he hadn't expected it to be so desolate. Finally, a dark shape appeared on the horizon as the steamer emerged through the gloom and sailed toward the pier.

"Wake up, the ferry's here," Tommy told Bern, who ignored him.

As a kid, Tommy had loved ships of all kinds, especially the steam-powered, iron-strapped wooden boats that carried passengers between the Islands. All the Zunft ferries seemed a little outdated now because the new volt-cells hadn't been incorporated into marine technology yet, at least as far as Tommy knew, but they were better than an old-fashioned sailboat. As the side-wheel steamer glided up to the pier, Tommy realized what he was missing. There was no one to say goodbye to. It wouldn't have been appropriate for Mrs. Trueblood to come, and his mother was long gone. On rare occasions, he still found himself missing her—or perhaps he was missing the idea of having a mother. When that happened, it felt like ripping a scab off a painful wound.

A young man swung the plank off the side of the ferry. It thudded loudly onto the cobblestones and startled Bern, who finally sat up and rubbed his eyes. Some of the lads had thrown a farewell party the night before, but Tommy had declined to join them. It seemed disrespectful to celebrate with the cottager violence so fresh in people's minds. Mrs. Trueblood and the other servants were still talking about arrests and death tolls. Tommy waited patiently until the man secured the plank to the pillar and tipped his cap.

"This all your gear, sir?" he asked Tommy in the lilting accent common among Aeren's cottagers.

"Yes," Tommy said, handing the man a coin as Bern brushed past them and stomped up the plank in search of a coffee.

Bern went into the lounge, but Tommy opted for a secluded bench near the boat's stern where he could avoid other travelers. He was too nervous about Seminary to try to carry on small talk with strangers. Of the four main islands, Aeren and Sevenna were closest to each other, so he anticipated it being less than an hour's run to the capital. If everything ran smoothly, Tommy would have time to eat potato pancakes at his favorite restaurant near Seminary Square before signing in with the head porter and seeing his new room. Though technically he could choose one of two specialties—jurisprudence or engineering—his father had made it clear ages ago that both boys were going to study engineering, even though neither had a natural aptitude for mathematics.

As he watched the green shores of Aeren fade in the distance, Tommy remembered a beautiful tune that Mrs. Trueblood had taught him when he was a boy.

"Alas, the emerald land of our fathers gone / Forlorn the empty hallowed home / King of Grief with golden crown / By the fields of Aeren, I am struck down," Tommy sang to himself.

A shadow fell across the deck and Bern stood next to him holding a copy of the *Chronicle*.

"Are you singing a cottager tune?" Bern asked. "I'd be careful with that if I were you. In fact, I'd forget everything Mrs. Trueblood ever taught you."

Tommy scanned the deck, but no one was near enough to hear what he'd said. Bern was right. He'd have to watch what he said now that he'd be living in the capital. On Aeren, he spent more time around cottagers than with other sons of the Zunft. That wouldn't be true anymore.

"What does the paper say?" Tommy asked.

"Father got the Ancestral Homes Act passed," Bern said. His brother sat down beside him to read the paper. He had to fold the pages in half to keep them from blowing in the wind.

"I heard Mrs. Trueblood talking about that," Tommy said. "They have to carry identification now, right?"

"Yes, but that's not really the point," Bern said. "He wants the cottagers to go back to working the estates. If an Aeren cottager is caught in Sevenna, he'll be sent home. I guess we won't have so many empty cottages along Miller's Road. Oh, and Hywel is still missing."

"There's no sign of him at all?" Tommy asked.

"I can't believe that he didn't go back to Sevenna for the Chamber session," Bern said. "How could someone neglect his duties in a time of crisis?"

"Maybe he got hurt," Tommy said.

Bern rolled his eyes. "Then why didn't he send a messenger to say so?"

"Can I see the paper?" Tommy asked.

Bern handed Tommy the *Chronicle*, and Tommy glanced at the headlines—"Trials Set for the Rebel Leaders!" "More Arrests Expected!" "The Grand Customs House to Reopen!" He handed the paper back to Bern.

"Did you hear that they let some girls into Seminary?" Bern asked. "They're supposedly math geniuses, and some professor wanted them in the engineering program. They had to close off an entire floor of one of the residence halls to accommodate three girls. It's a travesty."

"It says that in the *Chronicle*?" Tommy asked. He never read the society pages, which usually contained vapid news for ladies about social gatherings.

"No, one of the lads told me last night. It was some clause tacked onto Hywel's Open Education Act. No one really noticed until the *girls* started asking about their *domiciles*."

Bern spoke the last sentence in an annoying falsetto, batted his eyelashes, and used the newspaper as a pretend fan. Embarrassed, Tommy stood up to get away from his brother and noticed two dark shadows on the horizon.

"What's that?" Tommy asked, pointing in the distance.

"Uh, ships?" Bern said dismissively, but then the rumble of the steamer's engines abruptly stopped beneath their feet. The steamer bobbed up and down, drifting sideways. The black-haired porter dashed around the corner and barely acknowledged them as he barreled past.

"The captain wants all passengers inside the lounge," the cottager called over his shoulder.

Bern made a rude gesture at the porter's back. "Then the *captain* can tell me himself."

The two ships on the horizon sailed closer. Both were traveling at high speed. The ship in front was an expensive schooner, the kind favored by Zunftmen. Colston Shore himself had a similar model, which was the most expensive ship designed by the Bureau of Innovations. Strangely, the schooner was being tailed by a turret ship from the Zunft Navy, and only favorable winds allowed it to evade the more powerful navy ship for as long as it did. As the turret ship closed in, dozens of people gathered on the deck of the schooner. Someone began shooting at the navy ship with a single-shot rifle, which seemed insane considering the thick metal plating attached to its hull.

"Why is the schooner shooting at the navy ship?" Tommy asked. "Aren't they both Zunft? Maybe we should go inside."

"Let's go talk to the captain," Bern said, and they followed the railing around to the other side of the ferry and entered the lounge. Inside, the passengers were lined up at the windows, watching the strange spectacle play out a short distance away.

"I'm not sure it's much safer in here," Tommy muttered.

A passenger cried out as the turret ship launched a shot from the long cannon on its prow. The first cannonball missed the schooner and splashed into the waves, but the second cannonball struck the ship's side and ripped a smoking hole in her hull. The schooner tipped dangerously, and the people on the deck began jumping into the water. The captain appeared in the doorway, and passengers turned to him for answers.

"Everyone settle down," the captain said. "The navy is handling the situation. We'll be on our way soon."

"What is the situation?" Bern asked.

"Cottagers stole a ship," the captain replied. "The navy is recovering it."

Over the captain's shoulder, Tommy could see the schooner slipping below the water. The white prow jutted above the surface for a moment before it disappeared from sight. A whirlpool of white-capped waves churned where the ship had gone below. Numerous survivors thrashed in the water, trying to keep their heads above the rough seas.

"Are we going to help rescue them?" Tommy asked. The deck below him began to vibrate as the steamer engines rumbled back to life.

"Who?" the captain asked.

"The people in the water," Tommy said.

"Well, the navy is here to arrest them," he said. "We can't be involved in that."

"The captain has a schedule to keep," Bern said.

"Of course we do," the captain said. "This isn't the first stolen ship the navy has had to deal with. Since the Ancestral Homes Act passed, cottagers without paperwork are leaving the city in droves. They'd rather flee than face arrest."

When the captain left, Bern whispered to Tommy, "Like rats fleeing a sinking ship."

Tommy didn't laugh. He'd swum in the Aeren Sea many times and knew how cold the cottagers must be right now. The brothers' ferry continued toward Sevenna, and Tommy returned to his bench. He watched the turret ship, hoping to see the cottagers get rescued from the water. By the time the ship disappeared in the distance, not a single lifeboat had been launched. As their ferry sailed into Sevenna Harbor, Tommy wondered how long the cottagers would be able to endure the cold, rolling waves and whether they would finally be saved.

Inside the Seminary, Tommy closed the shutters of his dorm room to block out the sounds of the noisy city. His suite was on the top floor of Tauber Hall, which was in the western sector of the walled campus. From his window, he had a wide panorama of the city, with its smokestacks and ugly stone buildings. He could see the murky Lyone River snaking through the district, and he had a clear view of one of Sevenna's seven historic bridges, but he wasn't sure which one.

He hadn't spent much time in the city in recent years, and was surprised at how different it felt. When they arrived at the docks, throngs of cottagers were waiting for a place on the steamer back to Aeren. Zunft soldiers with chatter-guns patrolled the streets. On the carriage ride north through the city, Tommy counted dozens of beggars, including young children who stared at him with vacant eyes. He'd never seen beggars north of the Lyone River before, and he was surprised that the Zunft allowed them to cross the river into North Sevenna.

The Seminary campus was enclosed by high stone walls. Students had to enter through gates that were monitored by guards. Once inside, Tommy felt more relaxed. The Seminary had numerous grassy sports fields and immaculate gardens, which made it tolerable to live there, but all he had to do was look out his window to see the squalor and unhappiness of the rest of Sevenna. Tommy finished putting his books on the shelves and turned the gas fire down. His rooms were outfitted with the latest innovations, including heated water and an automatic fireplace. The small kitchenette even had an icebox, a hot plate, and a kettle. Tauber Hall had been recently refurnished, and he wondered if Bern's digs over in Sachsen Hall were as nice. Tommy assumed they must be. With the Zunft's acute sense of fairness, there would be riots if some boys got better accommodations than others.

Tommy put on his crimson Seminary jacket and headed into the corridor. It was nearly six p.m. and everyone was required to be in their seats in the dining hall before the bell chimed. Tommy trotted down the polished mahogany staircase, glancing briefly at the parade of oil paintings of various Zunftmen that hung on the wooden paneling. Earlier that summer, his father had commissioned his own official portrait. Before, it might have been hung somewhere like Tauber Hall, but now that he was chief administrator, his portrait would find a home in a government building, probably the Chamber itself.

At the bottom of the staircase, he was startled to hear the sounds of girls laughing. There were three young women heading out the front door. Two of them were blond, one tall and willowy and the other shorter with long, corkscrew curls. The third was a slender, black-haired girl with a thick braid down her back. Their laughter sounded nervous and excited, which was precisely how Tommy felt. At least he knew Bern and would have a familiar face to sit with at the first dinner of the new school year. These were the first girls ever to be matriculated in Seminary. The Zunft did not change easily, and the girls represented Hywel's politics of openness. Undoubtedly, there would be some students and professors alike who didn't appreciate their presence. Tommy thought about Hywel's legacy as he walked to the dining hall. Hywel had tried to accommodate the cottagers, and Tommy felt sad that his attempt had failed so spectacularly. Colston Shore would not be conciliatory toward them, of that Tommy was sure.

The dining hall was on the other side of the Green, a large grassy rectangle with elm trees planted along the perimeter. While in most gardens and other green areas of the Seminary grounds foot traffic was prohibited except along designated paths, the Green was open for students. The girls followed the path along the edge, but Tommy cut straight through the middle. Bern was waiting for him near the front entrance of the dining hall, where the heavy wooden doors were propped open to let in the cool evening air. There were twenty-four round wooden tables with white tablecloths. Tommy checked for name plates when they entered, but there were none. Apparently, you could sit wherever you wanted, but many of the tables near the front were already full.

"Come on, they're saving us a seat," Bern said, leading Tommy toward the front of the hall. A group of boys were laughing loudly, but they stopped as the brothers approached the table.

"This is your twin, Bern?" someone asked. "Maybe one of you got switched at birth."

"He's the evil half," Bern said. "They make 'em small and dark to blend in with the shadows."

This made everyone howl with laughter, and Tommy joined in even though it wasn't that funny.

"Kristoph. Giles. Frank. Dennett." Bern pointed at each boy in turn. "This is Tommy."

There was another round of hellos. Outside, the bells began to chime. Tommy took the empty chair between Frank and Giles.

"What hall are you in, Tommy?" Giles asked.

"Tauber," Tommy said.

"Oh, unlucky for you," Giles said.

"Why?" Tommy asked.

"The girls are in your hall," Giles said. "Your head boy, Richie Meagan, already said he wouldn't participate in the competition between halls because they're living under his roof. You're going to miss all the fun."

"That's stupid," Tommy said.

"Maybe you can ask for a suite in a different hall," Giles said.

Tommy had meant that Richie Meagan was stupid, but he decided not to clarify that to Giles. He didn't really care about the competition anyway. Bern had described it to him, and it involved playing games of shirtless Litball during rainstorms and other dumb pranks. Being assigned to Tauber Hall didn't seem so unlucky to him.

"Speaking of trouble," Giles said, nodding toward the entrance of the dining hall. The three girls from Tauber Hall had chosen seats at a table in the far corner near the door, but as soon as they sat down, the boys already at the table stood up en masse and walked away, leaving the three girls alone. The two blond girls looked mortified, but the black-haired girl was obviously furious. She stared defiantly around the hall, as if daring someone to say something to her.

"Of all the years to let them in, it had to be this one," Dennett said, staring at the girls. Like Bern, he had an athletic build, as if he spent a lot of time rowing or playing Litball.

"There's only one thing girls are good for," Frank said.

"And it isn't math!" Kristoph replied. The table erupted in laughter. Bern seemed to think it was the funniest thing he'd ever heard. Tommy's lips curled into a smile automatically because it was expected of him, but he turned his attention to the raised dais with a black ruffle where the professors sat facing the students. There were twelve men in black robes with blue stripes, which meant they were all tenured professors. The junior professors must eat somewhere else.

The headmaster of the school, a soft-looking man named Otto Olberg, stood behind a podium at the center of the table. Even though the hall had already quieted down, he rang a small bell to get the students' attention.

"Welcome, new and returning students," he said. "These are troubling times, and I'm grateful for the skillful leadership that has ended the violence and allowed us to open our doors on schedule, as we have for the past century."

A smattering of applause led by the professors echoed through the hall, but it was abruptly silenced when the side door opened. Two Zunft soldiers entered the hall, followed by Colston Shore. Immediately, everyone in the room stood up out of respect for this obviously important guest. Zunft leaders historically used the opening night of Seminary for important speeches, so this shouldn't have been a surprise, but Tommy hadn't expected to see Colston on his very first day in Sevenna. Having his father as the chief administrator was going to take some getting used to.

Headmaster Olberg waited until Colston Shore was next to him at the podium. He gestured for the students to sit down.

"Please welcome the chief administrator," Olberg said, and then he shook Colston's hand. This time the applause was more enthusiastic. Olberg took his seat, and Colston held his hands up for silence.

"I look at the young men of Seminary, and I see the future of the Zunft." Colston's voice rang out through the hall. "The rebels are trying to take the future from you. A future you deserve. A future that is your birthright!"

The hall erupted into thunderous applause again, and Colston waited until it died down.

"I believe in the traditions of the Zunft. I believe in hard work and fair play. I believe that it is the estate system that made us a prosperous and generous people. We need to return to the bedrock of our beliefs. We need to restore the glory of the Zunft!

"When I was young, cottagers slaughtered families in Aeren's central valley. I remember the specter of violence hanging over what should have been an idyllic childhood. I desperately wanted to save the next generation of children from those fears. The recent violence has revealed the cottagers' true nature. Some may hide their nature under a veneer of cooperation, but every one of them is capable of turning on us when we least expect it."

The generalization made Tommy uncomfortable. He'd seen the blast at Port Kenney, of course, but that was done by only a handful of cottagers. It didn't mean that every single one of them was violent. Mrs. Trueblood certainly wasn't. His father paused for dramatic effect and glanced around the room, making eye contact with students throughout the hall. Colston Shore was an accomplished public speaker and his words were having an effect on Tommy's fellow students.

"Toulson Hywel considers himself to be a compassionate man. But his cottager sympathies have diminished the strength of the Zunft, and if we don't stand together, we will fall to those who seek to destroy us. Hywel created a culture of dependency that *eroded* the cottagers' work ethic. When people begin to feel entitled to something that they did not earn, society falters."

Tommy thought about the cottager girl in the lavender dress. She had been on his mind a lot since the August Rising. Had she been a victim? Or the enemy? He wondered if she had healed from her injuries.

"The five surviving ringleaders of the August Rising have been apprehended. They will receive justice! The previous administration were apologists. Despite all of the accommodations, their policies were unjust because they asked more of cottagers than they are inherently capable of understanding. Our economy has been crushed under the weight of unsound policies, but no more. We will make sure that your legacy is strengthened.

"I won't lie to you. There will be some turmoil as I enforce the natural laws. You must not do anything that compromises the integrity of the Zunft. You all know what's expected of you. You know what kind of men you should be. Study hard and become the leaders you were meant to be."

When he said this, he was staring directly at his sons. Tommy felt like everyone in that hall was staring at him, judging him.

"Heritage, honor, good health!" Colston called the Zunft slogan from the podium.

Everyone stood up simultaneously and echoed the chief administrator's words: "Heritage, honor, good health!"

"Who provides these gifts?" Colston asked.

"The Zunft! The Zunft! The Zunft!" Tommy felt silly standing there shouting with all the other lads, but his father would see him if he didn't.

As the shouts died down, Headmaster Olberg accompanied Colston Shore off the dais. The two stood conversing by the door while everyone sat down. The men shook hands, and then Tommy's father left without another glance in his sons' direction. Olberg motioned to the headwaiter, and servers moved in from the archways with covered silver platters. The servers were cottagers, of course, and their faces were as still as statues.

9

THE SINKING OF THE *JUBILEE*

Seventeen people lost their lives when the Zunft Navy sunk the sailing vessel known as the *Jubilee*. The owner of the ship acknowledges that the cottagers worked for his estate but denies giving them permission to take the ship. The Zunft Navy reports their rescue efforts failed because the ship ran into a reef and sank too quickly.

—*JFA Bulletin*, September 3

The stack of dirty dishes teetered near Tamsin's elbow and she lunged to catch them before they fell. There wasn't nearly enough counter space to accommodate the mess created by the constant stream of patrons. Tamsin was working a shift at the Plough and Sun, and despite the hours of work ahead of her, she was thrilled to finally be up from her sickbed and able to pay the Leahys back for their hospitality. It was good to think about something besides how much she missed her family back on Aeren and how worried she was about her father locked up in the Zunft Compound.

Tamsin had been so occupied washing plates that she hadn't noticed the fire in the iron woodstove burning down to embers. She needed hot water for washing, but when she checked the box by the door, her wood supply was almost gone. Navid, who was supposed to be keeping her supplied with logs, had been called away on an errand. Slipping on her coat, Tamsin headed outside to get wood herself.

It was misty and cold, and the tiny yard was as muddy as a bog. Mr. Leahy had laid planks as a walkway to the woodshed, but the boards were slick from an earlier rain. She shouldn't be lifting too much weight, not with the sutures in her side, but Tamsin didn't want the fire to go out. She was leaning over awkwardly to lift one of the logs when she heard a voice behind her.

"Can I help?" asked a tall young man with glasses and brown hair that flopped over his forehead. He was standing near the gate and she couldn't make out his features. As he drew closer, she realized that it was Gavin Baine. He was the editor of the recently launched *JFA Bulletin*, the first attempt at a cottager newspaper since the August Rising, which had prompted the Zunft to crack down on all underground presses. Navid had pointed him out to her in the pub last week, but she hadn't been introduced to him yet.

"No, I can manage on my own," Tamsin lied. "You're Gavin, right? I'm Tamsin Henry."

"Yes—yes, I am," Gavin stammered. He seemed surprised that she knew his name.

"I think you worked with my father," Tamsin said. "Aren't you a journalist, too?"

"Um, yes," Gavin said. "I knew Michael quite well. I'm sorry for everything that's happened."

People had been saying that to her a lot lately. Everyone was so sorry about her father. She knew they meant well, but it always gave her a wormy feeling in her stomach.

"It's not your fault," Tamsin said.

"Are you settling in all right?" Gavin asked. "Do you need anything?"

That was the other thing people kept asking her. On Aeren, she was the one taking care of her little sisters. Here in Sevenna, she felt dependent on everyone else. She didn't even know where the nearest grocery was located. Not that she had any money to buy anything even if she did.

"Actually, I could use your arms. Would you mind carrying some wood?" Tamsin asked, and Gavin seemed relieved that she'd asked him to help her. Even though she lifted only one log at a time, she still felt a twinge in her wounded side.

"How do you like working in the pub?" Gavin asked.

"All right," Tamsin said. "Mr. Leahy has another job lined up for me as soon as I get papers."

"Right, I need to talk to you about that once we're inside," Gavin said. "One more log."

"Really?" she said doubtfully. He seemed to be swaying slightly under the load, but she balanced one more on his giant stack and then laughed because she couldn't see his face behind the pile of soggy wood. Together, they treaded carefully over the planks toward the rectangle of light from the open kitchen door.

"Have you seen the *Chronicle*?" Gavin asked, dropping the

logs into the box with a loud clatter. "The Zunft is blaming Norde cottagers for Hywel's kidnapping."

Tamsin nodded. "The fellows were talking about it in the pub. Just more Zunft lies. There's barely enough of us up there to do such a thing."

She hadn't meant it to be funny, but Gavin smiled. Norde had the lowest population of cottagers on all the Islands. People joked that Zunftmen from Norde were more tolerant of cottagers than from the rest of the Islands—there were so few cottagers to oppress that no one bothered to do it. Tamsin decided that Gavin had a nice smile and she found herself smiling, too.

"Extremists did it, or so they say," Gavin said. "We're investigating."

"Do you know anyone up there?" Tamsin asked.

"No, but if anyone does, it would be your father," Gavin replied. "Though honestly, I've never heard him talk about Norde much. Stokkur is the only city of any size there, but it's never been very political."

"Where can I get copies of the *JFA Bulletin* when they come out?"

"Most of our grocers will have them under the counter. Ask for an extra wrap and they will include one in your bundle."

"Why do you use the grocers' shops?" Tamsin asked as Gavin threw logs into the woodstove.

"It's a place where everyone goes," Gavin said. "I'm sure we have other sites, too, but I don't know about them. Other people organize it. It's safer if I don't know every detail."

"Clever," Tamsin said.

"That's how we handled it at your father's paper," Gavin said.

"Are they saying anything else about Hywel?" Tamsin asked. She swung the iron door of the woodstove closed and opened the flue slightly.

"The Norde cottagers are demanding guns and weapons, so this may be some criminal group profiting from the turmoil."

"I hope they get caught," Tamsin said. Criminals like that were only after material gain, and they gave all cottagers a bad reputation.

"It's only a theory," Gavin said. "It's not like we can trust what's in the *Chronicle* anyway."

"Do you need more writers for the *Bulletin*?" Tamsin said. She'd been thinking about writing articles like her father. Tamsin knew her mother would hate the idea because she wanted Tamsin to hide in a corner and do nothing. Well, too bad. Her mother had sent her to Sevenna, so Tamsin was on her own, free to make decisions for herself.

"Yes. Why, are you interested?" Gavin asked. "Oh, wait, I forgot something. We don't want the Zunft to know you're in the city. So Mr. Leahy asked me to get you this."

"What is it?" Tamsin asked, as he handed her a brown envelope.

"Fake identification card," Gavin explained. "Now you can get work anywhere and walk around Sevenna without being detained. According to the falsified records, you have a bond family here in Sevenna."

"Are they fake, too?"

"No, the Bradfords are an actual Zunft family that has sympathy for our cause."

"I didn't know there were people like that," Tamsin said,

sliding the envelope open. She read the name on the card and peered up at Gavin. "Emilie Johns. That's my new name?"

"Not as lovely as Tamsin Henry," Gavin said. "But it will do in a pinch."

"Thank you," Tamsin said. "What do I owe you?"

"Write an article for the *JFA Bulletin*," Gavin said. "If you're interested."

"Sure, but I think I should do more than that," Tamsin said.

"I'll let you know if I think of something," Gavin said, but Tamsin knew he wouldn't.

She smiled at him, and he made his way to the door. As he was about to leave, she called out: "What does *JFA* stand for in *JFA Bulletin*?"

"Justice for all," he said, grinning at her. She felt her heart leap. "Goodbye, Emilie. No, that doesn't quite fit you. Emmy? Emmy-lee? I know, Em!"

"You can call me Tamsin," she said, pretending to be cross.

"Angry Em!" Gavin joked. "It's the perfect byline for such a docile thing as yourself."

She hurled the wet dishrag at him, but he ducked through the doorway just in time. She could hear him chuckling as he went out the gate.

"Who can jest in times like these?" Tamsin asked the huge stack of dishes. She remembered her mother saying the very same thing on several occasions. Once, shortly after their father had left to work in the capital, she and her sisters had been tickling one another, giggling and rolling on the hardwood floor. Her mother's comment had immediately ended the fun. After Michael had left for Sevenna City, Anna's personality had changed. She'd begun to work all the time and expected the same from her daughters. Tamsin missed her mother's smile from the days before their family came apart.

"I sound like her," Tamsin told the dishes. "And we can't have that."

Tamsin rolled up her sleeves and began to work. But as she did, she sang an Aeren tune and thought about what she would write for Gavin.

10

HYWEL KIDNAPPED BY COTTAGER EXTREMISTS!

In shocking news, it was revealed that Toulson Hywel has been kidnapped by cottager extremists on Norde. Chief Administrator Shore announced that an investigation was in progress and there was every reason to believe that Hywel was still alive.

Chief Administrator Shore had this to say: "We received demands from the kidnappers last night. They are asking for substantial funds and a shipment of weapons. We will not be threatened by extremists, but every effort is under way to bring Mr. Hywel safely home."

Zunft Officer John Sanneral, who is in charge of the investigation, said there is evidence that Hywel was snatched on his way to Norde the night before the August Rising and has been in the clutches of the cottagers ever since.

—*Zunft Chronicle*, September 4, Morning Edition

"How did the Zunft overcome superstition?"

Professor Eugene Rannigan's question rang through the lecture hall and was met with resounding silence. The professor scanned the lecture hall from the stage and gave his new students a patient smile.

"What talkative lads," Rannigan said. "Well, we'll see about that."

Rannigan was an energetic junior professor who was a favorite among the students. He taught the History of the Zunft course, which was required for all first-year students. The only other history teacher was a droning old man who was known as the Sleepwalker, and everyone dreaded getting assigned to his class.

The lecture hall, which was one of the largest on campus, was almost full. The first three rows of wooden chairs were empty, except for the tall blond girl from Tauber Hall. She'd sat alone near the front, opened a leather-bound journal to take notes, and kept her eyes straight ahead as if the rest of the class didn't exist. Rannigan stood on the edge of the stage and gazed intently at the faces of his new students.

"History may not seem important to you," Rannigan said. "You can build a better tomorrow without understanding the past. But the story of the Zunft's triumph over ignorance and superstition? That's your story, gentlemen. One that profoundly affects how—and why—you do your work."

In a jagged scrawl, Rannigan wrote *The Age of Elevation* across the top of the blackboard.

"The Zunft victory in the War for Aeren marks the beginning of this era. The war ended the rule of the cottager clans and heralded the future successes of the Zunft. You have to understand what life was like when the cottagers tyrannized these Islands. People lived desperate and miserable lives. The cottagers *enforced* ignorance. They *prevented* progress. They encouraged belief in *magical* events, and this clouded the people's minds and made them simple and afraid. This was a world without ploughs, needles, or nails, gentlemen. It was a dark age indeed.

"Today, we are at the cusp of an Innovation Revolution. In recent years, we have seen the advent of horseless carriages, better weapons to keep us safe, and conveniences in our homes. To continue progress, we must have a strong economy. Everyone must do their share and maintain their proper place. A tower without a foundation is nothing but a pile of rubble. The estate system is the foundation of our tower. We are building that tower brick by brick, and at the top is the promise of peace and prosperity for all who have played their part.

"This year, we will study the beginnings of the estate system and learn about the men who had to forge the Zunft by becoming martyrs to the cause. You will see why your heritage is so important from a historical perspective. You will understand why the Zunft is a cause worth fighting for, although I'm sure you don't need me to tell you that. Given recent events, you have seen what can happen if we are not vigilant against the threat that lurks beneath our feet.

"You received the reading assignments from the steward last week," Rannigan said. "I trust you've done the reading."

Students shifted uncomfortably. Tommy suspected that very few of them had done the reading.

"Well, we shall see," Rannigan said, pulling out a sheet of paper from his binder. "Welcome to the question-and-answer session. We will do this periodically to support your personal reading. When I call your name, stand up."

The professor ran his finger down the sheet and called out: "Thomas Shore."

Tommy took a deep breath. With a last name like his, he was bound to attract attention. He'd done the reading, but he hoped he wouldn't make a fool of himself in front of the lads. Tommy stood at attention. He fixed his eyes on Professor Rannigan and did not fidget.

"Relax, Mr. Shore. You're not going to war," Rannigan said with a pleasant smile.

"Yes, sir," Thomas said.

Rannigan consulted his notes. "What was the Battle of the Hannon?"

Tommy felt a rush of relief. The reading had covered this, and besides, it was an event that took place less than ten miles from his home. His tutor had taken him to the site of the battle as part of his studies.

"It was when a small group of landowners led by Alexander Carver defeated cottager bandits who were killing women and children on the coast of Aeren."

"Who was Alexander Carver?" Rannigan asked.

"He is known as the father of the Zunft," Tommy said.

"And his name is the origin of the name of your father's political faction, the Carvers. Isn't that correct?"

There was a ripple of interest among the students. Colston Shore had published a manifesto of his beliefs a few years earlier, but it was never well circulated on the Islands. There were only fifty copies ever printed and a large stack of them were in his father's library on Aeren. As far as Tommy knew, that manifesto was the only place Colston had ever explicitly said where the name Carvers came from.

"Did you not know that?" Rannigan asked, addressing the entire lecture hall. "Yes, the Carvers are named for our forefather, Alexander Carver, who defeated the bandits at the Hannon. Many consider that moment to be the birth of the Zunft. Any questions?"

No one raised a hand, and Professor Rannigan nodded for Tommy to sit back down.

"Good job, Mr. Shore," Rannigan said, glancing down at his book again. "Let's see, who's next? Charlotte Ramsey."

The blond girl seemed to shrink into her seat for a moment. Then she stood up and the lecture hall became unnaturally silent.

"Did you do the reading?" Rannigan asked. When he was quizzing Tommy, he had sounded easygoing and cheerful. Now his tone was hard, like he was talking to a disobedient child.

"Yes, sir," Charlotte replied.

"Did you understand it?" Rannigan asked.

Charlotte hesitated and then replied, "Yes, sir."

"Why did you pause? Did you read it or not?" Rannigan asked.

"Yes, sir. I read it and understood it." There were titters among the students behind her. Tommy could see the side of her face and at the sound of laughter, her cheeks flushed red.

"Are you sure? There was some complicated material there."

"Yes, sir." This time, she didn't hesitate.

"Who was the leader of the bandits at the Battle of the Hannon?" Rannigan asked.

Tommy thought back to the reading. He didn't remember it saying anything about the opposing leader. He'd wondered how the bandits had amassed such a large force, but the reading hadn't explained that either. After a long uncomfortable silence, Rannigan shook his head in disgust and threw out another question to Charlotte.

"What was Alexander Carver's station at the battle?" Rannigan asked.

The reading hadn't said anything about that either. Tommy wasn't even sure what Rannigan meant by *station*.

"He was their leader, sir," Charlotte said.

Rannigan laughed derisively, and many of the students followed suit. "Yes, Miss Ramsey," he said. "As Mr. Shore pointed out, he was their leader. Do you know what I mean by *station?*"

"No, sir," she said quietly.

Rannigan slammed his hands on the podium. "I asked if you understood the reading!" he said loudly, and Charlotte flinched. "And you said yes. Yet here you are, utterly lost, wasting my precious time and the time of these students who are serious about their studies."

Tommy was shocked. He hadn't asked fair questions. Why was he giving her such a hard time? Charlotte bowed her head, and students snickered in the back.

"Women play a foundational role in the success of the Zunft, of that there is no doubt. It is an important role that must be protected and maintained. A tree must bear fruit for a healthy society. The women of the Zunft are the roots of that tree. What is the role of a tree's roots? They furnish the tree with what it needs. Everything has its appointed place, and if we alter that, then the tree begins to die."

Rannigan glared around the hall. His eyes deliberately avoided Charlotte, even though he was addressing her.

"Everything has its proper place. You understand that, don't you, Miss Ramsey? You're such a smart *girl* after all."

He said *girl* like he was saying something dirty. Charlotte's shoulders were hunched and she continued to stare at the floor. Tommy wondered how she had felt this morning as she got ready to come to class. He doubted she had expected this. Tommy's hand shot up in the air. "Sir?"

The entire class, even Charlotte, looked at him in surprise. Tears were running down Charlotte's cheeks. Tommy couldn't imagine anything more embarrassing than crying in the lecture hall, and he thought desperately for a way to divert attention away from her.

"Excuse me, Mr. Shore," Rannigan said. "I wasn't finished!"

"I was going to say that it's the same with the cottagers and appointed places. Natural laws . . ." Tommy trailed off as his classmates stared at him like he was insane.

"Well, yes," Rannigan said, obviously unsure how to respond to the son of the chief administrator. "That was the point I was getting to."

"The cottagers are trying to cut the tree down!" Tommy said, slamming his fist on the desk and making everyone around him jump. He had no idea what he was doing, and he could see Dennett and Giles staring at him like he was insane. Well, they couldn't argue with the anti-cottager rhetoric, and he'd distracted them from picking on Charlotte.

After a moment of silence, Rannigan seemed to warm to the situation. "Mr. Shore has an excellent point. It is your job to be

vigilant against transgressions wherever you see them. And sometimes they can be right in front of you."

Outside, the bell in the tower began to chime, signaling the
end of class. Charlotte, who was still standing, grabbed her
notebook and rushed toward the exit before anyone else moved.

"Miss Ramsey?" Rannigan called when Charlotte reached the
door. "A word, if you please?"

Charlotte froze near the entrance. By now, the other students
had filed out of their seats and toward the exit. They passed Charlotte as if she were nothing more than a chair or a hat stand.

"Don't forget to do the reading, lads," Rannigan called.
Tommy tried to catch Charlotte's eye on his way out, but she
stared at the floor with her back to Professor Rannigan. Tommy
crossed the threshold into the weak morning sunshine. He suddenly imagined what Charlotte might have looked like when she
was a little girl, sitting at her mother's knee while her mother
brushed her golden hair and wished all good things for her beautiful daughter.

COLSTON SHORE, ILLEGITIMATE LEADER?

In light of the new information regarding the kidnapping of Hywel, the administration of Colston Shore should be called into question. Hywel was unable to attend to his duties at the Chamber because of violence and imprisonment, and yet his faction deserts him and flocks to this questionable leader. What, exactly, did Shore offer them for this treasonous behavior? Until Hywel is safely returned, all acts passed by Colston Shore should be null and void, and the administration of Hywel continue in absentia. Shore's Ancestral Homes Act is a blatant attempt to deport cottagers from the city and turn them into slaves for the profit of the estate system.

—Angry Em, *JFA Bulletin*, September 12

A soggy newspaper lay in the gutter. It was an illegal cottager paper and like all the others, it would probably disappear quickly.

The paper was cheap and the ink smeared, but Tommy could still make out the words of the headline denouncing his father. Hywel had been advocating freedom of the press before he was kidnapped. That was yet another issue that made Tommy's father hate the former chief administrator. Embarrassed to see his family name in such a state, Tommy ground the paper with his boot until it was a pulpy mess.

"What are you doing?" Bern asked impatiently.

"Making father proud," Tommy muttered, but Bern didn't hear him over the roar of rover engines. A convoy of army vehicles bumped past them on their way to the Zunft Compound at the edge of the city, and everyone had to wait until they were gone to cross Linden Boulevard. Their street corner was getting crowded with commuters and Tommy studied the men waiting with them. Zunftmen in bowler hats with the *Chronicle* folded under their arms, heading home to the residential districts in North Sevenna. On the other side of the street, it was probably cottagers about to return home to South Sevenna.

The twins were headed to a dinner party at their father's town house a mile northwest of Seminary. Colston had sent a soldier to hand them each a personal invitation, or a be-there-or-else summons, as Tommy preferred to think of it. They'd been at school nearly a month, and this would be their first visit with Colston. It would also be the farthest that Tommy had ventured into the city since classes had begun. Mostly, he stayed inside the Seminary walls. The library had the books he needed. The dining hall provided the meals, and anything else he could buy at the grocer's on the corner of Dawson Street. There was a large newsstand at the north end of Seminary Square near the front gates. Sometimes he went there to buy the *Zunft Chronicle*. He'd strolled through the shops along Dawson Street and up to the pocket park called Sebastian's Circle, but mostly he was too busy with classes to explore.

"What's your best class?" Tommy asked his brother.

"Not the History of the Zunft," Bern said. "The Sleepwalker makes me want to jump off a cliff. You're so lucky you got Rannigan."

Tommy thought about telling Bern how Rannigan had treated Charlotte, but the last rover bumped by and the boys set off for their father's again. Linden Boulevard was one of the main thoroughfares of the city, and it ran all the way down to the Lyone River across Fourth Stone Bridge and into the cottager district. This was the only section that was paved with cobblestones, but the rovers had tracked mud from the south along the road and by the time the brothers reached the other side, Tommy's trousers were speckled with mud.

Once the boys crossed Linden, they officially left the city center and entered the North District, which was the wealthiest quarter of the city. Most Zunft politicians and high-ranking officers kept their town houses in the North District. It was the only part of the city where the streets were well maintained. The noise of the city faded as they strolled up the tree-lined avenues. The immaculate town houses and ornamental gardens formed a perimeter that blocked any view of the poor southern districts. From here, it was easy to pretend they didn't exist.

"Has Father *ever* hosted a party before?" Bern asked. "This is going to be hilarious."

Hilarious was not the word Tommy would have chosen when

describing a formal evening with high-ranking Zunftmen and their bored families.

"I hate this sort of thing," Tommy mumbled. His collar was too tight around his neck. He felt like he was choking every time he tried to turn his head.

"Why?" Bern could never understand Tommy's aversion to social events.

"I've got things I need to do," Tommy said. "Don't you have loads of homework?"

"Oh, that reminds me—quit refusing the invitations from the lads," Bern said. "It makes me look bad."

"How does it make *you* look bad?" Tommy asked. "It doesn't have anything to do with you."

"You're the son of the chief administrator," Bern chided him. "You have to do certain things. Act certain ways. And if you don't, people will notice quicker than if you were a nobody."

"I'm busy studying," Tommy said. He didn't want to say that his engineering classes were much harder than he had expected and twice as boring as he had feared. "Surely that's an acceptable thing to do as a Seminary student."

"Not if you're a social outcast," Bern said. "Father is having to adjust, too. He's not exactly a social person either, but Hywel hosted regular parties, and now Father feels like it's expected of him."

"Talking to these people makes my brain go numb," Tommy said.

"You're being judgmental," Bern snapped. "You have no idea if these people will be boring. You haven't met any of them."

"What do you mean?" Tommy said. He was expecting to see

the same group of men as always—the stalwart Carvers who had supported Colston for years.

"After the cottager violence in August, Hywel's men became part of the Carver faction. Remember how Father warned everyone that a cottager rebellion was coming? The cottager violence gave him credibility. And once the Zunftmen were finally listening to him . . . Well, you know how good he is at striking fear into the hearts of men. Their allegiance is the point of tonight. By attending, people are publicly declaring their loyalty to Father."

"No one will actually say that, though, because that would be too obvious," Tommy said, switching to an obnoxious voice: "I hereby join the Carvers because I am opportunistic and fickle."

"Watch your mouth, Tommy," Bern said. "Don't say stuff like that."

"Now that they know Hywel was kidnapped, why are they still loyal to Father? It's not Hywel's fault."

"Actually, it *is* his fault," Bern scoffed. "Hywel coddled the cottagers, and they turned on him anyway. Father's in charge now, so it's smarter to stick with the Carvers. The chief administrator gets to assign positions in government, after all."

Tommy sighed. So some of the new Carvers were terrified and some were greedy—either way, his father had majority control of the Chamber. The boys turned on Piper Lane and could see their father's home at the end of the street. Like most of the town houses in the North District, it was a three-story rectangular building with a flattop roof and a high wooden fence around the property. The town house had recently been painted light blue with white trim around the tall windows. The door was still a glossy black but the golden Shore crest had been replaced by a silver Zunft symbol, which hung above the knocker. Tommy found himself wishing for an explosion or an earthquake— anything to get out of the festivities.

A servant met them at the door and escorted them to the library. The last time that Tommy had been here, an oversize mahogany desk dominated the room. Now that was gone, and a smaller cherrywood desk was tucked in the corner. One wall had been ripped out and replaced with glass doors that opened onto the garden terrace. Leather-bound tomes filled the floor-to-ceiling bookcases. They had been acquired by Tommy's maternal grandfather, who had been an avid naturalist and mapmaker. Colston kept the books because they were rare and expensive, but Tommy doubted he'd ever read them.

A uniformed officer and a Zunftman in a tailcoat were seated on two new couches that had been placed in a cozy arrangement in front of the marble fireplace. The two men rose when the boys entered the room, but Colston remained seated. The Zunftman in the tailcoat offered his hand and greeted each of the boys. The officer nodded at them but kept his distance.

"Right on time," Colston said approvingly. "Let me introduce you to my guests. This is Officer Sanneral, a Zunft army investigator, and Mr. Anderson, a member of the Zunft Chamber. These are my sons, Bernard and Thomas. They are both students at Seminary this year."

Tommy had never seen Mr. Anderson before, but he seemed like the sort of ally you'd want in your camp. A handsome blond man with a boyish face, Mr. Anderson had a booming voice with a distinct Norde accent. In contrast, Sanneral reminded him of a weasel with his pointy chin and small eyes.

"Pleased to meet you, sirs," Bern said quickly, and Tommy nodded, not sure whether he was supposed to repeat the sentiment or not.

The twins remained standing while the men continued with their conversation.

"The suspects are communicating through a series of couriers," Sanneral said. "We're monitoring them, of course, but no one has led us directly to Hywel."

"You're from Norde," Colston said to Mr. Anderson. "What are your thoughts on the native cottagers?"

"As you know, it's quite different up north," Anderson said. "We don't have the large agricultural holdings like you have on Aeren. Many of our cottagers have never been associated with an estate at all."

"Do you have problems with criminal elements like we do in the city?" Sanneral asked, and Anderson looked thoughtful.

"A lot of them are hunters who live in the forest," Anderson said. "They still call themselves Rangers up there and are more savages than criminals."

"Savages who would kidnap the chief administrator?" Colston asked.

"Perhaps," Anderson said. "Although they don't seem to pay much attention to our affairs. There aren't any schools outside of Stokkur, and I doubt any of the people can even read."

"What language do they speak?" Colston asked.

"Old Aelin, actually," Anderson said. "The forests of Norde are the only place where it's still spoken on the Islands, or so I'm told."

"It's hard to imagine that there are such backwaters left,"

Sanneral said. "They've probably never seen an autolight or a rover."

"Most of us on Norde haven't," Anderson joked, earning an appreciative laugh from Colston.

"We'll do our best to change that, Karl," Colston said. "We can't have our brothers in the north shivering in the dark."

"Good man," Anderson said. "At night, it's darker than a cottager district up there."

"Turn on a few lights and we might find Hywel himself cowering in the shadows," Colston said.

"What are the latest demands from his kidnappers?" Anderson asked. "Have we heard anything more?"

Unexpectedly, Colston smiled into his port glass. "Oh, the kidnappers have made a new demand. They demand the *dissolution* of the estate system. Prepare to hand over every acre to the fools in their flat caps."

There was shocked silence, and then Sanneral and Bern burst out laughing, but Anderson seemed perplexed.

"Surely this wasn't planned by someone on Norde," Anderson said. "I don't think our cottagers appreciate how our legal system works."

"Well, you're correct," Colston said approvingly. "I suppose it's time to give them the news, Sanneral. Despite the early reports, our investigation has revealed that the kidnapping happened here in the capital. Hywel was then transported to Norde and probably taken to a remote location in the wilderness."

"There are huge areas of unexplored wilderness in Norde," Anderson said. "How will you search for him?"

"The kidnapping was masterminded by a radical who lives

here in Sevenna," Sanneral said. "We'll compel him to reveal his Norde connections."

"It's these Norde connections who have Hywel?" Anderson asked. "That's who you're getting demands from?"

"Apparently," Colston said. "Because the mastermind is in jail."

Sanneral snorted and Colston smirked. The two men were enjoying a private joke, but everyone else was obviously confused.

"You've arrested the mastermind?" Anderson asked. "Where did you find him?"

"He was already *in* custody," Sanneral said. "We arrested him at the customs house during the August Rising."

"Michael Henry masterminded the kidnapping of Hywel," Colston said.

"He must have planned the kidnapping as a fail-safe in case his rebellion failed," Sanneral said. "I guess it occurred to him that men with flat caps can't really fight men with guns."

"I know that name," Anderson said. "He's that cottager journalist from Aeren who makes all the street speeches."

"A rabble-rouser with pretensions to power," Colston said. "Hywel even took pains to accommodate this bastard. And see where it got him."

"Now that you know Henry was involved, what are you going to do?" Anderson asked.

"Shoot him for treason, eventually," Colston said. "But first, we need to get Hywel back."

"Do you really think Henry will talk?" Anderson asked. "His kind will martyr themselves for any reason."

"It doesn't matter whether he does or not," Colston said. "I'm ending the bread subsidy in response to the kidnappers' demands. If the cottagers have a single intelligent man among them, they'll realize that the rebels are making their lives more difficult. Hopefully, someone will turn on them, and we'll learn the whereabouts of our colleague."

"What about a reward?" Sanneral said. "Do you want to offer a reward for his safe return?"

"No, I'm not spending a coin if I don't have to," Colston said. "They want me to dismantle the estate system. Well, they can bully me all they want. I won't dismantle anything. I'll make it stronger—and untouchable—for future generations."

"Hear hear!" Sanneral and Anderson raised their glasses, and Tommy and Bern quickly did the same.

There was a knock at the door, and the butler announced that dinner was being served. As they filed into the dining room, Tommy whispered in Bern's ear: "How does ending the subsidy help make the estate system stronger?"

"For reading so much, you don't know anything," Bern whispered back. "The subsidy has made the cottagers lazy. Now Father's going to make them work for a living and blame the extremists for their situation at the same time. It's really brilliant."

"Uh-huh," Tommy agreed, feeling stupid because it didn't make sense to him, yet it all seemed so clear to everyone else.

At the long banquet table, the guests had prearranged seats. An officer's wife to Tommy's left and a politician on his right— and neither was interested in talking to Tommy. After the requisite pleasantries at the beginning of the meal, Tommy sat silently through cranberry salad, lobster bisque, and duck-in-orange. He wondered who had chosen such modern fare. His father preferred more traditional food—roast and potatoes—but maybe that would feel too provincial to the Sevenna crowd.

At the far end of the table, Bern was seated next to one of the girls who lived in Tauber Hall. Not Charlotte from Tommy's history class, but the girl with blond curls and a wide smile. Bern made no attempt to talk to her, which surprised Tommy. If she was here, that meant she was related to someone important. Tommy figured that would count for something, at least in Bern's twisted logic. But no, Bern spent all his time talking to Officer Sanneral on his right, and the girl looked as bored as Tommy felt. After she caught his eye for the second time, he made himself stop watching her. When the guests finally finished their dinner and were free to mill around before dessert, Tommy tried to find her.

She was standing at the open balcony doors and she startled when he said hello.

"I'm Tommy Shore," he said. "I've seen you at Seminary. I live in Tauber Hall, too."

"Yes," she said pleasantly. "Kristin Anderson. I'm pleased to meet you."

"Anderson . . . I think I met your father earlier. He was in my father's library when I arrived."

"Yes, I met your father as well," she said. Then she whispered: "Your father is scarier than mine."

Her unexpected comment made Tommy laugh, which he tried to turn into a fake cough. He was embarrassed, but Kristin looked pleased with herself. She handed him a goblet of water from the refreshments table.

"You all right, Tommy?" she said. She had a mischievous sparkle in her eye.

"Did you enjoy dinner?" he asked when he stopped coughing.

She squinted at him. "Sure, if you enjoy being ignored, it was great."

"My brother's not so friendly, huh?" Tommy said.

"Your brother and all the other lads at Seminary," Kristin said. "I must admit, it caught me completely off guard."

"What did?" Tommy asked.

"How the lads treat us," she said. "I didn't think they'd welcome us with a giant party, but I thought they'd play fair. Isn't that what they drill into us as children? That's what it's like on Norde anyway."

"It's the same on Aeren," Tommy said. "Whenever we went to children's parties, no one was allowed to be excluded or have anything better than anyone else."

"Everyone got the same present and the same-size cake." Kristin laughed.

"Everyone believed they were superior to their peers, but you weren't allowed to say it out loud," Tommy continued, enjoying the conversation.

"When Ellie Hywel and I were studying last night, she called them—" Suddenly, Kristin stopped with a horrified look on her face.

"Ellie Hywel?" Tommy asked. "One of the other girls is related to Hywel? Who, your black-haired friend?"

He'd heard Charlotte's surname and it wasn't Hywel. So Ellie must be the slender girl with the braid. Hywel was a widower, but Tommy had heard that the former chief administrator was childless, which was frowned upon by the Zunft. One of the Zunft policies was for each family to have at least two children.

"I meant Ellie Sommerfield," Kristin mumbled.

"You said Hywel . . ." Tommy said, and then it dawned on him why Kristin was so upset. She was standing in a room with Carvers, who disliked Hywel whether he'd been kidnapped or not. "Don't worry. I won't tell. I didn't know Hywel had a daughter."

"He doesn't!" Kristin said. "She's his second cousin or something like that. When her father died, she became his ward. She was more like his personal secretary than a family member."

"Why doesn't she want anyone to know?"

Kristin scowled at him. "Are you serious? Everyone hates us because we're girls. It would make it that much worse if people knew she was related to the cottager-loving Hywel."

"I don't hate you," Tommy said, glancing around to see if anyone was watching. Fortunately, no one seemed to be paying any attention.

"Half the students are 'new' Carvers, like my dad," Kristin said, reaching for a water glass. "Hywel isn't a good name to have now. She asked that we all use her mother's name, which is Sommerfield."

"I won't say anything," Tommy promised. "And I'm sorry about how people treat you."

"Ellie says the lads act that way because they're like sheep, too stupid to think for themselves," Kristin said. "You should talk to her sometime. I've never met anyone like her."

Tommy didn't know what to say, so he waited while Kristin took a drink of water. "One time, my brothers and I were playing out in the garden when a fox came out of the bushes," she said. "It must have been ill because it walked sideways. The gardener put this crate over it and trapped it, and it went crazy, slamming itself against the plank and screaming. I didn't know animals could scream, but they can."

Tommy felt confused. "Are we still talking about Ellie?"

"It's a metaphor, dummy," Kristin said playfully. "I'm trying to be philosophical."

"So Ellie is like the screaming fox?" Tommy guessed.

Kristin laughed. "She's like the fox the moment they put the crate over its head. I always have the feeling that she's about to *start* screaming."

"Because of how the lads act?" Tommy asked.

Kristin nodded. "She's really unhappy with the state of the world."

A few Zunftmen crossed the room to the drink table. Tommy tipped his head toward the balcony and the two walked into the chilly night air. Kristin took a deep breath.

"At home the sky is crystal clear," Kristin said, staring up at the stars. "I hate Sevenna's yellow haze. It's like seeing the sky through cheesecloth. Have you ever been to Norde?"

"Only to Stokkur Town on a sailing trip," Tommy said. He hadn't been very impressed by the squat ugly buildings and fishermen's huts, but the sweeping expanse of stars had been riveting.

"Stokkur isn't anything like the rest of Norde," Kristin said. "Our manor house is on a cliff overlooking a valley. The forest goes on *forever*, Tommy. I don't think my father even knows where his land ends."

"It sounds nice," Tommy said. "Nice and cold."

"You get used to it," Kristin said. "It's better than Sevenna's humidity."

"Are you all from Norde?" Tommy asked. "You, Ellie, Charlotte?"

"We were all born there," Kristin said. "But Charlotte was tutored in Sevenna. And Ellie has bounced around from relative to relative."

"That's hard," Tommy said.

"She doesn't let anything scare her," Kristin said. "Charlotte is about to snap from the way the lads treat her, but not Ellie."

"Charlotte's in one of my classes," Tommy said. "Or at least she was. I haven't seen her lately."

"She sits in her room day after day. I don't think she's going to lectures. One of her professors was a total bastard to her. He said things to her that you shouldn't say to a dog."

"Professor Rannigan?" Tommy asked.

"How did you know?" Kristin asked.

"He was giving her a hard time in class," Tommy said.

"Ellie and I are really worried about her," Kristin said. "I think she should go home, but she's afraid her parents will be mad at her. They were so proud of her when she was accepted."

Kristin nodded toward the room that was now crowded with boisterous Zunftmen. Her father stood next to Tommy's and they were both watching Bern as he animatedly told a story. He made his fingers into claws that swiped at the air, and the roomful of people burst out laughing.

"Do you wish you were in there?" Kristin asked.

"Not even a little bit," Tommy replied. They watched as Mr. Anderson clapped Bern on the back. Then Colston began speaking and everyone quieted down in rapt attention.

"It was my father's idea for me to go to Seminary," Kristin

said after a moment. "He wanted me to have the best education possible. That was back when he was a staunch supporter of Hywel and his views on open education. But he was shocked by the cottager violence. I think it made him feel vulnerable, and that's unacceptable for a man like him. Now that he's a Carver . . . I suspect my days in Seminary are numbered."

Later, the butler led the guests toward the small ballroom where a piano had been set up for the evening's entertainment, but Bern intercepted Tommy and hustled him into the kitchen.

"What?" Tommy asked. Not that he was keen to listen to the piano, but his conversation with Kristin had been interesting. If he had to spend the rest of the evening at his father's house, he wanted to sit next to her.

"Father gave us permission to leave," Bern said. "I told him we had plans with the lads, and he supports our attempts to develop connections with our future colleagues."

"What are you talking about, a pub crawl?" Tommy asked. He had no intention of going out with the lads, but he followed Bern down into the cellar where there was a door that led into the back garden. Leaving was fine with him. It wasn't like he would never talk to Kristin again. She lived in the same dormitory.

"Pubs are so passé," Bern told him. "We're going to a cabaret."

"What's that?"

"Live performers doing skits," Bern said. "It's pretty hilarious. You should come with us."

"Hilarious" must be Bern's new favorite word, thought Tommy. His brother placed a high value on being entertained.

"Well, not tonight," Tommy said. "I want to get some work done."

"What were you and that girl talking about?" Bern asked.

"Who, Kristin?" Tommy asked. "The one you were sitting next to for three hours?"

"How should I know her name?" Bern asked.

"Didn't you introduce yourself?" Tommy said. "Weren't you saying something earlier about doing what's expected of you?"

"I was talking about people who matter," Bern said.

"She's the daughter of Karl Anderson," Tommy pointed out. "He matters. Bloodlines matter. You do the math."

When they came out of the cellar into the back garden, they startled one of the cottager servants, who was throwing away platters of uneaten food from the party into the trash bin near the cellar door.

"Do you know anyone who wants that?" Tommy asked the woman. "It seems like a waste to throw it away."

"Shut up, Tommy," Bern said.

"She could take it if she wanted," Tommy said.

"Who are you?" she asked, looking uncertainly between the boys.

"He's no one," Bern said. "Come on, Tommy."

"I'm Colston Shore's son," Tommy said. "There's no reason to waste that food."

"I was told I had to throw it away," she said. "But if I'm allowed to take it, I will."

"You're so stupid, Tommy," Bern said. He turned to the servant. "Keep doing what you were told."

"If she wants to keep it, then she should," Tommy said. He

was furious that Bern was contradicting him. Bern always had to be in control. He always had to be right.

Bern grabbed Tommy's arm and dragged him out the gate and down the path. Near the gate, he shoved Tommy hard. Tommy stumbled over the curb and fell into the deserted street. When Tommy got up, he could see past his brother and through the gate to the backyard. The servant was standing there, staring at them helplessly.

"She was given an order—don't confuse her," Bern said. He strode into the street and cuffed his brother's ear. Humiliated, Tommy stalked off down the road, rubbing his sore wrist and hating Bern for being bigger and stronger than he was.

12

MICHAEL HENRY MASTERMINDS KIDNAPPING OF HYWEL

The rebel Michael Henry is responsible for the kidnapping of Toulson Hywel. Officer John Sanneral, head investigator for the state, said that Henry planned the crime as a fail-safe in case his August Rising rebellion was quelled. Henry is already in custody for his role in the destruction of the Grand Customs House.

"Given the continued demands of the extremists, there is every reason to believe that Mr. Hywel is still alive," Sanneral said. "We'll find them. It's only a matter of time."

—*Zunft Chronicle*, September 25, Evening Edition

As she stepped into the alley, Tamsin blinked her eyes uncomfortably. After hours inside the dark cabaret, her eyes were having trouble adjusting to the light of dawn. The sun was rising, and the sky was a pale orange in the narrow opening above her. Tamsin remembered mornings on Aeren, hiking the ridge above Port Kenney under a sky like this. She longed for her sisters and the quiet of the forest. She missed waking up in the morning and not feeling angry at the world.

The coins earned from her shift at the Estoria felt heavy in her pocket, but Tamsin had been sending her wages back to her family on Aeren and knew it wasn't nearly enough to provide for them. Before her father had been arrested, he'd been the one to send money back to Aeren. Now the responsibility was hers. Only the thought of her little sisters being hungry could have compelled her to work in a place like the Estoria, a cabaret that occupied a sprawling cellar near the waterfront. It was wildly popular with Zunftmen, especially students from Seminary but also with off-duty military from the compound.

So far, Tamsin had been assigned to kitchen duty, but she'd asked to be trained as a barkeep, which would mean better pay and better opportunities to hear what the Zunft officers had to say about politics after they'd had too much to drink. Even from the kitchen, she'd already heard conversations about the sinking of the *Jubilee* and the high number of arrests and deportations since the passage of the Ancestral Homes Act. She didn't know what good such information would do her—except to fuel her rage—but it made her feel like she was doing *something*.

As she left the alley, someone touched her shoulder. She jumped in surprise, but it was Gavin, who had been waiting for her on the busy street near the entrance.

"Tamsin? I didn't mean to startle you." Gavin's cap was pulled down low over his forehead and his bangs nearly covered the right lens of his round spectacles. He was wearing a white shirt with the sleeves rolled up under a dark wool vest. There were circles under his eyes like he hadn't slept in a while.

"Sorry," Tamsin said, lowering her hands.

"Were you going to hit me?" Gavin asked.

"If you had been a Zunftman, maybe," Tamsin said.

"Do you know how to box?" Gavin asked.

"Papa taught me a little," Tamsin said. Before he'd been a street speaker, Michael Henry had been a brawler. "He used to show me how to fight. Even if he hadn't left, Mama would have made him stop teaching me."

"Why?" Gavin asked.

"Because I'm not a boy," Tamsin said.

"If I had daughters, I'd teach them how to fight," Gavin said.

"I would, too," Tamsin said. "But Mama likes to hide, not fight. She thinks it makes her safe."

A pained expression crossed Gavin's face. "Can we talk?" he asked.

"Sure. Were you waiting for me?" Tamsin asked, but she already knew the answer. He'd waited for her after work at the Plough and Sun several times. They'd gone for tea twice in the last week alone, but this was the first time he'd met her at the Estoria.

"Do you want to get breakfast?" Gavin asked. He seemed worried, and Tamsin realized that his unexpected presence meant that something bad had happened. She was tired of being blindsided by one thing after another. It seemed like life was a relentless wave of tragedies and injustices.

"If there's news, please tell me," Tamsin said.

"Let's go down to the café on the pier," he said. "My treat."

"Gavin, please tell me," Tamsin said. She could tell by his forced cheerfulness that something was terribly wrong. "Is this a conversation you want to have in front of an audience at the café?"

"I guess not. If you don't mind a short walk, we can talk on my front porch," Gavin said.

"You have a front porch?" Tamsin asked. "Such things don't exist in the city."

"You'll see," he said. "It's close."

She followed him through the crowds along Linden Boulevard. They turned right at Shadow Bridge and then took the North Wall Quay until they reached a block of low-rent flats near the harbor. They ducked inside one of the small covered markets that sold mainly rugs and cheap wooden furniture. Gavin led her through the crowded stalls and out the back into a dingy corridor that led to a public stairwell. At the top of the stairs, they crossed a rickety walkway over an alley that ended at a private stairwell up to the roof. Gavin used two separate keys, one for the door at the bottom of the stairs and one for the door at the top.

They came out on the flat roof of a one-story building squeezed between two taller buildings. A small shedlike building with a blue door stood at the far corner of the narrow roof. There were no windows on either of the neighboring buildings, only redbrick walls towering on either side. A large kitchen garden planted in wooden boxes dominated the center of the roof. Two carved benches faced each other with an outdoor fire pit. She wondered if that was Gavin's only way to cook hot food.

"Your front yard is lovely," Tamsin said sincerely. This secret little place felt like another world.

"It's hard to grow a garden up here. With these walls, I only get sun for a few hours a day, but you should come back in the spring. I'm not a bad gardener, when I find the time."

"You live in there?" she asked, pointing to the shed.

"I sleep in there. It's basically what it looks like, a shed with a cot. I'd offer you tea, but there's no water."

"I'm fine," she assured him as they took a seat on a bench next to the fire pit. "Please, talk now."

"I wanted to be the one to tell you." He reached into his vest pocket and pulled out a folded piece of paper. "They're blaming your father for the kidnapping of Hywel."

"What?" She unfolded the paper, which was torn from the *Chronicle*. It described the charges against Michael Henry. Tamsin stood up and wandered a few steps toward the brick wall that was the side of the neighboring building. She wanted to hit something or stomp something to pieces with the soles of her boots. She wanted to destroy . . . something. She squeezed her eyes shut, but she could feel that Gavin had come to stand beside her.

"I feel so helpless," she said.

"You're not helpless," he said.

"I want to scream from the rooftops," she said. She finally opened her eyes. Gavin was staring at her with so much concern, she wanted to shove him away and embrace him at the same time. "But who would care if I screamed?"

"You'd probably get us both arrested," he said. "Come on, sit down."

"They arrested Father at the customs house," Tamsin said furiously as Gavin led her back to the bench. "How could he have been there *and* kidnapping Hywel at the same time?"

"I don't think they care much about logic," he said. "I read the legal charges. They're saying he orchestrated it before the Rising."

"That's a lie!" Tamsin cried.

"I know," Gavin assured her. "We all know."

"He respected what Hywel was trying to do," Tamsin said.

"That's what he told me as well," Gavin agreed.

"Before this, there was a chance he wouldn't be executed," Tamsin said. "It was a small chance, but no Zunft died in the fire, right?"

Gavin gave her a funny look, but Tamsin continued. "And making martyrs of leaders hasn't worked in the past. I mean, the War for Aeren might never have happened if the Zunft hadn't slaughtered the rebel leaders."

"Except that war turned out well for the Zunft," Gavin pointed out. Both the cottagers and the Zunft consider the War for Aeren the decisive event that ensured the Zunft's control over the Islands. Beyond that, the two sides' accounts of the war vary a great deal."

"I know!" Tamsin said defensively. "We lost the war, sure, but more cottagers joined our side when the Zunft began executing our leaders and made martyrs out of them. Their brutality turned sympathizers into rebels! I hoped maybe . . ."

"He wasn't ever going to get a pardon," Gavin said. "You have to be realistic about that. They weren't going to forgive and forget."

"I have dreams of destroying the Zunft," she said. "I see an army of cottagers overrunning Seminary Square. We march up to the prison compound, and I smash open the gates and Papa strolls out of there. I dream about walking with him on Giant's Ridge, across a free Aeren."

"Oh, Tamsin," Gavin said. "Those are the fantasies of a child, not the realities of our time. Your father had dreams like that, too, and—"

"I know!" Tamsin interrupted. "I *know* the world isn't like that. He's going to be tried for treason, whether they're pinning this kidnapping on him or not."

"Let's not give up hope yet," Gavin said. "Mr. Leahy is talking to his contacts. Maybe if the kidnappers hear that your father is taking the blame for their actions, they'll release Hywel. It's not much, but it's something."

"I wonder who these 'cottager extremists' are," Tamsin said. "They want money and weapons, which makes them sound organized. But we don't know anything about them."

"They've made a new demand," Gavin said. "They're asking for the dissolution of the estate system in exchange for Hywel's life."

Tamsin shook her head miserably. "They might as well ask for the moon on a silver platter. I want to see my family. I want things to be fair."

"Since when is the world fair?" Gavin asked.

"What's that supposed to mean?" Tamsin said.

"If *fairness* is your benchmark, you'll spend your life bitter and angry," Gavin said.

"Then what should be my benchmark?" Tamsin said. "You're the editor of an illegal newspaper. If you're not going for fairness, then what are you doing?"

"I'm trying to get the truth out there to as many people as will listen," Gavin said. "I don't expect all wrongs to be righted and then we'll all live happily ever after."

"What do you want your life to be like?" Tamsin said. "Are you going to cower like my mother and hope for the best?"

"Why do you think your mother is cowering?" Gavin asked.

"She isn't out there on the streets trying to make a difference, not like Papa," Tamsin said.

"She's taking care of her family," Gavin said. "Raising you. And she's been doing a damn good job of it."

"It's not enough," Tamsin said.

"I disagree." Gavin shrugged. "Bringing children into the world and doing your best to make them happy and safe—that seems pretty noble to me."

"The world isn't happy and safe!" Tamsin practically shouted. "That has to change first."

"Do you mind another walk?" Gavin asked her after an uncomfortable silence. The sun had gone behind the building and she was visibly shivering. "I want to show you my backyard."

Tamsin smiled weakly. She was embarrassed by her tirade, but Gavin didn't seem angry at all. "Front porches. Backyards. Such things don't exist in Sevenna," she said. Gavin smiled gently and offered her his hand. "Wait and see."

Gavin took Tamsin to the secret offices of the *JFA Bulletin*, which were located in a cavernous cellar beneath an abandoned glassworks factory. A blocky printing press took up one entire wall. The contraption was about twelve feet long and seven feet high and mounted on a metal frame. Two huge rollers were suspended above a mesh cage, which caught the pages while they were still damp with ink. A complicated system of ink troughs, pipes, and vats buttressed the rollers. A long wooden table stood against the far wall. It held the cases of lead type and composing sticks. Rolls of cheap brownish paper were stacked up near the entrance, ready for the printing of next week's *Bulletin*.

"Where do you get your paper?" Tamsin asked. Paper was extremely expensive and cottagers were prohibited from buying or selling it without a permit.

"There's a mill south of the city," Gavin said.

"Bookless?" Tamsin asked. Bookless meant off the books, a nonregistered business that operated outside official channels of commerce. A bookless shop had to piggyback onto a sanctioned business, so it was like two stores running out of one building. In Sevenna, all cottager businesses had to operate this way or risk being shut down by the Zunft. In his articles, her father called this a two-headed economy. One head smiles and nods at the master. The other keeps its eyes down and its mouth shut.

"No, Mr. Leahy's uncle works there," Gavin said. "He tells the owners that he buys it to sell to the fish markets."

On one table, piles of handbills were waiting to be folded. An imperfect portrait of her father smiled up at her under the words: *Justice for the August 5! Come to a Demonstration on Saturday in Mast Square. Speak Out Against the Ancestral Homes Act!*

"Nice portrait," Tamsin said, trying to sound positive, but the image of her father made her homesick. "Who does your art?"

"A kid named Theodore," Gavin said. "He does these amazing story pictures, too. You should see them sometime."

"Story pictures," Tamsin repeated, not sure she knew what he meant.

"It's stories told in a sequence of pictures instead of words," Gavin explained. "He sells a monthly packet of them with Navid and his friends."

"Hasn't the Zunft outlawed them yet?" Tamsin asked. Every time a new art form became popular, the Zunft tried to regulate, squash, or otherwise hinder the cottagers' creation of it and access to it. It was even illegal for cottagers to buy paint because the Zunft said they would use it to deface public buildings.

"Well, they probably would, except Theodore's not political," Gavin said. "He draws talking animals with clothes and flying rovers—that sort of thing."

"My sisters would love it, but it doesn't help our cause," Tamsin said.

"What kind of stories would you tell?" Gavin asked.

"True ones," Tamsin said. "Like what the Zunft did to Navid's hands or the sinking of the *Jubilee*."

"You should write another treatise for the *Bulletin*," Gavin said. "A longer one, about whatever you want. Or come on Saturday to Mast Square. Say a few words at the demonstration."

"My mother doesn't want people to know I'm in the city," Tamsin said.

"If you change your mind, let me know. It might help sort things out in your own mind," Gavin said.

"It's amazing what you've done here," Tamsin said, abruptly changing the subject. She didn't want to give a speech. People would expect her to be amazing, like her father, and she wouldn't live up to him. "I can't imagine how hard it was to get those presses."

"Your father did that," Gavin said. "He knows a mechanist

out of Norde. He helped us get the last three presses after the Zunft confiscated our other ones from us."

"Back on Aeren, we used to get shipments of machine parts from Norde," Tamsin said. "Mother would show us how to break them apart and sew the pieces into her stuffed toys."

"The ones she sells at Abel's Toys?" Gavin asked.

"You know about that?" Tamsin asked.

"Samuel Abel is one of our allies. We send messages through him all the time."

"We shipped the metal letters for the presses in toys, too," Tamsin said, pointing to the case with lead letters organized alphabetically in compartments. She picked up a tiny *a* and held it up in front of her eye.

"Each of these was carried across the Midmark Sea in a toy," she said. "Your spies are stuffed antelopes and fluffy raccoons."

"*A* is for antelope? *B* is for bunny?"

"I don't think we were that systematic," Tamsin said. "And I cheated once. I was tired of sewing, so I stuffed sixteen of these into a cat."

"Using toys as couriers was one of your family's more inspired ideas," Gavin said.

"Have you heard anything about the prison visit?" Tamsin asked. It had been Gavin who submitted the tangle of paperwork to request a visit with Michael Henry. So far, there had been no reply from the Zunft officials.

"I used your mother's address in Black Rock," Gavin said. "And the name of a relative. Your aunt, I think. If your mother hears something, she'll be in contact with you."

"Maybe my mother should go," Tamsin said. "Then she can yell at Papa herself instead of expecting me to do it."

"I don't think that's what she wants you to do," Gavin said. "Her feelings about the Rising can't be simple."

"Why didn't you join Father in the customs house?" Tamsin asked.

"Do you hate me for that?" Gavin asked.

"Why would you think that?" Tamsin said.

"Your father is my mentor," he said. "And my friend. He is the closest thing to a leader that we've ever had. But I believe the August Rising was misguided. He thought that he would make this grand gesture and all the cottagers would follow him."

"Why didn't they?" Tamsin asked.

"Well, on a very mundane level, not enough people knew what was happening," Gavin said. "I talked to him right after the Rising started in Port Kenney. It caught him by surprise, but he said it was an opportunity to show solidarity with the Aeren cottagers."

"That's what he told you?" Tamsin said, surprised to learn that her father had lied to Gavin. Michael knew all about what was happening in Port Kenney. He'd orchestrated it, and Tamsin herself had struck that match. Gavin obviously didn't know about her involvement either.

"Yes, he wanted me to join him and occupy the Grand Customs House," Gavin said.

"And you didn't?" Tamsin asked.

"No, Tamsin, I didn't," Gavin said. "Your father was angry with me about it, and I'm very sorry about that. But we weren't organized enough to make a grand gesture like that. I told him it was suicide."

"You think he made a mistake," Tamsin said.

"I understood his motivations," Gavin said. "He felt betrayed by his contacts in the Zunft, and he made an impulsive decision. It was a courageous gesture on the part of a good man."

Candlelight. She thought about the feel of the stone and the match in her hand. Had it been futile? Had anything been gained in that explosion of power and flame?

"I don't know why I did it," Tamsin said, choking on her words.

"Did what?" Gavin asked.

"I can't talk about it," Tamsin said, realizing how stupid that sounded since she was the one who had brought it up.

"It's all right," Gavin said. "I understand."

"Someone told me to do something and I didn't question it," Tamsin said. "I didn't stop to ask why. I did it. People got hurt. And I might have been wrong. What does that make me?"

"Some people live their whole lives and never ask why," Gavin said. "You're doing that now, Tamsin. And that means something. You've got to give yourself that, at least."

Tamsin stared at the case of metal letters. Gavin asked her what stories she would tell. Right now she felt like a blank page. She could sit back and let the world stomp all over her. But Tamsin didn't want it to be like that. She didn't want to be a passive observer like her mother. She wanted to write her own story and stamp it on the world.

13

SPEAK OUT FOR
THE AUGUST 5

A vigil will be held at eleven a.m. on Saturday in Mast Square to show support for the men arrested during the August Rising. These men should be treated fairly, allowed visits with their families, and given counsel to help them with their trials.

—*JFA Bulletin*, September 27

It was a beautiful autumn morning. Instead of studying, Tommy kept staring out of the open window at the old oak trees planted along the inside of the Seminary wall. Their leaves had changed late and they were now a picturesque band of crimson against the gray stones and the city beyond. It was unseasonably warm, and the birds were chirping as if they had forgotten that winter was coming. Tommy couldn't bring himself to focus on the schematic that he was supposed to draw by Monday.

A knock at the door startled him. Bern was usually the only one who visited his room, and he was on a walking holiday in the northern woods with some of the lads. When Tommy opened the door, Kristin and the black-haired girl, Ellie, were standing in the corridor. Kristin gave him a cheery smile. Ellie looked uncomfortable—Ellie, whose real last name was Hywel, but Tommy wasn't supposed to mention that.

"Hello," Tommy said, realizing that he hadn't brushed his hair or changed his clothes from the night before, when he fell asleep in his armchair in front of the fire. Seminary rules prohibited him from entertaining girls in his room, so he stood in awkward silence.

"It's a beautiful Saturday," Kristin said. "What are you doing inside?"

"Banging my head against my math homework," Tommy said, earning a little smile from Ellie. Bern had said she was a math genius, so she probably flew through assignments.

"We're going to see Mast Square," Kristin said. "You have to come with us."

Mast Square was a historical site on the south banks of the Lyone River. A large sailing ship stood at the heart of a courtyard surrounded by tenement buildings. The circumstances of its grounding were lost to history, and for years it had lolled on its side as if flung from the harbor by a giant's hand. Recently, it had been hoisted upright and turned into an open-air museum. Tommy had read about the ship's renovations, but hadn't had a chance to visit yet. That sounded like more fun than sitting in his room drawing a plan for a better icebox.

"You don't have to, if you're busy," Ellie said.

"I've always wanted to see it," Tommy said. "Let's go."

As they headed toward the front gate, Tommy felt an unexpected surge of happiness. He noticed a few glances from passing lads, but didn't really care what they thought. Strolling with the girls through the campus was the first time he'd felt like a real student, not just Bern's brother tagging along with some group that didn't want him. Ellie had a copy of *The Streets of Sevenna*, a pamphlet-size book of street maps. She kept flipping the pages as they crossed Seminary Square and through the shadow of the giant statue of the Vigilant Zunftman, a twenty-foot stone man with both fists raised above his carved shoulders.

"Why are his hands raised like that?" Kristin asked.

"I think he's giving a speech to the masses," Tommy said.

"It must be a very dramatic speech." Kristin laughed.

"I think it looks like he's holding an invisible rifle," Ellie said, still not looking up from her maps.

"You're right, it does," Kristin agreed.

"That's the last thing we need: soldiers with invisible guns," Tommy said.

"Maybe that's just what the cottagers need," Ellie muttered.

"Ellie!" Kristin scolded her. "You have to watch what you say."

"I'm not inside the Seminary walls," Ellie retorted. But then her eyes flicked to Tommy, as if she had remembered she was talking to the son of Colston Shore.

"No worries," Tommy assured her. "Which way do we go?"

"This way," Ellie said. They headed toward the harbor district, which was on the north side of the river but had a large population of cottagers living near the docks. She led them into a narrow alleyway lit only by sparse shafts of sunlight. Planks had been laid between the buildings to form a makeshift floor above the alley. Shabby furniture was visible through the gaps, and people paced the rickety boards above. At the end of the alley, a flight of crumbling granite steps descended into a long tunnel that doubled as a market. The air smelled like lantern oil and oranges, and the noise of the crowd echoed off the mossy walls. Despite the narrowness of the tunnel, it was jammed with wooden carts selling cabbages, salted meats, wreaths of dried flowers, and red tulips. Each cart sported a lantern, casting shifting shadows along the length of the passage.

"What is this place?" Kristin asked as they struggled to navigate through the crowds.

"A creepy carnival," Tommy said.

"It's a shortcut," Ellie replied.

"Are you sure?" Tommy asked. "How old is that book?"

"I think this is Piper Leaf Market," Ellie said. "My book only lists official Zunft sites, so it's not in here."

"We're in a place that doesn't officially exist?" Tommy said. "How did you know about it?"

"Hywel talked about tunnels that run under the city," Ellie said. "Most of them are old coal tunnels, and have been sealed off. He had some idea about transforming the tunnels into a transportation system that anyone could use to get around."

After Ellie mentioned Hywel, the conversation died away. The news that the cottagers had kidnapped the former chief administrator had broken very recently, and Tommy wasn't supposed to know Ellie's connection to Hywel anyway. They reached the end of the tunnel, climbed another set of crumbling steps, and emerged near Regent's Bridge. Built from reddish limestone, it had distinctive lion's-head carvings at both ends of the span.

"That's Mast Square," Ellie told them, pointing south across the Lyone where masses of people were spilling out of the square and into the street. "Maybe there's some kind of gathering."

"Let's go see," Kristin said. Fortunately, they were wearing ordinary street clothes with nothing to identify them as Seminary students. The girls had on long wool coats over their flowered dresses. If anyone studied their knee-high leather boots, they would see how expensive they were, but hopefully no one would be paying attention.

When they reached Mast Square on the opposite bank, they pushed their way through the crowd at the entrance. Once inside the large courtyard, there were so many spectators that it was hard to move at all. Solid blocks of tenement houses formed both the eastern and western walls, and scores of onlookers leaned out of windows, waving green handkerchiefs. The curved side of a majestic ship rose above the heads of the spectators. Seeing the old-fashioned sailing vessel perched in the heart of the city was even more impressive than Tommy had imagined, and he wished he could have seen it without all the people around. He couldn't imagine what circumstances could have brought such a ship so far inland.

"What are they celebrating?" Kristin asked.

"Maybe it's some kind of street performance?" Ellie wondered.

The crowd quieted as a woman stepped forward and raised her hands. From his angle below the prow, Tommy could only see the side of her face and the black curls tumbling down her back. She looked like she was in her forties, with starbursts of lines at the corners of her eyes.

"Fellows," she called out, her voice echoing around the silent square. "Please forgive me, I've never made a speech before. For

127

those who don't know me, my name is Meg Stevens. My husband is Jack. My son was Christopher."

She paused as a murmur of recognition rippled through the crowd. Her voice wavered a little, and she was gripping the edge of the prow as if she might fall over.

"They won't let our children get an education. They won't let us publish a newspaper. They won't let us own our homes. Now they threaten to send us to the estates to work as slaves and bleed us for a loaf of bread. What choice did the August 5 have?"

"Who's Jack Stevens?" Kristin whispered to Ellie and Tommy.

"One of the cottager rebels," Ellie whispered back.

"Our people are disappearing!" Meg Stevens raged. "Did you wake up one morning and find your mother, or your uncle, or your son had gone missing? Colston Shore expects us to believe that these people have trotted back to their ancestral estates like good little slaves. Well, that's a lie!"

"People are disappearing?" Kristin asked. "What is she talking about?"

"I don't think we should be here," Tommy whispered.

"We are the Children of the Islands!" Meg Stevens shouted. Her voice wasn't shaking anymore. "The rightful heirs to all the land. *We* are the warriors of old. *They* are fattened lambs. We are stronger than they'll ever be. And we will not be silenced!"

"We need to leave—" Tommy started to say. But the onlookers roared enthusiastically and drowned out his words. Suddenly, the cheers turned to shouts of warning, and people whirled toward a commotion near the entrance of the square. There was a flurry of movement, and the crowd surged, knocking Ellie to her knees. Tommy pulled her to her feet and strained to see what was happening. He couldn't see over the heads of the people, but he could hear rovers rumbling in the street in front of the square.

"What is it?" Kristin cried.

Tommy grabbed the girls' hands. "The Zunft!" he shouted over the crowd. But the frightened people crushed together and there was nowhere to run. The terrified mob pushed in all directions as Zunft soldiers riding black horses galloped into the square. Tommy struggled to stay on his feet while the soldiers spurred their excited mounts into the mob, swinging heavy truncheons indiscriminately.

Holding hands and moving in a tight huddle, Tommy, Ellie, and Kristin tried to force their way through the crowd. Nearby, a man tumbled to the ground in front of a line of mounted soldiers. Several people came to his aid, but the soldiers closed ranks, trampling several more people under the hooves of the riled animals. Tommy heard the thud of a truncheon and a young man wheeled backward clutching his bloody head. As the soldiers drove the crowd against one side of the square, they became so tightly surrounded that Tommy couldn't even lift his arms. The pressure of the bodies made it feel like his ribs were crushing his heart. Around him, everything seemed to be moving abnormally slow. The quivering mob paused for breath, and Tommy felt like a cornered fox run to exhaustion by dogs.

An eerie quiet descended on the square. One of the horses danced sideways as a guard pulled hard on its reins. The soldiers advanced on the small crowd that was now trapped against the wall. Beyond the line of skittish horses, the square was empty except for the injured lying on the ground. Suddenly, a gunshot rang out and then another. A man in a flat cap crouched on the roof of a nearby tenement building. He cradled a rat gun on his shoulder. At the sound of the second bullet whizzing through the air, the mob sprang to life and rammed forward into the line of soldiers. The horses reared back as the soldiers tried to rein them under control and drive them against the crowd.

In the confusion that followed, Tommy lost his sense of direction. He heard screams and the clatter of hooves. Terrified that they were going to fall and be trampled to death, he clung to the girls' hands with all his strength. Suddenly, Ellie yanked his arm painfully, and he followed blindly, dragging Kristin behind him. Ellie's head was down and she was dodging people and darting through holes in the crowd.

Kristin's hand was ripped from his. Tommy spun around as a mounted soldier loomed above her with a raised truncheon. He swung it down as if he meant to crush her skull. Tommy rushed toward her, but there were too many people between them. Kristin stood frozen, staring up at the soldier like she couldn't believe that he wanted to hurt her. At the last second, a young man pushed her out of the way. The truncheon cracked down on his shoulder and he fell to one knee. The soldier tugged on the reins and circled his horse around.

The young man struggled to his feet. His flat cap had been knocked off, and Kristin bent down and picked it up off the cobblestones as the soldier struggled to get his horse under control. Tommy grabbed Kristin's sleeve.

"Get out of here!" the young man shouted.

Tommy dragged Kristin into the crowd in the same direction that he'd seen Ellie disappear moments before. They clawed their way to the edge of the mob and caught sight of Ellie near the entrance to the square. She had climbed onto a low window ledge and was desperately scanning the crowd. She jumped down when she saw Tommy and Kristin, and the three of them didn't stop running until they reached Regent's Bridge. Tommy's muscles were quivering and his legs were unstable. When they reached the middle of the bridge, Kristin held out the man's flat cap. The cloth was covered in blood from where it had fallen on the ground. Kristin tossed the cap in the river without saying a word. They watched as it floated down the current, and Tommy thought about the anonymous cottager who had helped Kristin. *Gain five hundred honor points for saving a stranger from a crushed skull.*

"Act casual," Ellie said as they strolled back through Seminary Square. That struck Kristin as hilariously funny and she started giggling, which made Ellie and Tommy start laughing, too. For the rest of the walk back to the Seminary, one of them would start laughing nervously and the others would follow suit until Tommy felt light-headed from all the laughing. Once they reached Tauber Hall, they paused under the elm outside the entrance. Tommy marveled at how normal things looked: the lads playing Litball on the Green, the ivy-covered walls of the dormitory, and the birds chirping on the branches of the trees with crimson leaves.

"Well, thanks for the outing," Tommy said, and they started laughing again. But now the shock had worn off and it dawned on them all at the same time: there was nothing funny about the situation. The Zunft soldiers had attacked a peaceful demonstration. People had been hurt, and maybe killed.

"If my father finds out I was there, he'll be furious," Kristin said. "Your father would probably kill you, Tommy."

"Let's not tell anyone else," Tommy said. "Or talk about it again."

"At least not where anyone else can hear," Ellie whispered as they trudged up the stairs and into Tauber Hall.

14

FIFTY INJURED
IN MAST SQUARE

Mounted soldiers attacked a peaceful demonstration in Mast Square today. More than fifty people were injured. Four women sustained life-threatening injuries. There were at least ten arrests, including Meg Stevens, the wife of Jack Stevens, who is currently incarcerated and charged with treason for his involvement in the August Rising. "The Zunft gave no warning," said one man who wished to remain anonymous. "They didn't ask us to disperse. They charged in, hitting women and children with clubs."

—*JFA Bulletin*, September 29

"Mama, I'm here," Navid called down into the root cellar. From the top of the stairs, he could see a flicker of candlelight among the stacks and barrels. "Ma-ma! Do you need help?"

Katherine Leahy appeared at the bottom of the steep wooden

steps with a heavy sack of potatoes to make stew for the evening crowd. Navid scampered down partway and helped haul up the heavy load.

"How was school?" Katherine asked. Navid was too old for state-sponsored school, which ended at age ten for cottagers. But Gavin Baine and some of his friends ran a small school for a couple of hours during the day, which kids like Navid attended around their jobs and chores.

"It was math day," Navid said, dragging the sack into the kitchen.

"Well, you're good with your numbers," Katherine said.

"I like writing days better," Navid said. "Or politics days, when we read the newspaper."

"Maybe you'll be a journalist," Mrs. Leahy said. "Like Michael Henry."

"Some of the fellows said he kidnapped Mr. Hywel. Is that true?" Navid asked.

"Who was saying that?" Katherine asked.

"Some of the boys at school," Navid said.

Katherine looked hard at him. "It's not true. It's more Zunft lies."

"Well, they thought Mr. Henry did the right thing," Navid said. "They said Mr. Henry should have shot him, and *bam*, one less Zunftman."

"I don't want to hear you talking like that," Katherine said sternly. "Death is never that simple."

"I know, Mama," Navid said. "Do you need help with the stew?"

The pub was half-full even though it was only early afternoon. By four o'clock, the tables would be filled with hungry patrons.

"Not with dinner, love. The pies are already cooking," Katherine said. "This is stew for tomorrow, but I do need you to run some errands for me."

Navid nodded in agreement. He'd much rather do errands than help in the kitchen. He loved running through the streets, taking secret shortcuts that no one knew but him.

"You're such a good boy." Katherine smiled at him proudly. "Hold up two fingers."

Navid did. This had been their system for years.

Katherine tapped his first finger: "Head to Seminary Square. Visit Abel's Toys. Talk only to Samuel Abel. Say, 'I would like to buy a deer. A purple deer. I will name her Anna.' Repeat."

"I would like to buy a deer. A purple deer. I will name her Anna."

She tapped his second finger: "Go to Ash Street Garden. Sign my name for two packages. Leeks and carrots."

"Leeks and carrots."

Katherine kissed him on top of his head. "Thank you, love. See you at dinner."

Before she even finished talking, Navid was already out the door, flying across the teetering boards laid across the muddy yard, through the open gate, and into the alley behind the pub. On Killough Street, he stuck close to the wall as he dodged pedestrians and slow-moving wagons. Navid crossed Shadow Bridge and ran down the Strand. When he reached the crossroads at Linden Boulevard, a Zunft soldier stopped all foot traffic for a line of rovers that crawled south. Navid waited impatiently, like a horse before a race. He paced along the wooden fence, which was plastered with posters in support of the August 5: Michael. Brandon. Hector. Kevin. Jack. He knew them all personally.

They'd sat in his home or in the pub, eaten with his family, laughed with him. He and Jack regularly played kick ball in the alley behind the pub. Their ink-drawn faces stared out at him, larger than in real life. Navid wondered if one day his face would be on a poster like that. Maybe he didn't want to be a journalist like Michael Henry after all.

When the rovers finally passed, Navid darted across Linden and then ducked into Long Alley, which ran all the way into the city center. Long Alley was the collection site for Zunft merchants' trash, and the smell was unbearable, but it was nearly deserted and made for quick travel. Besides, Navid carried a scarf for these occasions. He covered his nose and mouth and ran as fast as he could.

At the end of Long Alley, the layout of the city changed. The city looked like a pretty painting, with white-stone buildings, trimmed lawns, and well-dressed people.

Zunft soldiers would target a cottager kid in Seminary Square, so Navid had to be careful there. His parents had never registered Navid's birth with the Zunft, and he didn't carry identification. The Zunft gave one bag of flour per year for every child, so by not registering him, the Leahys had less to eat. But his parents believed it was better to be anonymous, and Navid was happy to be a nonperson in the eyes of the Zunft.

Abel's Toys was in a shopping district near the Seminary. In the northern districts, the buildings were farther apart, so navigating the roofs would be more challenging, but Navid was an excellent jumper. As he scampered up the fire ladder in the alley and onto a town house roof, he planned his route. He would face three dizzying jumps and two scary ledges—still better than being harassed on the ground. He could see the walled Seminary with its pavilions and green fields for playing Litball. From his bird's-eye view, it looked like paradise. He imagined the lads in their crimson jackets, each sporting his team's colors on a scarf around his neck. Navid wouldn't admit it to anyone, but he envied their easy lives as sons of the Zunft.

When he was two blocks away from Abel's Toys, he shimmied down a drainpipe, went two blocks out of his way to avoid the Records Hall, and finally relaxed when he reached Dawson Street, where both cottager and Zunft merchants sold their wares. The Zunft had the shops, but the cottagers had the open stalls, and the crowds frequented both. Buskers played music along the street, and Navid wished he had a coin to toss into the fiddler's hat in front of Abel's Toys.

Navid pushed the heavy gilded door open and was greeted by the scent of cedar and vanilla candles. Abel's Toys was the most famous toy store on the Islands. Its owner, Samuel Abel, had been an important Zunftman who left the Chamber to become a toy maker. He had a reputation for high-quality craftsmanship and whimsy, and almost every Zunft baby had an Abel's stuffed toy in the crib from birth. They ranged from palm-size to life-size, and they were every living—and fantastical—creature you could imagine.

Mr. Abel was helping a Zunftwoman, so Navid clasped his hands behind his back to show that he was well behaved, and gawked at the shelves until the woman left with her package.

Samuel Abel turned his attention to Navid. "Good afternoon, young fellow. What can I do for you?"

Navid smiled shyly at the floor. He had been to Mr. Abel's shop many times before, and the toy maker knew exactly who he was. Mr. Abel was like a big kitten, but you had to pretend that he was as mean as any Zunft shopkeeper. Of course, most Zunft shopkeepers wouldn't have let cottager children inside their shop.

"Good afternoon, sir," Navid said. He pulled off his cap to be polite. "I would like to buy a deer. A purple deer. I will name her Anna."

Mr. Abel nodded. "I'll be right back," he said, and disappeared into the storage room behind the carved door.

While Navid was waiting, another Zunftwoman with two young girls came into the toy shop. She impatiently rang the bell on the front counter while her children poked at the stuffed animals, knocking over a display of fuzzy mice.

Mr. Abel returned with a brown package, which he thrust at Navid. "Tell Mr. Smith to place his order earlier," he said grumpily. "I'm not made of time."

"Yes, sir," Navid said, tucking the lumpy package under his arm. He cringed as one of the girls tipped over a blue horse while her mother ignored her entirely. Then the door shut behind him, and Navid was off running again. He took side streets until he reached the Lyone, darted up the quay, and crossed Seventh Stone Bridge. When he was finally back on safe ground in South Sevenna, he narrowly dodged a wagon, waved as the driver cursed at him, and sprinted toward Ash Street Garden.

Navid was approaching the large flour mill at the corner of Ash Street when he heard shouting. A group of people, most of them holding empty flour sacks, were yelling at a woman standing on the steps of the open doorway, her hands on her hips defiantly.

"You're a foul-mouthed bastard!" she shouted at one of the people in the street.

Navid sidled up beside a boy of about seven, who looked worried as he watched the adults arguing in front of the mill. An Aeren seashell hung from a piece of twine around his neck, a sure sign that his family was political. Navid had seen him with his parents at the Plough and Sun, but he couldn't remember his name.

"What's going on?" Navid asked the boy.

"They don't have flour to sell, and the man is saying they sold it to the Zunft instead," the boy said.

Several men shouted at the woman, who turned a deep shade of red. Navid assumed they were insulting her, but he didn't know what the words meant.

"Why do they think she did that?" he asked the boy.

"You're a traitor!" a blond man yelled. His fists were balled up at his sides. Someone else—Navid couldn't see who—threw a rock that barely missed the woman's head.

"Bastards!" she yelled again. She quickly ducked inside and slammed the door and the sound of a metal lock sliding shut rang across the cobblestones.

"Now we're turning on one another?" yelled another woman in the crowd.

There was a scuffle, and the blond man punched another man in the face. The victim stumbled back, regained his footing, and charged at his attacker. As soon as the two tumbled down into the gravel, more men started brawling in front of the flour mill. Navid and the other boy glanced at each other in alarm. A fight was no place to be if you were shorter than everyone else.

It seemed like more people were arriving every moment and the street corner was getting crowded. Navid tapped the boy on the shoulder and jerked his head to indicate it was time to leave. They ran together until they reached the end of the street, then the smaller boy veered off on McCall Street, waving goodbye to Navid.

"See you!" Navid called. Then he looked back at the fight, which had grown to a dozen people scuffling as the crowd around them jeered and shouted. Navid wondered how big it would get before the Zunft arrived, but he wasn't stupid enough to wait around and find out.

He was out of breath by the time he reached Ash Street Garden, a communal garden available to anyone who would put the hours into helping it grow. It was the only reliable source of vegetables for most cottagers who lived in the city, and Navid spent at least ten hours a week doing chores for the head gardener, a tiny, white-haired woman named Nova James. The garden was the size of a city block and completely walled in. Nova told him it had once been a prison, but they'd taken down everything except the walls.

Navid ducked in the little gate on the north side, which was the only gate that was ever unlocked, even during the day. He loved crossing from the gray, bustling streets into the quiet of the garden. Real glass houses lined the perimeter, and inside them summer plants thrived in the hot, moist air. In the growing seasons, the beds outside were planted in a spiral pattern with circular paths that wound toward a raised tier of earth. An elaborately carved wooden pillar marked the heart of the garden, which was now a lonely sentinel among the brown leaves and untilled soil.

Nova was coming out of one of the houses, sweat beading her age-lined face. Navid knew lots of people who were good with their hands, but Nova was a true master. She could make anything grow anywhere, and always seemed to find an extra bunch of carrots or bag of potatoes for a family in need. Nova smiled at him and handed him a basket filled with leeks and carrots.

"How'd you know?" he asked.

"Magic." She smiled. "Now run home. Your mother is expecting you."

"There's no magic, Nova," he told her. It was a running discussion between the two of them. She insisted that she could cast spells. He told her there were no such things as witches.

"What about my glass houses?" she said. "I make things grow even when it's cold."

"Glass isn't magic," he said.

"No, but it's very expensive," she said, laughing and tousling his hair.

"I'll see you tomorrow," he shouted as he darted back to the north gate.

Before he plunged into the teeming streets of Sevenna, he glanced back at the garden and imagined a purple deer leaping through the lengthening shadows.

At dawn, Tamsin finished scrubbing the sticky filth off the tables at the Estoria and headed back to the Leahys' row house at the end of her shift. She was a bartender now rather than a dishwasher, so the money was better. But now she worked constantly, often for days on end without a day off. Forget about writing anything for

Gavin—there was no time left between shifts. Her father used to say that the Zunft made the cottagers work long hours so they wouldn't have time to rebel, and she believed him. The more she worked, the more money she had to send home, but increasingly her life felt like a hangman's noose with a knot she was tying herself.

Ever since the riot in Mast Square, there had been patrols along the Shadow and Seventh Stone Bridges. She hoped to avoid the soldiers if she crossed the butchers' district and took the quay to Hanged Bridge instead. She hated that she couldn't go where she wanted without fear of being arrested. She was exhausted, and the thought of having to go nearly a mile out of her way made her furious. Lately, she'd been angry so often that it felt like a poison she alone was drinking. Something had to change. She couldn't spend her life serving Zunftmen in the Estoria, but she couldn't stop either—money had to be sent to Aeren or her sisters would suffer. "Trapped. I'm trapped," Tamsin whispered to herself with every step through the butchers' district.

The area was a maze of small shops and slaughterhouses, and the air always seemed thick like broth. Tamsin wondered if the blood of the animals somehow hung in the air. As she turned a corner, she caught a glimpse of herself reflected in a shop window. She hadn't looked in a mirror since she moved to Sevenna, and she almost didn't recognize herself. She was thinner than when she was back on Aeren, probably because she didn't have any milk here. Her mother kept goats, and Tamsin and her sisters drank milk at every meal. As she stared at her reflection, she realized that her fifteenth birthday had come and gone. She'd been so busy serving drinks to the Zunft that it had never occurred to her that she was a year older.

She reached up and loosed her long hair from its braid. She still wore the long hair of her childhood—at least that hadn't changed. She thought of her sister Eliza, and how they used to braid each other's hair before bedtime. What was Eliza doing right now? How were the little ones holding up without her? And her father, what was he thinking about as he sat in some dark cell in the compound? Tamsin felt like an outcast from the warmth and safety of her mother's house. She was furious with Anna for that. But if she was honest with herself, Tamsin knew it wasn't her mother who had put the match in her hand in Port Kenney. Tamsin had done that all by herself.

When she reached the Leahys' row house, she found it was empty for the first time since she'd moved to Sevenna. Tamsin stood in the foyer, breathing in the silence. In her new life, she was never alone. She was surrounded by people at the cabaret, at the pub, and even at the row house. Tamsin hung her coat on a peg, and went to the kitchen. Usually, she did the cleanup when she got home, but today the kitchen was spotless. There was a note from Mrs. Leahy: *No chores for you today. Get some rest. There's a package on your bed.*

Tamsin built a fire in the woodstove and lit a candle to take to her dark room. She dragged herself up the stairs, so tired that she felt dizzy. The tiny room was frigid, although heat was steadily rising through the grate in the floor. In the glow of the candle-light, she saw a brown paper package on her pillow. She tore off the paper and found a finely crafted purple deer from Abel's Toys. Her mother made stuffed animals for Abel's, and Tamsin knew right away that this was her mother's handiwork. She felt her heart pounding faster at the prospect of a note from her family. Particularly a note carried in secret and not through the censored post. Maybe her mother had forgiven her and wanted her to come home.

Tamsin yanked her sewing basket from under the bed. Using a needle, she gently broke the seam under the deer's chin. A tiny roll of paper had been stashed inside the head. Then she eagerly unrolled the note: *Prison visit. October 5, 9 a.m. Mary Henry.* Mary Henry was an aunt who had died a few years earlier. Tamsin pushed the stuffing around and found her deceased aunt's identification card. Now she had the paperwork to be a dead woman.

She pressed on every corner of the purple deer to see if she had missed anything, but that was it. Angrily, she threw the purple deer against the wall. Her mother could have written her a letter and given her news about her sisters. She could easily have said more, but she chose not to. Tamsin set the note alight with the candle, nearly burning her fingers. She swept the ashes into the candleholder. She unfastened her worn ankle boots and threw the quilt over herself.

But after a few seconds, she climbed out of bed and picked the deer off the floor. She sewed the seam closed under its chin and placed it on her bedside table. Then she blew out the candle and curled up under the quilt again. She was going to see her father, and that's all her mother had to say.

15

LABOR SHORTAGES IN WAKE OF ANCESTRAL HOMES ACT

With rumors about deportations swirling around Sevenna, have some residents chosen to return to their ancestral islands rather than risk detention in the Zunft Compound? The owner of a paper mill in the Sevenna southlands reports a labor shortage from the loss of workers who disappeared soon after the passage of the act.

Labor activist Beth Harl doubts that the shortages are truly from people leaving the capital voluntarily. She believes that the Zunft are behind their disappearances and has been seeking information about her missing brother, Devon. "We talked to my neighbors up and down the row," Miss Harl said. "Everyone knows someone who's gone missing. My brother would never have left Sevenna by choice. He doesn't know any other island."

—JFA Bulletin, October 4

On a bleak day in early October, Tamsin climbed the steep road that led to the Zunft Compound. It had taken her an hour to cross Sevenna as she dodged the crowds and traffic. Now she was a solitary figure approaching the Zunft's seat of military power, and she felt an unexpected surge of confidence. In her pocket, she carried a dead woman's name. No one would know that Tamsin was the one who had blown up the warehouse in Port Kenney. All they were going to see was a scrawny cottager girl with a bag of apples, not a defiant rebel.

Constructed on a windswept plateau above the northern edge of the city, the compound was surrounded by high stone walls with spikes embedded in the top. Two austere towers rose above the wall and into the rainy sky. She couldn't yet see the main building where her father was imprisoned. Her boots made crunching noises on the gravel as she approached, and the two guards watched her with their hands on their chatter-guns. The iron blast doors were wide open and the teeth of the portcullis showed above them. Inside the courtyard, lines of guards marched in formation, while an officer shouted commands in time with their steps.

"Name?" asked a guard with a notebook.

"Mary Henry," Tamsin said.

"Here to see?" the guard asked.

"Michael Henry," she said.

They checked her identification, peered into the bag of apples that she carried, and confirmed her appointment in the ledger. To her surprise, the guard waved her through with no more trouble. Tamsin was relieved until she realized that was only the pre-checkpoint to get to the main checkpoint. Once inside the prison, she was shown to a windowless room, told to undress completely, except her shift, and to lay everything out on the table. Her confidence evaporated as she stood in the corner, half-naked, while a burly guard inspected her clothing, especially the seams. He slammed the apples around until they were covered with mushy bruises, and inspected her fake identification card several times.

Finally, the guard threw her clothing on the floor at her feet and stared at her for a long moment. First, she felt like a cow on an auction block, but the longer he considered her, the more his interest began to feel more sinister.

"Can I get dressed?" she asked.

"Did I tell you to speak?" he barked.

When he moved toward her, she flinched. He had the authority of the Zunft behind him. The circumstances of her birth afforded her no rights. From the moment she was born, men like this guard felt like they deserved power over her. She clenched her hands into fists but before he reached her, the door swung open and another soldier stood in the threshold. He frowned at the sight of her. "Get dressed, girl," he said. "Your brother is in the visitors' room."

The burly guard loomed over her for a moment longer. He was standing on her clothes with his filthy boots. Tamsin knew she shouldn't, but she tipped her head up and met his gaze. He despised her, she could tell by his eyes. Hurting her wouldn't trouble his conscience at all. The other soldier had moved into the corridor, but he was still in hearing range. Finally, the first guard spun on his heel and marched out, giving her privacy to put on her now-muddy clothes.

The visitors' room was a long, low-ceilinged space that

reminded her of a stable. Instead of stalls, there were rough-cut wood tables along the walls. The room was abnormally bright from the numerous volt-cell lights attached to the walls and Tamsin felt disoriented under their harsh glare. The tables were empty except for the one in the center where her father sat with his hands chained to a metal loop. At thirty-five years old, her father was bald headed and muscular. He'd always looked more like a boxer than the journalist he actually was. Tamsin had seen him speak before, and he *dominated* people's attention. Hundreds turned out for his speeches, and it was like he knew what to say to get people screaming for action, for change.

But two months in prison hadn't been kind to him. He looked like a faded version of himself. His complexion was sallow and his strong jawline had begun to sag. The guard led her to the table, indicated that she should sit across from her father, and dropped the apples unceremoniously on the table. He marched back to the door where he stood at silent attention. Tamsin peered closely at her father, who disarmed her with a boyish grin. Despite the grim conditions, he still exuded powerfulness. As a child, she'd always felt safest around him. She'd hide behind him during their play fights against imaginary bears. Tamsin and her sisters would squeal with mock terror as their father swung the broom valiantly against the shadows on the wall of the cottage. Nothing could hurt her when her father was around.

"You brought apples." Michael smiled. The chain around his wrists was long enough that he could pick one up. He took an enthusiastic bite. "My favorite."

"They're mush," Tamsin said, remembering how she and her father used to pick apples together from the orchard off Miller's Road. Even though she had promised herself that she wouldn't cry, tears pricked her eyes. She tried to blink them back, but they leaked down her face.

"Ah, my love, I think they're perfect," he said happily. "It tastes like Aeren on a windswept autumn day."

"I miss you so much," she whispered.

"Let's cry for one more minute," he said gently. "And then let's put our tears away and get down to business."

Tamsin wiped her face on her sleeve. "A minute is too long to bother with weeping."

"That's my girl," he said. "How is my family?"

"I get letters from Eliza and she says they are doing well. Iris turned seven last week, and Eliza said she's as strong as a horse."

"And your mother?" Michael asked.

"I don't know, Papa," Tamsin admitted. "Mama hasn't written me."

"Your mother is a woman of few words," Michael said. "And she's had to stay very strong."

"I think she's angry with me," Tamsin said.

"If she's angry at anyone, it's me," Michael said. "She would never blame you. She loves you immensely. I know she is doing what she can to help us."

"Maybe," Tamsin said.

"And how are you?" Michael asked.

"I am . . . angry," Tamsin said. "At the world," she added in case he thought she meant she was angry at him.

"I have heard of the charges against me and I am angry at the world as well."

"At first they said it was extremist factions," Tamsin said. "That's what we all thought."

"Love, there are no extremist factions. There are only angry and confused cottagers who hate being slaves. None of them are responsible for what has happened to Hywel."

"People are going missing every day," Tamsin whispered. "There are rumors they are leaving to join the extremists, but I don't believe that. Are they being brought here? Have you heard anything?"

"No, I haven't," he said. "But those rumors are lies. The Zunft are kidnapping those people. I could have stopped such tragedies. I could have saved those people."

"Papa, I'm confused," she said. "If I say *candlelight* and *no candlelight*, do you know what I'm talking about?"

"Yes," he said quietly. "Be careful, though."

The room had a low ceiling with wooden rafters, and their voices didn't echo. There was one guard near the door at the far end, but he didn't seem particularly interested in them.

"I feel like I'm at a crossroads between these two paths," she said. "I have a friend who doesn't believe in 'candlelight.' You know him. He worked with you before."

"What's his name?" Michael asked.

"Gavin," Tamsin whispered.

"Ah," Michael said. "Of course. And what of 'candlelight'? Is there someone leading you down that road?"

"Just myself. And you."

The door opened and another guard entered the room. The two stood there talking and glancing over at Tamsin and her father. She'd been warned that the visit might be short because the guards started her allotted time from the minute she arrived at the gate, not when she first saw her father. But she couldn't bear to have it end so quickly. She'd barely had time to talk at all.

"We don't have long," Michael said. "But I want you to stay away from Gavin. He's a traitor who deserted me in my time of need. If men like Gavin had stood with me at the Grand Customs House, I'd be leading Seahaven right now instead of rotting to death here."

"Gavin betrayed you?" Tamsin said. Gavin had told her that he hadn't participated in the Rising because he thought it would be suicide, but she had no idea that her father was angry about it or considered her friend a traitor.

"You're clever," Michael said. "People flock to you. You have this energy, like an inner flame that people want to be near. You've been that way since you were young. There was always a string of children following you no matter what you did."

"I was the eldest," Tamsin said. "That's why."

"No, you're a natural leader," her father said. "You take after me. We're destined to be leaders. We're worthy of legends."

"What do you want me to do?" Tamsin asked.

"You must continue what I started," Michael whispered. "You must use whatever means necessary. Seek out the families of those arrested with me. They will rally to your cause. Do not spend time with turncoats and cowards."

The guards moved toward them with a sense of finality. The meeting was over.

"Go quietly, without saying goodbye," he whispered, his eyes flashing with anger. "Take up my sword, daughter. Don't let me die in vain."

16

CRIME RATE FALLS IN SEVENNA

The city of Sevenna is enjoying the lowest rates of cottager crime in almost a century. Incidents of larceny, assault, and arson have all fallen dramatically. Zunft officers attribute this success to increased patrols and the decisive leadership of Chief Administrator Shore.

—*Zunft Chronicle*, October 5

"Hey!" the guard shouted, putting a hand up to stop Tommy from entering the lecture hall. "Where's your student's card? And why aren't you wearing your uniform?"

"Oh, sorry," Tommy said. He reached into his jacket and pulled out the folded paper that had his name, his physical description, and the official Zunft seal. No one had ever checked his card before a lecture and he'd never heard of wearing school uniforms to ordinary classes. But inside the hall, the lads were decked out in their Seminary attire.

"If you're not wearing your uniform, then I have to see your identification," the guard explained.

"Did something happen?" Tommy asked.

"More cottager violence in Mast Square," the guard said crossly. He brusquely took Tommy's card, but when he read the name on the card, his demeanor changed. "Are you the chief administrator's son?"

"Yes," Tommy said. "I'll wear my uniform next time."

"Off you go," the guard said with forced cheerfulness. "Have a nice day!"

Rannigan was striding up the steps to the podium as Tommy slid into an open seat near the door.

"So now you have to wear uniforms to prove you're Zunft," Rannigan said, surveying the lecture hall. "You lads look . . ."

". . . smarter than usual," someone piped up in the back, and everyone laughed.

"I couldn't have said it better myself," Rannigan said. Then he opened his lecture book, signaling the end of informal banter. Tommy didn't really see why the uniforms were a solution to cottager violence. It seemed more like posturing than an actual safety measure.

"Continuing from our discussion of the estate system from last week," Rannigan said, picking up his wooden pointer from the podium. "We talked about how the system reflects natural law. How a man's land and manor are inherited by birth. We talked about how cottagers owe labor to the Zunft in exchange for use of the land. The Zunft Chamber was set up after the War for Aeren. The Zunft had secured its power, but now it was embroiled in factional discord and infighting. A great power struggle emerged among the ten great estates."

Rannigan unclipped the map of Seahaven that hung from a roller above the stage. It was a detailed map drawn by a master cartographer. Tommy loved maps, particularly the old ones that listed all the ruin sites and standing stones. He sat up straighter as Rannigan took his pointer and tapped Norde, the largest island in Seahaven. Before the professor could speak, a student hooted and called, "Norde forever!"

There was a moment of silence while everyone waited to see if Rannigan would punish him, but the professor smiled. "Apparently we have a Norde man with us today. Any others? If you hail from the land of pine trees, fish, and frozen toes, raise your hand."

All the boys from Norde stomped their feet and whistled. With an amused expression, Rannigan pointed to Catille, which had a distinctive half-moon shape. Tommy had read about the steep mountains rising out of its rugged coastline, but he'd never visited the island himself.

"What about the mysterious southern isle of Catille?" Rannigan asked. "Do we have anyone from the wild, dangerous jungle?"

A lone boy sheepishly raised his hand, and Rannigan acknowledged him with his pointer. "Good man. You're the future of the Zunft down south."

Rannigan smiled directly at Tommy when he said, "And to our west, the green hills of Aeren—"

About twenty of the students in the class were from Aeren, and they clambered to their feet, whooping like excited children. Tommy clapped with them until Rannigan motioned for everyone to sit down.

"Lastly, we have Sevenna Island, seat of knowledge, home to civilization," Rannigan said, but he raised his hands before the students from Sevenna made any noise. "Let's show our allegiance to this great island by sitting quietly and listening to the rest of this lecture."

The students laughed and Rannigan tugged the bottom edge of the map and sent it spinning up around the roller. Rannigan paced along the edge of the stage before diving back into the history lesson.

"After the War for Aeren, the Islands were divided into two estates. If you want to learn more about these families, read *The History of the Ten Families* by Alexander Carver. It's an excellent book. Also, you should note that of all the lads in this room, only two of you are members of the original ten families: Thomas Shore and Dennett Crane.

"By the beginning of this century, those ten estates had been broken into smaller entities, but at its inception, the Zunft Chamber was established to ensure fairness among the ten estates. An adjudicator would see to it that all houses be heard in the Chamber. The houses would appoint one member as the chief administrator, a position that would shift depending on political alignments. No one person should be chief administrator indefinitely because that would lead to corruption and, ultimately, the downfall of the Zunft. Today, the Chamber is much larger. We have fifty estates represented in the Chamber.

"The system is simple yet it represents the apex of political thought," Rannigan said. Tommy couldn't help but think this was anything but simple. How could there be an apex of thought?

Wouldn't people keep thinking of new things as old ideas morphed into new ones?

"Chief Administrator Shore is enlightened and compassionate. He knows that the market cannot survive under the heavy hand of subsidies. By ending the sale of cheap bread, he is ultimately protecting all of our futures. No doubt we will continue to see unrest, like the bread riot last week in Mast Square. The problem is simply this: the cottagers are being forced to work harder than they've become accustomed to doing. Their reactiveness is sad but not surprising."

Rannigan launched into a mind-numbingly detailed story about a mill and the process through which grain was stored and then divided according to a complicated equation based on the growing capacities of the ten oldest estates . . . and Tommy stopped paying attention. Rannigan had called the violence in Mast Square a bread riot, which wasn't true at all. *Lose fifty honor points for lying to your class.*

"So that's your assignment for the week, gentlemen," Rannigan said. "An essay on the economic benefits of ending the subsidy. Have it on my desk by the start of next week's class. You're encouraged to visit shopkeepers and include interviews as source material."

Tommy filed out of the lecture hall with the other boys, who were laughing about some wild match on the Litball field the night before. The boys crowded together as they exited the hall, and hemmed in on all sides by bodies, Tommy had a flash of fear as he remembered the horses running the crowd into the wall in Mast Square.

"Tommy, we're heading to the dining hall. You in?" Kristoph asked. He was one of Bern's friends. He was also a foul-mouthed boy who criticized anyone and anything, as long as they weren't within hearing range. Ellie and the other girls were some of his favorite targets.

"Thanks, but I've got another lecture," Tommy lied. The students were still bunched up at the door waiting for their turn to exit. Tommy resisted the urge to shove everyone out of the way and sprint into the sunlight.

"We'll see you at the Estoria?" Dennett said. They had finally exited the hall, and now outside, Tommy felt himself relax.

"Yes, tonight," Tommy agreed. He'd promised Bern that he would go out to a cabaret with him and his friends. It was the third time that Bern had asked him. Tommy had made excuses twice before and didn't think he was going to get away with it again without serious grief from his brother.

Tommy planned to go back to his room and study, but there were people milling about in front of Tauber Hall. Zunft soldiers guarded the entrance and a rover was parked near the outer wall. A group of boys who lived in his dormitory stood huddled in a tight group near the door. Ellie was standing by herself under the large oak in front of the hall.

"Could we go into our rooms already?" a student shouted.

The doors flew open and a man in a long coat and bowler hat burst through. He was immediately followed by two guards carrying a stretcher, which was loaded into the passenger compartment on the rover. The person on the stretcher was covered by a sheet up to their neck, and Tommy couldn't see their face.

"Finally!" one of the lads yelled as the soldiers moved away from the entrance. Tommy, who had been paying attention to the guards, jumped because Ellie was now standing inches away from his elbow. Her eyes were red, like she'd been crying.

157

"Are you okay?" Tommy asked. "What's wrong?"

"Can you go for a walk?" Ellie asked.

Tommy worried what Kristoph and the other lads would say if they saw him, but he knew they should be in the dining hall by now. Besides, he had been dying to talk to Ellie and Kristin about what had happened on Saturday in Mast Square, now that he'd had time to sort through it in his head.

"Sure. Let's go," he said, leading her toward Dawson Street Gate, which was the farthest entrance from the dining hall. The guard at the gate nodded to them as they left the confines of the Seminary and crossed onto Dawson Street, which was crowded with shoppers. A fiddler played in front of Abel's Toys, and the lively music followed them as they headed toward Sebastian's Circle, the little park that was known for its tulips in the spring.

"That was Charlotte on the stretcher," Ellie said.

"Is she sick?" Tommy asked.

"She's weak," Ellie said furiously. Then her face softened. "Sorry, I didn't mean that. She can't take being an outcast. Everyone hates us, and she blames herself. She says she feels sick all the time. I can't remember the last time she ate more than a slice of bread."

"I'm sorry," Tommy said. "I wish the situation was different."

"Really?" Ellie retorted. "Then why don't you do something about it?"

Tommy felt his cheeks go red. Why was she mad at him?

"Sorry," Ellie said, resting her hand on his arm. "That was rude. I'm worried about Charlotte."

"Just because I'm Colston Shore's son doesn't mean that I can snap my fingers and make things different," Tommy said.

"I know," Ellie said. "I really didn't mean it."

There was an awkward silence and Tommy tried to think of something to say, but Ellie spoke first: "Kristin told you who I was, right?"

"Hywel's relation?" Tommy said. "Don't worry. I won't tell anyone. I wanted to ask you how you were holding up on Saturday, but . . ."

"Things got incredibly insane?" Ellie finished his thought for him.

"It didn't seem real until a few hours later, and then I realized I was covered in bruises," Tommy said.

"Did you see Kristin?" Ellie said. "She must have gotten hit on the side of the head and didn't even know it. Her ear puffed up and turned purple."

"Is she all right?"

"She pretended to be sick to avoid a family gathering," Ellie said. "She didn't know how she would explain it to her parents."

"In class today, Rannigan was talking about what happened in Mast Square," Tommy told her. "He called it a bread riot."

"Well, he's a bully and a liar, so I guess we know how much his thoughts are worth," Ellie said.

When they reached the park, they crossed under a wrought-iron trellis and into the stillness under the trees. Ellie wandered over to a bench that was partially hidden from the path by a hedge. Tommy sat down on the other end of the bench. He leaned forward and rested his hands on his knees. A pair of squirrels played chase around the trunk of a tree, and they watched in companionable silence.

"I saw how Rannigan treated Charlotte," Tommy said finally.

"Kristin said it was even worse when they were alone together. Can't she report him or something?"

"To whom?" Ellie asked. "He's a likable guy and friends with all the other professors. If she told anyone, they either wouldn't believe her or wouldn't care."

"There have to be decent men among them," Tommy said.

"Maybe," Ellie agreed. "But being decent isn't enough. Someone would need to be brave enough to stand up against Rannigan."

"Will Charlotte go home now?" Tommy asked.

"She doesn't have much choice," Ellie said bitterly. "I hate the smug justifications of the men in power. They make the rules, so trying to argue with them is pointless. They create their own logic."

"What about you and Kristin?" Tommy asked.

"Thankfully, I don't have a professor like Rannigan breathing down my neck," Ellie said. "And I'll never leave voluntarily. They'll have to kick me out."

"You'd rather put up with the grief than go home?" he asked.

"Well, considering I don't have a home," she said. "I was Hywel's ward, not a close relation. With him gone, it's not like I can stay in his house."

"Have you talked to that investigator, Sanneral? Is there any progress?"

"You know him?" Ellie said. "The man couldn't *investigate* his way out of a paper bag. I can't believe our system favors men like that."

"I met him at the same party where I first talked to Kristin," Tommy said.

"I was called to the headmaster's office a few weeks ago," Ellie said. "He asked me a few questions. Dumb questions. He struck me as exceedingly incompetent."

"I'm sorry you have to go through this, Ellie," Tommy said.

"Honestly, it doesn't seem real," Ellie said. "I have to remind myself that Hywel is a prisoner somewhere. I can't get my head around it. I didn't know him very well. I was only his ward for a few months before he vanished, but the thought of him trapped somewhere is horrible."

"I hope he's okay," Tommy said.

"I'm not sure your father does," Ellie snapped. There was an awkward silence, and then she spoke again. "Sorry, I tend to open my mouth without thinking."

"You don't need to apologize," Tommy said. "Whenever we're not in Seminary, you can say whatever you want. About my family. About my hair. About the horrible state of the world."

"I've been meaning to talk to you about your hair," Ellie said.

Tommy's hands flew up to the sides of his head while Ellie laughed.

"Kidding! You're such a girl!" she howled. She was the least self-conscious girl Tommy had ever met. Most Zunft daughters tried to act formal or flirt in this really forced way. Even Kristin had seemed a little unnatural, at least at the dinner party. But there was nothing false about Ellie.

"Can I tell you a secret?" he asked.

"Do you think you can trust me?" she said.

"Actually, I do," he told her sincerely.

"Why?"

161

"Because you know what it's like to have your father be the chief administrator," Tommy said.

"Hywel is *not* my father," Ellie said. "But that aside, you can tell me whatever you want. It's safe with me."

"I was in Port Kenney during the Rising," Tommy said. "Someone had blown up a Zunft warehouse, and soldiers chased me into the forest. I got away from them, but I found this girl lying under a tree. She had burns, as if she'd been in the fire."

"A cottager?" Ellie asked. "Do you think she might have been one of the rebels?"

"I don't know," Tommy said.

"What did you do?" Ellie asked.

"I took her to the nearest cottage and left her on the porch," Tommy said. "Soldiers were patrolling the woods, and I was scared we'd get caught."

"Did you ever find out who she was?" Ellie asked.

"No, but I worry about her sometimes," Tommy confessed. "You know what scares me? That I didn't do enough or didn't do the right thing."

"What would your father have told you to do?" Ellie asked.

"Report her to the passing soldiers," Tommy answered. "Let them figure out what she was doing there."

"Where was your father that day?" Ellie asked.

"At the manor," Tommy answered.

"On Aeren? With you and your brother?"

"Yes. Why?" Tommy asked.

Ellie picked at a thread on her black skirt. Her leather boots were scuffed and unpolished, and the cuffs of her jacket were frayed. Either she didn't care about her appearance or she didn't have enough money to care—either way, Tommy found her all the more endearing.

"I think you did the right thing," Ellie said after a moment. "It's not like you could take her to your manor house with your father there. And if there were patrols in the woods, you didn't have a lot of time to think your decision through."

Tommy felt a strange sense of relief. It felt good to finally tell someone about the cottager girl in the lavender dress. Beside him, Ellie frowned as she peered over his shoulder: "Speaking of patrols," she said.

Three Zunft soldiers entered the park and headed down the path in their direction. The soldiers weren't paying any attention to them, but Ellie was obviously uncomfortable.

"Let's head back," she said. "I need to check on Kristin and then go to the hospital to see Charlotte."

"Of course." Tommy understood, but he felt disappointed. When they stood up, she linked arms with him, like they were old friends on an outing. He wondered if the gesture was for the benefit of the soldiers so they would pay less attention to the two of them.

"Let's make a pact," Ellie said as they strolled back down Dawson Street. "That bench is the safe zone where we can talk about whatever we want. We're going to come back there someday."

"I can't wait," Tommy said, and he meant it.

17

END OF BREAD SUBSIDY CAUSES GRIEF

The end of the bread subsidy has triggered riots among the hungry populace of South Sevenna. "People are unable to feed their children," said one shopkeeper who refused to give her name. "I feel their pain, but I can't afford to give the bread away."

—*JFA Bulletin*, October 6

Later that night, Tommy sat in the Estoria. Squeezed between Kristoph and Dennett, Tommy was miserable. The red-light lanterns cast a disturbing glare on the black walls, and the weird shadows distorted people's faces into creepy masks. The other lads—including Bern—were smoking reets and drinking some sickly sweet wine out of long-stemmed glasses. A fake floral scent hung in the air, and it was making Tommy nauseated. Onstage, male performers in aprons warbled in falsetto while the crowd—an odd mix of students, professors, and Zunft officers—laughed uproariously at the bawdy jokes.

The painted actors finished their tune, bowed, and shuffled off the stage. Another group of lads stumbled onstage wearing wigs and dresses that resembled the traditional garb of cottager girls from Aeren. The jests in the last skit had made Tommy uncomfortable, and he wasn't interested in hearing them make fun of cottager girls. Tommy stood up abruptly and mumbled something about finding the washroom, but Kristoph grabbed his wrist.

"Get me another of these, would you, old boy?" Kristoph said, pushing his glass into Tommy's hand.

At the back of the crowded cabaret, there was a smoking lounge with a bar. It was quieter in there, and the tables were only half-full. The server was taking a tray of drinks to a table, so Tommy waited at the gilded bar for her to come back. In the background, he could hear the performers' mocking tone. There were small brass flamingos placed along the bar, and Tommy picked one up, fiddling with the tiny hinged wing.

"Can I help you?" a woman asked from behind the bar.

When Tommy saw her face, he dropped the flamingo. It fell with a thud and pockmarked the shiny wood surface of the bar. The woman's long red hair was pulled back in a thick braid, but her face was unmistakable. Even in the dim light of the bar, Tommy could see the shadows of the burn marks above the collar of her dress. It was the girl in the lavender dress that he'd seen in the forest the day of the August Rising.

"You," he said in disbelief. "I remember you."

The girl's eyes grew wide and she glanced around quickly. Tommy wasn't sure if she was looking for an escape or if she was afraid that someone would hear them talking. But they were the only two people at the bar.

"Wait," Tommy said, leaning forward and talking softly. "I was the one who helped you. I mean, I think I did. I thought the porch would be safer than the forest."

The girl had regained her composure. She stared at him, her face expressionless.

"I've been worried that you were all right," Tommy said. He wasn't making much sense, but he kept talking because he wanted her to understand. "I didn't know what to do, but I couldn't leave you out in the storm for the soldiers to find."

"Thank you," she said, but she seemed to be speaking through clenched teeth.

"No, don't thank me." Tommy was feeling flustered. "I wanted to ask . . . If I did the wrong thing, I'm sorry."

She picked up a cloth and began drying a glass, but her eyes continued to scan the room over his shoulder.

"I'm Thomas. Tommy. And I'm glad to see that you're all right."

"You're an estate boy, right? There's only one estate in that area." The girl knew full well that she was talking to the son of Colston Shore.

"I didn't mean to bother you," Tommy said. He felt embarrassed that she knew who he was. "I'll let you get back to work."

He turned to go, but she said, "Emilie."

"Excuse me?" he asked.

"That's my name," she said. "And thank you. Really, I mean it. Getting caught would have been a disaster."

"That storm was a bad one," Tommy said. The girl tipped her head quizzically, and he realized she had meant getting caught by the Zunft.

"Right, getting caught by the storm would have been a disaster," she said. "Ocean storms are the worst."

He got the feeling that she was trying to joke with him, but her face remained humorless. Still, it made him relax a little. At least she didn't seem mad at him anymore.

"Remember the deluge last December?" Tommy said. "That was the worst one I've ever seen."

"The waves were practically lapping at your door," the girl said. "We could see the flood from the top of the ridge."

"And then it started snowing," Tommy said. "It was the thickest snowfall I'd ever seen. And then thunder that nearly burst my eardrums. It was so surreal."

"Typhoon, flood, and blizzard—all in one day," she said.

"They say that was the storm of the century," Tommy said. "I hope it was more like the storm of the millennium."

Emilie laughed at his joke, but his comment hadn't been that witty. Tommy wondered if he should let her work, but didn't relish the idea of going back and sitting with the lads. He waited for her to say something, but she was staring intently at the glass in her hand.

"Well, I should be getting back," Tommy said.

"There's a pub a few blocks south of the river," she said. "It's called the Plough and Sun. You go over Shadow Bridge, take a right at Connell, and go two blocks east."

"Is that your local?"

"You should drop by some Saturday night," she said. "If you don't see me, ask for Emilie Johns. Let me buy you dinner as thanks for not leaving me in the woods."

"You don't have to buy me dinner," Tommy said. "You have to put up with too much, working at a place like this, to spend your coin on me."

"If you don't like this *entertainment*, why are you here?" she asked.

"Mocking people doesn't qualify as entertainment," Tommy said. "At least not to me."

"Well, you're the first estate boy to say that, I think," she said.

"I got dragged here by my brother and his Seminary friends," Tommy said. "I didn't know what it would be like or I wouldn't have come."

"Ah," Emilie said. "Well, the offer for dinner still stands."

"Sure," Tommy said.

"I'm always there on Saturday nights. Emilie Johns. Don't forget."

"Saturday nights," Tommy said, feeling a little confused both by the invitation and by her persistence. "But would I be . . . I mean, would it be all right?"

"Well, don't wear a Seminary uniform," she said. "Or announce your name at the door. But if you act normal, you'll be fine."

"Normal," Tommy repeated. "I'll do my best."

A Zunft officer appeared at Tommy's shoulder and rapped impatiently on the bar with his knuckle.

"If you want to have a seat, I'll bring you that drink, sir," she said to Tommy even though he hadn't ordered anything.

As he returned to his seat, Tommy ran the conversation through his mind. He couldn't believe that the girl in the lavender dress was here in Sevenna. Her name was Emilie, and she was all right. He hadn't done anything wrong that day after all. Maybe he *would* go to the Plough and Sun some time. Why not? He bet his brother had never gotten an invitation to a cottager pub. If nothing else, he would have a good story to tell Ellie and Kristin.

When they finally left the cabaret, Tommy sucked in deep breaths of cool air to chase the scent of sweat and smoke from his nose. He couldn't wait to get back to his room and climb into the clean sheets. But instead of heading north to the Seminary, the lads headed toward the Lyone River.

"Isn't this the wrong way?' Tommy said.

"Isn't this the wrong way?" Dennett mimicked in a snotty voice.

"My brother has an acute sense of direction," Bern said. The other boys, including Bern, had had too much to drink. They stomped down the middle of the deserted road like drunken conquerors.

"It's a short detour," Kristoph assured Tommy.

"To the cottager district? Why?"

"No worries, Tommy," Bern promised heartily. "You'll like this."

Tommy wanted to take off and go back alone, but leaving the group would be considered bad form, and Bern would never let him hear the end of it. They crossed the Seventh Stone Bridge onto the quay. By this hour, the lanterns had burned out and Tommy kept tripping over the ruts in the rough road as he followed the other lads. There was a singed smell to the air, as if there had been a recent fire. Someone had pasted rows of large posters along the wooden fences. They showed pen-and-ink portraits of different men, each with a name: *Michael. Brandon. Hector. Jack. Kevin.* And then: *Save the August 5.* Tommy remembered the black-haired woman who spoke in Mast Square. She had said she was the wife of one of the rebel leaders.

"Kidnappers and murderers," Kristoph said, looking at the posters. Dennett pulled out his pocketknife and slashed a long cut through the faces of the men on the posters as he walked. Tommy glanced around nervously. He really hoped they wouldn't run into any cottagers. Bern slowed down a little, and Tommy did as well. Soon there was some distance between them and the other boys.

"This is stupid," Tommy said. "Let's go back."

"I heard you were with one of the girls from Seminary," Bern said. "Holding hands on Dawson Street."

"We weren't holding hands," Tommy said.

"But you were with one of the girls?" Bern asked. "Seriously, Tommy, where is your sense of self-preservation?"

"I'm not the one who suggested coming down to the cottager district," Tommy pointed out.

"I meant with the lads," Bern said.

"Oh, I thought you meant with the cottagers who are going to come out and pound us," Tommy said. "And it's none of your business who I spend time with."

"Are you serious?" Bern said. "Father is going to kill you if he finds out."

"Kill me for walking with a girl?" Tommy said. "Why are the lads being so disrespectful to them anyway? Aren't we supposed to protect the daughters of the Zunft? I seem to remember Father saying that."

"It wasn't even one of the cute blondes, was it?" Bern asked. "It was that scrawny dark one with the braid."

Dennett had stopped in front of the wooden fence to inspect a poster. It showed skeletons wearing flat caps shuffling into a factory shaped like a fanged mouth. Clouds of black smoke billowed out of smokestacks in the background and formed the words *The Great Devourer*. Tommy pressed his fingertip against the poster. The paste was still damp.

"The Great Devourer," Dennett scoffed. "Such idiots."

"There were more attacks in Norde last week," Kristoph said. "They hit another guard station. Stole all their weapons."

"I heard they killed a farmer and his young sons," Dennett said. "Burned down his house and stole all his animals."

"My mother's family has lived in the northlands for generations," Kristoph said. "It's gotten so bad they have to bar the doors at night or the cottagers will kill them in their sleep."

"Kidnapping Hywel has gotten them nowhere," Bern said. "They thought it would bring them all this power. But now they're desperate and on the defensive. My father has them on the run."

"Well, maybe he could move a little faster," Kristoph said. "They should all be rounded up, like stray dogs."

"Do you think Hywel is still alive?" Tommy asked.

"Probably not for much longer," Kristoph replied. "They'll dump his body in some alley in Stokkur."

"Then they'll have no power and no options," Bern said. "I think they'll keep him alive awhile longer."

A few blocks down the road, they came to a high stone wall. The lads stopped in front of a whitewashed gate secured with a large rusty padlock. While the others talked softly among themselves, Tommy peered at the faded wooden sign above the gate: *Ash Street Garden*.

"You're here to see a garden?" Tommy asked doubtfully.

"No, we're here to pay our respects," Dennett said sarcastically.

The wall was about six feet high. Dennett gave Kristoph a boost, and he pulled himself up and perched on top of the wall. After a few moments, he motioned for the other boys to follow. Bern and Dennett disappeared on the other side while Tommy waited on the street.

Soon, Bern's head reappeared above him. "Get up here, Tommy."

"Thanks, but I'll wait here," Tommy said.

"You're going to get jumped by thugs standing there by yourself," Bern pointed out. He leaned down and offered his hand. Tommy grabbed it, and Bern hoisted him to the top of the wall.

"Lose fifty honor points for breaking into a garden," he told Bern.

"Nah, it's gain fifty for not being a pansy coward," Bern replied.

Tommy hopped off the wall and into the garden. The

moon had emerged from behind the clouds, and its pale light illuminated the open ground inside the walls, which was more expansive than he had expected. The high walls enclosed the entire block and there were no structures except greenhouses along one wall. They were dark inside, but in the light of the moon, Tommy could see the lush green growth through the misty panes of glass. It was winter, so the rest of the garden was barren, but the beds had been made in a spiral pattern with circular paths that wound toward a raised tier of earth. An elaborately carved wooden pillar marked the center of the garden. Tommy wished he could see the garden in the heart of the growing season. It would be breathtaking.

Near the front gate, Kristoph inspected a vine-covered trellis. He grabbed one support and shook it. Then he pushed against it until the trellis crashed to the ground, splintering the delicate latticework. Nearby, Dennett picked up a rock that had been neatly laid along the edge of the garden bed. Someone had painted the rocks. Tommy could see the faded outlines of childish scrawls.

As Dennett reached back to throw the rock, Tommy realized what he was going to do. He ran forward, catching Dennett's arm.

"It's a garden," Tommy said. Dennett shook Tommy's arm off and moved again to throw the rock at the greenhouses. This time, Tommy stepped in front of him.

"Move!" Dennett shouted.

"Seriously, these people don't have as much food as we do," Tommy said.

"Back off, Tommy," Bern called.

Dennett dropped his rock. Tommy glanced toward his brother and the next thing he knew, Dennett charged at him. Tommy was caught off guard, and Dennett easily shoved him to the ground. Tommy tried to get up, but Dennett kicked him in the ribs. Shocked by the pain in his ribs, Tommy doubled up on the ground and Dennett moved to kick him again.

"Easy," Bern said. He stepped in front of Tommy to block Dennett's next strike. "We're all friends here."

Tommy struggled to his feet, a sharp pain in his side. Kristoph left the destroyed trellis on the ground and stood beside Dennett.

"I don't like your brother, Bern," Kristoph said.

"What happened?" Dennett asked. "Did your mother shag a cottager, and he came out?"

"How dare you—" Tommy began, but Bern clamped his hand on Tommy's forearm. His fingernails were like claws digging into his skin, and Tommy closed his mouth. Bern didn't even try to defend their mother and Tommy hated him for that.

Dennett bent down and picked up the rock. He moved to throw it again, this time making a dramatic show of it. He pulled his arm back in slow-motion as if taunting Tommy to try to stop him again. Tommy shook off his brother's arm, lunged forward, and caught Dennett's arm. Dennett dropped the rock, but Kristoph clobbered Tommy in the back of the head. Tommy stumbled around, unsteady on his feet. Before he regained his balance, Kristoph swung at him again, this time hitting him in the face. Tommy felt the skin of his cheek swell up, and his field of vision narrowed. His eye felt like it was burning on the inside.

"I'm not going to fight you," Tommy said, holding up his hands. "But it's stupid to destroy food."

Kristoph and Dennett moved to attack him again, but Bern grabbed Tommy's arm and dragged him away.

"I'm taking him back to Seminary," Bern said. "You two have your fun."

"Don't bring him next time, Shore," Dennett yelled.

Bern practically threw Tommy over the wall. Standing on the street, Tommy could hear the sound of shattering glass as the lads destroyed the greenhouses.

"That was crap, Tommy," Bern said. "They come from important families. Find them tomorrow and make nice."

"No way," Tommy said.

"You're destroying your future in the Zunft," Bern said. "You'll be an outcast."

"I don't care anymore," Tommy said.

"Are you insane?" Bern said. "You might be in the Zunft Chamber with those two someday. You might work with them in the bureau or in the army, or whatever losers like you manage to do. Stop trying to fight what should be easy for you!"

"Maybe it shouldn't be so easy for you," Tommy said.

"You realize that this hurts Father," Bern said. "You're being incredibly selfish."

"You're calling *me* selfish?" Tommy asked. "Did you think about the people who depend on that garden for food? People like Mrs. Trueblood?"

"It's people like Mrs. Trueblood who are trying to take our land and kill us in the streets," Bern said.

"People are so hungry they're rioting," Tommy said. Images of Mast Square flashed through his mind. That hadn't been about bread, at least not directly. He wished Bern could have seen the panic and desperation in those people's eyes.

"Father is trying to fix that!" Bern shouted. "Everything he

does, it's ultimately because he cares about us, and you're mess-
ing everything up."

"They insulted our mother, and you did nothing," Tommy
said. "I'll never forgive you for that."

For the first time, Bern's bravado faltered. But then he scowled
with anger. Expecting to be punched again, Tommy took a step
back. Instead, his brother spoke with icy calm.

"By siding with the cottagers, you're the one who is betraying
her memory, not me," Bern said. "Now get away from me."

"Happily," Tommy said, and turned to leave.

"Tommy?" Bern called. "When bad things happen to you
from now on, just remember you deserve them all."

I8}

VANDALISM AT ASH STREET GARDEN

The greenhouses of Ash Street Garden were destroyed in an early-morning act of vandalism. Nova James, the steward of the garden, says that more than thirty-five families receive most of their subsistence from the garden. "I expect the food shortages to be even worse," James said. "This is utterly senseless, a tragedy for the community." Ash Street Garden is asking for donations of plate glass. Please contact Nova James if you have information.

—JFA Bulletin, October 7

"Happy birthday! Fifty years young!"

It was Katherine Leahy's birthday, and the Plough and Sun was packed with well-wishers. The crowd cheered when Brian Leahy put his arm around his wife's waist and danced her around the table.

"She hasn't changed since the day I married her!" Brian called.

Katherine swatted her husband on the shoulder playfully. Brian gave his wife a bear hug, picked her up, and spun her in a circle. Tamsin held the kitchen door open, and Navid carefully carried in a lopsided two-layer cake with real frosting. Tamsin had traded some fresh vegetables for the sugar, which was impossible to afford at any Zunft markets and unavailable at the bookless shops.

"Cake for everyone!" Navid called, and people cheered even though there wouldn't be nearly enough for all the patrons. So the children crowded around, and Tamsin cut slivers while Navid passed them out. Soon the cake was gone, but no one seemed to mind. Tilo Locke and his band set up near the fireplace. Everyone moved the tables out of the way, and even though the dance floor was triple its normal size, it was jammed with dancers.

Tamsin was about to head back into the kitchen when Gavin sidled up to her. He looked so sheepish that she wanted to laugh.

"What's on your mind, sir?" she jested although she had a pretty good idea.

"Do you want to dance?" he asked.

"I need to get to the dishes," she said.

"No, you don't," Katherine said. She had appeared out of nowhere at Tamsin's elbow. "Go dance. Have fun."

"What do you think, Miss Henry?" Gavin asked.

"Why not?" she said. He took her hand and led her onto the dance floor. The band was playing a slow dance, and Gavin put his hands awkwardly on Tamsin's waist. She hadn't seen him since she'd visited her father in the compound and she wasn't going to tell him that Michael Henry had called him a traitor. But she was afraid he would want to talk about it. Sure enough, when he opened his mouth, he asked, "How was the visit with your father?"

Tamsin chewed on her lip. Gavin was tall enough that he couldn't see her face unless she lifted her chin. So she stared at the buttons on his spotless white shirt instead. She and Gavin were barely moving to the music, and she could feel the eyes of the dancers watching them curiously.

"Tamsin?" Gavin asked. "Are you all right?"

Take up my sword, daughter. Don't let me die in vain.

She was saved from answering when the song ended and the band began a quick jig. The dancers formed into small circle dances and there wasn't any more time for talking. The jigs continued for a good half hour, and Tamsin forgot about everything else but the dance. After a particularly fast song, everyone was out of breath and the set ended. She glanced at Gavin, and his eyes were on her, too. She hadn't expected her father's feelings about Gavin to affect her, but she realized she felt differently about her friend. Michael Henry hated him. How was she supposed to feel?

Before he could say anything to her, the sound of a lone pennywhistle quieted everyone in the pub. It was the beginning of a familiar tune that dated back to the War for Aeren. Tilo began to sing in his beautiful tenor voice. He sang about green fields stained with the blood of the innocents, and the heart of Aeren, broken in battle. Everyone stopped dancing and stood in reverent silence.

When the song ended, Mr. Leahy climbed up on a bar stool.

The top of his head brushed the rafters. He raised his glass, and everyone looked at him expectantly.

"To the ones we lost," he said somberly, and everyone in the room raised a glass or a hand in memory of the fallen.

"To the ones they have taken from us," he said. "To Brandon and Kevin."

"Brandon and Kevin," echoed the crowd.

"To Jack and Hector," Mr. Leahy said, raising his voice even louder.

"Jack and Hector," the crowd echoed again.

Across the dance floor, Tamsin glimpsed Hector's young wife, Adele, with her arms tight around their seven-year-old daughter, Marina. Tears were streaming down both their faces.

"To Michael Henry!" Mr. Leahy shouted.

The crowd exploded with whistles and shouts of support, but all Tamsin could think about was the fury in her father's eyes when he told her to take up his sword. She had the urge to flee the crowd, but at the same time she didn't want to be alone. Tamsin grabbed Gavin's hand and pulled him out of the pub, through the kitchen and outside, into the back alley. She took deep breaths of cold air while Gavin watched her with concern and confusion. They weren't wearing their coats, and Tamsin was shivering uncontrollably. She regretted bringing Gavin with her. She wasn't sure how she felt about him anymore.

"Is it really so late?" Tamsin asked. It was a cloudless, windy night. The air felt cleaner than usual and the stars were almost as bright as they were on Aeren. "I think dancing with you is the first time I've lost track of time since I came here."

"Are you angry with me?" Gavin asked. "It seems like since you went to see your father, you've been avoiding me."

"I haven't written the treatise for you yet," Tamsin lied. "I feel bad for letting you down."

"Oh," Gavin said. She could tell that he didn't believe her. They shivered without speaking for a while, and she thought he'd let the issue go. But then he spoke again. "That doesn't make a lot of sense, Tamsin. I'd rather you be honest with me than tell me something you think I want to hear."

Tamsin couldn't bring herself to tell Gavin that her father hated him. Or how her father expected her to take up his mantle and crush the Zunft in his name. She couldn't bring herself to talk about Michael Henry and how the weeks in prison had grayed his hair and softened his jawline. Instead, she decided to share an idea that had been fermenting in her mind since the night she met Tommy Shore.

"I met someone at the Estoria the other night," Tamsin said. "I met Tommy Shore, one of the sons of the chief administrator himself."

Gavin didn't say anything for a long moment. When he spoke, his voice sounded strained. "I don't think you should work there anymore," he said. "I'm sorry to be so direct, but I don't."

"He doesn't know who I am, but he knows I'm from Aeren," Tamsin said. "I told him to come here sometime, asking for Emilie."

"Why would you do that?" Gavin sounded incredulous.

Tamsin took a deep breath. She knew what she was about to say would sound atrocious to Gavin. It had started as a germ of an idea after she met Tommy, but it had grown hour by hour until she could hardly think about anything else. She had run through scores of other scenarios in her mind, but none of them could help her father. Then she formulated this plan, and though it was coldhearted, she believed that it was the only thing that would work.

"We could make a trade," Tamsin said. "Him for Papa. And Jack and the others."

Gavin took a step backward and stared at her, and his silence was terrible. Part of her wanted to take the words back and reverse time. Another part of her felt defiant, proud that she'd shocked him. She knew that her father would be proud of her. It was a plan he would appreciate even if Gavin did not.

"You're talking about a human being, Tamsin," he said. "It doesn't matter who his father is. He has the same rights as every other human being."

"We wouldn't have to hurt him!" Tamsin said. *Unless they hurt Papa.*

"But you'd consider it?" Gavin asked. "It's something you would actually entertain?"

"Nothing else will save Papa," Tamsin said. "They're lying about his involvement with Hywel, and he's going to die for it."

"He's facing a charge of treason for the August Rising," Gavin said.

"We rose up against an unjust system!" Tamsin cried. "We rose up against people who treat us like slaves!"

"I want nothing to do with violence," Gavin said. "I want change as much as you do, but I will not be a part of this."

"Why do we always have to be weak?" Tamsin demanded. "Why not do the things that will make us as strong as them?"

"You're putting your life at risk," Gavin said. "You're putting your mother and sisters at risk even talking about this. Is this who you want to be?"

"You tell me another way to be, then," she said. "A way that isn't powerless. A way that actually changes things!"

"I never said I had all the answers," Gavin said. "But I know that subjecting another human to violence is wrong. I would rather die than hurt someone else."

"You only say that because you're not in jail, too," Tamsin said. She was so angry she could barely see straight. "You were too much of a coward to put your life on the line."

"That's how you really feel, isn't it?" he said sadly.

If she wanted any friendship with this man, Tamsin knew she should take back what she had said. But somehow she meant it. Maybe he *was* a coward to let men like her father face the firing squad while he printed his books and bulletins. After an intolerable silence, Gavin walked away, and she let him.

19

THE ZUNFT CHAMBER
TO BE REFURBISHED

Chief Administrator Shore has commissioned a renovation of the Zunft Chamber. His aide says substantial funds have been set aside to re-create a replica of the Chamber room when it was first established following the War for Aeren nearly a century ago. His plans include commissioning an artist to refurbish the mural *The Victory at the Hannon*, which commemorates the Battle of Aeren.

—*Zunft Chronicle*, October 8

The appearance of the Zunft Chamber had changed drastically since the day Colston Shore took power in August. The two tiers of chairs that had faced each other were gone. Now there was only one platform with chairs against the north wall. The chief administrator's podium had been raised to a height above the chairs, and the adjudicator's seat had been moved off to the side. As before, the loft only had a smattering of people viewing the proceedings. Gavin recognized the same official journalist who wrote for the *Zunft Chronicle*. He was sitting in the same chair and acted as bored as he had last time.

The old man, Kaplan, appeared to be snoozing in the adjudicator's chair. Colston Shore stood at the podium before the Zunftmen who had assembled for the Chamber. From the loft, Gavin could only see the back of Shore, but he had a clear view of the faces of the Zunftmen as they watched their chief administrator with rapt attention. Gavin sensed something else, too. Many of the men looked tense and worried, even men who had chosen to align with Shore after the August Rising. In the last session, Colston Shore's new supporters had acted like cocky victors. Now that arrogance was nowhere to be seen. Even Anderson was pale and withdrawn as he sat silently waiting for the session to begin.

"After a brief hiatus, the Chamber is back in session," Shore said. Kaplan opened his eyes and sat up straighter. The opening rituals were supposed to be his job. Almost immediately, his eyes drooped and he slumped back in his chair and swiped his arm across his face. Gavin wasn't sure if he was trying to raise his hand or wipe drool from his mouth. It was such an awkward motion that Gavin wondered if the old man might be drunk or drugged.

"The investigation of the disappearance of Mr. Hywel is progressing," Shore said. "As we speak, Zunft officers are closing in on a compound in Norde where we believe he is being held. If our information proves true, we hope to have him returned to the capital within days."

There was a tepid round of applause among the Zunftmen,

and Shore continued. "I'm pleased to announce that the revenue resulting from the end of the bread subsidy—"

Richard Shieldman stood up abruptly. He stamped his foot on the riser, a reverberating noise that halted Shore's speech. The men around him seemed astonished at his affront.

"With all due respect, *sir*," Shieldman said. "You are not following proper procedures of the Chamber. Adjudicator Kaplan should be directing the process. I have properly submitted a petition, which must be addressed under the hallowed rules of the Chamber. Under Statute 289.3b, I am calling into question the passage of the Food Purveyance Act . . ."

As Shieldman was speaking, Shore motioned to the guard at the door. Briskly, the guard opened the door and four armed soldiers marched in. The slam of the door and the thud of their boots drowned out Shieldman's voice. People glanced around in confusion, and someone shouted, "Kaplan!" But the old man merely opened his eyes a fraction and let them fall again. The guards stopped at the edge of the riser, near where Shieldman was standing. He tried to keep speaking, but when the guards closed in, his voice faded away.

"What is the meaning of this?" Shieldman asked Shore.

"A loyal Zunftman brought your recent activities to our attention," Shore said. "We conducted an investigation and found you guilty of treason."

At the word *treason*, there was a shocked silence in the Chamber. Gavin saw several people glance toward the revolvers strapped on the soldiers' belts.

"You are under arrest, Mr. Shieldman," Shore said.

"I have the right to face my accuser," Shieldman said.

"You have the right," Shore repeated. "Very well. Mr. Anderson?"

Karl Anderson stood up abruptly. Anderson had been a supporter of Hywel prior to the August Rising, but had quickly become a vocal supporter of the Carvers. Gavin had written an article about him, calling him a "plump sheep in the company of wolves." At the thought of the articles he had written, Gavin was struck by fear. He realized how much risk he'd put himself at by being here. Maybe no one had noticed him, but he felt as if a beam of light were shining down on his head. Gavin suddenly realized that he hadn't brought a false identification card. If he were stopped, he would have to hand them a document with his real name. Gavin cursed himself for his stupidity. He'd barely slept after his argument with Tamsin and his fatigue had made him careless.

"During the debate over the Open Education Act, Shieldman approached me about voting for the act," Anderson said. "He told me that there would be financial reward should I vote for the act and that he himself had received payment from cottager elements."

"You're a liar!" Shieldman yelled.

"Did you take such a reward, Mr. Anderson?" Shore asked, ignoring the outburst.

"I did not," Anderson said.

"You voted for the act!" Shieldman shouted.

"Richard Shieldman is under arrest," Shore said. "You're to be held until such time as a trial is scheduled and your sentence is determined."

At those words, Shieldman seemed to deflate. He turned back

toward his peers and colleagues, but most averted their eyes from him.

"First the cottagers, now one of your own?" Shieldman asked the Chamber. "Aren't you afraid you'll be next?"

Of course the Zunftmen were afraid they were next, Gavin thought. That was why no one spoke in support of Shieldman. With one hand, Shore had played the fearmonger card while the other hand shelled out rewards to his loyal followers. Shieldman's earnest idealism was no match for Colston Shore. A guard put his hand on his gun and moved toward Shieldman. Resignation crossed Shieldman's features, and he let the guards take him into custody without incident. Gavin surveyed the faces of the men as Shieldman was removed from the Chamber. Their expressions ranged from the smugness of the veteran Carvers to the undisguised horror on the faces of the few remaining men who stayed loyal to Hywel. There was fear in many of the new Carvers' faces as well, but they were doing their best to conceal it.

When the door of the Chamber slammed shut and Shieldman was out of sight, Kaplan lumbered to his feet and weakly stamped the floor for attention. All heads turned toward the aging adjudicator. Shore walked over to the man's chair, leaned down, and whispered in his ear. Kaplan stood up straighter.

"In light of the recent political unrest and with the revelations of corruption in the Chamber, I move to dissolve the Chamber for a period of not more than six months," Kaplan said, slurring his words. "During that time, Colston Shore will have full legislative powers and the authority to prosecute those who are found to have participated in this bribery scandal. We will vote by secret ballot."

In response to this, two of Hywel's men stood up and left in protest. When the men had reached the door of the Chamber, Shore motioned to one of the guards to follow them. Gavin wondered if they would even make it out of the building before being detained.

The remaining Zunftmen wrote their votes on scraps of paper that were put into a silver bowl. Kaplan left the Chamber to count the votes. He returned in less than five minutes.

"The decision was overwhelmingly in favor of the emergency legislation," Kaplan announced. "This Chamber is officially dissolved."

Colston Shore stood up, but there was no applause. "We will hold a mass trial for the rebel leaders this week," he said. "Justice has been delayed for too long."

This time, no one disagreed. After all, they had witnessed what had happened to Shieldman, the only man courageous enough to speak out against the mass trial back in August. Now that Shore had full legislative power, there was no way to compel him to reconvene the Chamber. In effect, power was completely in his hands. Gavin decided it was time to leave. He avoided the main entrance by ducking into a side stairwell, which led down to the lower level and into an alley. But when he turned the corner, he saw that a checkpoint was set up in front of the side doors. The soldiers motioned to him, and now that they had seen him, there was no way to go but forward.

"Identification card, please," the guard said gruffly.

Gavin's hands trembled as he handed over his card. He was mere steps away from the door. A beautiful autumn day beckoned him to come outside, but these men were like an impassable wall.

Gavin felt a rising sense of panic as the soldier read the card carefully and jotted down information in his ledger.

"Gavin Baine," the guard read. "What's your profession?"

"Machinist," Gavin lied.

"Is this your current residence?" the soldier asked, peering at the address printed on the small piece of paper.

"Yes, sir," Gavin lied again. The address on the card was actually an empty warehouse in the butchers' district, but the numbers and street name were a plausible place for a cottager to reside.

The soldier jotted more notes in the ledger. It seemed to take forever, and every once in a while, he'd consider Gavin critically and then make another note. Finally, after a tense silence, the man spoke.

"You're free to go," the soldier said.

Gavin had to restrain himself from sprinting into the street. Now that they had his name, he wondered how much freedom he had left.

20

MASS TRIAL FOR REBEL COTTAGERS BEGINS

The mass trial of the rebel leaders has begun at the Zunft Compound in Sevenna City. While the good people of Port Kenney try to rebuild the ruins of their village, they call for justice to be done. The families of the soldiers murdered in the August Rising demand action! Chief Administrator Shore has heard their cries and he has answered: justice will be done!
—*Zunft Chronicle*, October 21, Evening Edition

On Saturday, Tommy entered the dining hall as the bell rang to signal the beginning of the evening meal. Across the sea of tables, Kristoph and Dennett were laughing together as they sat at their usual table with Bern. When Tommy entered the dining hall, Bern glanced at him and quickly turned his attention elsewhere. The two brothers hadn't spoken since the night at Ash

Street Garden, and Tommy had mostly avoided the dining hall. But he was tired of lukewarm soup and crackers. He didn't want to avoid his brother anymore. Tommy had been in the right, not Bern and his buddies.

Tommy wove his way between the tables toward the back of the hall and stood behind the chair next to Ellie's. As always, Ellie and Kristin were the only students at the large table near the entrance to the kitchen. The servers were so accustomed to this arrangement that they only put out two place settings instead of eight. Tommy stood there, waiting for an invitation to join the girls, but they both stared at him like he had two heads, which oddly hurt his feelings.

Everyone in the hall stopped talking and stared. Tommy pulled a chair out to sit down, but the legs screeched against the floor. The noise reverberated loudly in the hall as Tommy plunked down in his seat. With everyone watching him, everything seemed overly loud and overly dramatic. It was so silent that Tommy could hear the clink of the dishes from the kitchen as the servants prepared the meal. The blood rushed to his face as he felt all eyes on him.

Kristin tossed her blond curls and laughed. "I don't know if there's room for you, Tommy. This table is pretty crowded."

"Is it all right if I sit here?" Tommy asked. "I should have asked first."

"Of course, Tommy!" Kristin said. "You don't have to ask."

Finally, the students returned to their eating and chatting—probably about Tommy—but at least the racket felt like a shield around them. He glanced over at Ellie, who was frowning at him.

"What?" he asked.

"This is where Zunft careers come to die," Ellie said.

"Ellie!" Kristin said.

"I'm sorry," Ellie said. "But he has to know what he's doing."

"No problem. I already ruined my political future by disagreeing with the lads," Tommy said.

"Is that what happened to your eye?" Ellie asked. Tommy still had a faint black eye from Kristoph's fist. Tommy shrugged as if it wasn't important. Ellie and Kristin glanced at each other, and then they both grinned at him.

"Well, then, welcome to the table where the fun never stops," Kristin said.

"We put the 'fun' in funeral," Ellie said, and Kristin groaned. It took Tommy a second to get her joke.

"Ugh, Ellie, that was terrible," he said, and she laughed, delighted with herself.

"Ellie is the master of bad puns," Kristin told him.

"My father was this incredible genius who was tickled by dumb humor like that," Ellie said. "When I was little, I would get him laughing with the silliest jokes."

"What did your father do?" Tommy asked.

"He was an engineer with the Bureau of Innovations," Ellie said.

"He has the patent on volt-cells, right, Ellie?" Kristin said.

"Your dad invented the volt-cell?" Tommy asked. He suddenly remembered the name Peter Sommerfield from his engineering book. He was considered the father of the industrial revolution.

"His original model was incredibly unstable," Ellie said. "But it's the foundation of what they make now. That's why they let me into Seminary—to carry on his legacy or something."

"Both Ellie and I come from *notable* families," Kristin said. "We're smart, sure, but our dads have *spectacular* pedigrees. It was Charlotte who was the true genius. Her dad's a nobody, and they still let her in."

Kristin had a funny inflection every time she talked about the Zunft. To someone who didn't know her well, it made her sound ditzy. Tommy had come to understand it as a layer of sarcasm. She wasn't as overt as Ellie about her disdain for the Zunft, which was definitely the safer choice.

"How is Charlotte doing?" Tommy asked as a server arrived with plates of chicken and fresh bread.

"I haven't had a letter from her in a while," Kristin said.

"Not since her mother took her back to her grandparents' house on Norde," Ellie said. "Apparently, she's going to stay there. Probably for the rest of her life."

"Poor Charlotte," Kristin said. "She thought her grandparents' manor house was haunted. She's going to be miserable."

"Charlotte left Seminary for good?" Tommy asked. He actually wasn't surprised. He hadn't seen her since the day she was ill and went to the hospital. The same day that he and Ellie had walked around Sebastian's Circle.

"Did you hear what they did for Rannigan?" Ellie said. "They rewarded him with a full professorship and a shiny new office on the top floor of the administration building."

"Did she leave because of Professor Rannigan?" Tommy asked.

"The rest of the students weren't exactly friendly," Ellie said. She and Kristin exchanged glances. "But he targeted her specifically. There was a bet among some of the professors about who could get us to leave."

Tommy glanced up at the row of men eating at the head table. Sure enough, Rannigan was now wearing the stripes of a full professor on his black robes. He was talking to Headmaster Olberg, who was seated on his right. Even from a distance, Tommy could see Rannigan's self-important smile. It was amazing to him that anyone could congratulate himself for bullying a girl—a girl he was supposed to be teaching and helping find her way in the world. And his colleagues had rewarded him for his efforts. Tommy stared down at his chicken. Suddenly, he wasn't hungry anymore.

"Well, the issue of girls in Seminary is being examined in the Chamber now," Ellie said. She lowered her voice. "Not that there is a Chamber anymore."

"Ellie!" Kristin hushed her. "Not here."

"I can talk about the facts," Ellie retorted. "The chief administrator dissolved the Chamber. All power now resides with him."

"It's a temporary thing, right?" Tommy said.

Ellie scowled at him. "Your father crowned himself the metaphorical king of the world. Do you really think he's going to willingly hand his scepter back to the peasants—ever?"

Tommy felt annoyed and he wasn't sure why. Maybe it was her tone of voice. "It's not like the 'peasants' ever had any power."

"Did you think I meant the cottagers?" Ellie retorted. "Your father treats his own faction like peasants. And you know what? They're starting to desert him. He's taken his power trip too far, and it doesn't matter how much he tries to pay them off, they don't want to be second-class citizens to King Colston."

"Uh-oh," Kristin said softly. She tilted her chin toward the front of the hall. A group of lads were approaching their table. Kristoph, Dennett, and Frank were among them, but Bern had disappeared from the hall.

"They're swaggering," Ellie whispered.

"Swagger alert," Kristin agreed.

"Like cocks showing the hens what's what," Ellie whispered back, and Kristin made barely discernible chicken noises under her breath. *Cock-a-doodle-do!* Tommy realized that the girls were rehearsed at this. Maybe it made them feel better, but Tommy wasn't laughing.

The lads lined up along the edge of their table. The dining room was surprisingly empty considering the meal had been served only a short while ago. Kristoph and Dennett lifted the edge of the table up and dropped it back down with a loud bang. The three water glasses tipped over, and the rest of Tommy's food was ruined. Ellie was about to speak, but Kristin shot her a warning glare, and Ellie closed her mouth.

"What is it with you and food?" Tommy asked.

"I think you dropped something at the garden," Dennett said, and the other boys snickered. "Your balls, Tommy. Some kid is playing with them in the garden."

Tommy mopped up the water in front of him with his napkin. The hall had grown quiet again. At the front, a few of the professors excused themselves and left the dining hall. The rest made a point of talking among themselves and pretending to ignore the situation. Rannigan was the only one who was watching openly.

"We've been talking about you," Kristoph said.

"You've got nothing better to do?" Tommy replied.

"And we've decided that you must be a pansy boy," Kristoph continued. "That explains why you're such a fruitcake."

Tommy wasn't sure if he should stand up and leave or sit there and take it. Either way, people would think he was an idiot. Across the table, Ellie was red faced and furious. Kristin was staring at the entrance like she was wishing she was somewhere else.

"Pansy boys should really wear some face paint and ribbons," Kristoph said. "Why don't you ask your girlfriends for some?"

"Shut up, Kristoph," Ellie, who couldn't keep quiet anymore, said.

"Close your trap, dog face," Kristoph said.

"Hey!" Tommy stood up abruptly, pleased to see that Kristoph took a step backward. "Leave her alone."

"You know what your brother told us?" Kristoph retorted. "Your father thinks you're a pansy, too."

Tommy hesitated. Either Kristoph was skilled at saying the right things to hurt someone or Bern had talked about Tommy to his friends. Colston Shore probably *did* think Tommy was a misfit, but it was a betrayal that Bern would actually reveal that to anyone else.

Kristoph spun around to address the hall, speaking loudly so the remaining students and professors could hear him, "There ought to be a law. No pansy boys in Seminary. Will someone please take out the trash?"

There was a smattering of laughter among the rest of the students. Suddenly, Tommy wanted to kill Kristoph. Throw him down on the ground and smash his face. But if he swung at Kristoph, he'd get himself expelled. So instead, he turned and walked away.

"A pansy *and* a coward?" Kristoph called. "Pathetic."

When he reached the door, he could still hear the lads laughing at his expense. Tommy wished he could enjoy the irony of Kristoph calling him a coward. Here was a rich kid who destroyed a poor man's garden in the dead of night. As Tommy yanked the door open and hurried down the stairs, he wondered if he should wait for the girls. If they didn't follow him, he would look even more like an idiot. It was getting dark and he wasn't supposed to leave the Seminary at this hour. He was going to have to slip out a side gate to avoid being stopped by a guard. If he got caught, it would mean trouble, but with his face still burning with humiliation, he really didn't care. He wanted to get out of there—beyond the walls of Seminary. He wanted to be beyond the reach of any Zunftman.

Go over Shadow Bridge, take a right at Connell, and go two blocks east. That's what Emilie had told him that night in the cabaret. He found the Plough and Sun, a pub with a wooden sign swinging in the cool breeze. Warm firelight glowed under the door, and even from the street, he could hear lively fiddle music and laughter. When Tommy stepped inside, he was met with a blast of heat. He surveyed the room anxiously, but no one paid any attention to him. He was just another body in the already packed establishment. A crowd of people danced on the open floor in front of the roaring fireplace. The inside of the pub was bigger than it looked from the street. There were high-backed booths along the far wall and long tables and benches in the center of the room.

Tommy was happy to see that, like him, most of the men wore brown trousers and long-sleeved shirts. Many had their vests on and their sleeves rolled up. Tommy shoved his green scarf in his pocket and loosened the buttons on his jacket. He gingerly navigated the crowd and waited patiently in the crush of people near the bar. After ordering shepherd's pie and a mug of cider from the harried barkeep, he asked her about Emilie Johns, but he could barely make himself heard over the noise. So he found an empty alcove in a far corner away from the boisterous dancers and waited for his food. It was dimly lit and colder in the back of the pub. A half-burned candle flickered in the center of the scarred tabletop.

Tommy poked at the base of the candle, leaving fingerprints in the soft wax pooling in the tin holder. A shadow fell across the table and he jerked his hand away, expecting to see the server. But it was Emilie. Her long red hair was loose around her shoulders tonight. She seemed happier and more relaxed than she had at the Estoria. She set a covered crockery dish in front of him. Steam wafted out from under the lid, and Tommy realized how hungry he was.

"Don't look so guilty," she said. "It's only candle wax."

"Hey," he said. "It's a Saturday night, so . . . Here I am."

"I didn't think you would come," she said.

"Is it all right that I'm here?" he asked.

"Why *did* you come?" she asked, sliding into the booth across from him.

"The entertainment is better here," Tommy said, nodding toward the band, which had just finished a set. They were stowing their instruments back in their cases, and the dancers were heading off the floor for a break. The noise in the pub settled down to a dull roar.

"Better than the Estoria?" She laughed. "Well, at least we agree on something."

"How did you know I was here?" Tommy wondered.

Emilie nodded toward the bar. "Jeanie said you were asking about me."

There was an awkward silence while Tommy took a bite of the pie, which was delicious.

"Wow, this reminds me of my childhood," Tommy said appreciatively.

"Your childhood on Aeren," she repeated thoughtfully.

"Yes. I miss Mrs. Trueblood. She's our—"

"Mrs. Trueblood is my relation," Emilie interrupted. "I've actually heard her talk about you before. She said you were the sweet one."

"I don't think anyone in the world would ever call my brother sweet," Tommy said.

"She said you liked to read, and you used to share your books with her," Emilie said.

Tommy shrugged. "She was welcome to any of the books. She liked archaeology as much as I do."

"You helped her in the kitchen," Emilie said.

"Sure. That was the best room in the house." Tommy was a little surprised at how much Emilie knew about him. He knew nothing at all about her. "What about you—"

"She said your father was a monster to you," she interrupted again, ignoring his question.

"Well, *monster* is probably too strong—"

"She said he made you stand in the corner with weights tied to your ears for hours for interrupting him when he was speaking to you."

"Oh, well, maybe that's why they stick out so much." Tommy tried to make a joke. "The good thing was that he wasn't there much. Mrs. Trueblood was."

The girl stared at him intently. She had a slight furrow between her eyebrows, and Tommy squirmed under her intense scrutiny. This felt like an interrogation and he didn't really like it.

"Have you heard anything about Mrs. Trueblood?" Tommy asked.

"She has a first name," the girl said, with a trace of annoyance. "Do you know what it is?"

"Greta," Tommy said.

"Why don't you call her that?" she asked.

"Do you call your mother by her first name?" Tommy asked.

"She's not your mother," the girl said.

"I guess not," Tommy said. "But when I was a child, it felt like she was. It's not that I don't know her name. I call her Mrs. Trueblood out of respect."

The girl picked at the candle wax. "That makes sense. Sorry, I didn't mean that the way it sounded."

"Do you miss Aeren?" Tommy asked her.

"Every day," she said.

"Did you ever climb to the top of Giant's Ridge?"

"Sure, we live along Miller's Road. My sister and I would go up there on Sundays after chores were done."

"It's amazing that we never ran into you, because Bern and I used to go up there on Sundays, too," Tommy said. "We practically grew up next door, and I never saw you."

"Well, not really next door. We went to school on the other side of the ridge, down in the valley."

"All the way down in the valley?" Tommy asked. "How long did that take?"

"An hour each way," the girl said. "And we did see you sometimes on Miller's Road, Tommy. We made sure you never saw us."

"Why?" Tommy asked.

"Your brother treated us like imbeciles," she said. "Even though Mrs. Trueblood said you were different, I didn't believe her."

"It's hard to believe she doesn't work at Shore Manor anymore," Tommy said. "When I go back home, she won't be there."

"Well, she's not dead," Emilie said. "She's safe and sound."

"I didn't think she was dead," Tommy said.

Emilie said nothing for a long moment. "Why did you help me that day in the woods?"

"It was raining and there was a rover driving up and down Miller's Road," Tommy said.

"But you must have known I was a cottager," the girl said.

"If they had found you, they would have arrested you," Tommy said. "It wouldn't have mattered what you were doing, you would have been in trouble."

"Did you think about what happened in Port Kenney?" Emilie asked.

"Not at the time," Tommy said. "If I shouldn't have come here, I can go. I was humiliated in front of my classmates and teachers, and I wanted to be somewhere that the Zunft weren't."

"I want to show you something," the girl said. "Will you come with me?"

"What is it?" Tommy asked, taking another bite of his pie.

"Will you come?" she asked again.

"It's not like I'm in a hurry to get back to Seminary," he said. "The lads are probably trashing my room as we speak."

"Why? Did you tell someone that you were coming? Your brother?"

"No. And my brother is the last one I'd tell."

"Can you give me a few minutes?" Emilie said. "I need to finish something up in the kitchen. You finish your pie, and I'll be back in five."

"Where are we going?" Tommy asked.

"To see Mrs. Trueblood," Emilie said. "She doesn't want the Zunft to know she's in Sevenna, but she'd make an exception for you."

"She's here in the city?" Tommy exclaimed. "Why didn't you say so? Of course I'll wait! Take your time."

Emilie gave him a bright smile and disappeared into the kitchen while Tommy settled back and happily finished his pie.

In the kitchen, Tamsin searched for the sharpest knife she could find. After digging through a drawer of dull table knives, she found a long, narrow carving knife that was the perfect size to slide inside her boot. She was holding it up to check the sharpness when the kitchen door opened and Gavin stepped inside. She didn't even try to hide the knife, and from his face, she could tell he knew exactly what she was planning to do.

"Is that him out there in the booth?" Gavin asked. "That slender kid with black hair? Try to think of life from his perspective, Tamsin. I'm sure it isn't easy being the son of someone like Colston Shore."

"Shut it," Tamsin snapped. "I know what I'm doing."

"What's the plan?" Gavin asked. She could tell by his voice that he was angry, but his face was a mask of calm. "Are you going to drag him into a back alley and cut his throat?"

"No!" Tamsin said. "I'm going to . . ."

"What?" Gavin pressed when she paused. "Overpower him? Lock him in a basement? Make demands for his release? Isn't that how these things go? I notice it's worked so well for Hywel's kidnappers. Maybe you should go into business with them."

"I don't know how this works, but it's something!" Tamsin said. "Papa's trial has started. He's got a week at most before they find him guilty and shoot him and the others."

"That's right," Gavin said. "He knew the risk of what he was doing."

"He knew the risk?" Tamsin repeated. "Is that all you can say?"

"I want you to stop and *think* about the consequences," Gavin said. "Who else are you dragging into this?"

"Think about the consequences if I do nothing!" Tamsin insisted.

"Remember what you told me that night in the *JFA* office?" Gavin asked. "You had been told to do something, and you didn't question it. That's what you said, remember?"

"Yes, but—" Tamsin began.

"You thought I didn't know what you meant, but I did," Gavin said. "Your father involved you in Port Kenney. I think he involved you in the uprising knowing full well that you might die."

"You don't know what you're talking about," Tamsin said.

"People lost their lives that day, and you're partly responsible," Gavin said. "You have to bear that burden, but your father's burden is much worse. He should do everything in his power to *keep* you safe, and instead he put you in harm's way."

"But it was for the greater good!" Tamsin argued.

"Tamsin, I know your father better than you do," Gavin said. "He is an amazing man, no doubt, but he wanted glory. He wanted the August Rising so he would be elevated above the common man, to be a leader worthy of legend. It was more about him than the greater good."

"You don't know that!" Tamsin protested. *Leaders . . . worthy of legends.* Her father had said something similar during her visit to the compound.

"Please stop this madness and leave with me," Gavin said.

"We *need* a leader worthy of legend," Tamsin insisted. She leaned down and slipped the knife into her boot, but for the first time since the plan took shape in her mind, the path suddenly wasn't as clear.

"Why people do things is as important as what they do," Gavin said.

"Get out of my way," Tamsin said, trying to sound tough.

"Your father told me that he was willing to sacrifice you," Gavin said. "Bury you young in the green fields of Aeren. He wanted them to sing songs about it. It was all about him, Tamsin."

Tamsin hesitated. She thought about Eliza and her other sisters. How she would feel if it had been them in the warehouse in

Port Kenney. Little Iris tucked behind the workbench, holding the match, waiting to be consumed by fire. The image infuriated her. Why hadn't her father felt that same revulsion at the thought of her death? But then she remembered Michael Henry with his hands chained to a rough-hewn table. She imagined him blindfolded in front of a wall as an executioner readied his gun. Her father was powerless, but she was not.

Gavin was watching her carefully, and she could see hope in his eyes. He thought she'd changed her mind. But she pushed past him and went to retrieve Tommy Shore.

21

WHEN EMILIE GOT BACK TO THE TABLE, she seemed angry. She kept glancing at the kitchen door while Tommy put on his coat. Over her protests, he laid enough coin on the table to pay for two meals.

"Do you still want to go?" he asked. He really wanted to see Mrs. Trueblood, but Emilie was a strange girl. When they were talking earlier, it was more like an interview than a conversation. And now she seemed jumpy and ready to bolt.

"Yes," she said. "Definitely."

The pub was less crowded now, and as they headed to the door, Tommy could feel the eyes of the other patrons watching them. Maybe everyone here knew everyone else, so he stood out as a stranger. Whatever the reason, he'd had enough of being stared at for one night. He was happy when they left the pub and headed out into the darkened streets.

"See how the lights flicker?" Emilie asked, pointing to the gaslight at the end of the street. "It always happens at this hour. The lanterns are about to run out of fuel."

"It's creepy," Tommy said, watching the light dance along the sides of the buildings and wooden fences. It looked like the shadows of monsters skulking down the muddy road.

"Better than that horrific glare from the autolights in your section of the city," Emilie said. "How do you sleep with that harsh light coming through your window at night?"

"Curtains," he said. He didn't agree with Tamsin that the oppressive darkness of the nighttime was better. He was sure he was going to twist an ankle in a pothole as they navigated the rutted street. "Where does Mrs. Trueblood live?" Tommy asked.

"A few blocks south," Emilie said. "I should warn you, Tommy, it's not in a nice area. And that's part of my motivation for bringing you to see her, even though it's so late."

"What do you mean?"

"She's not doing very well. She's having a hard time making ends meet. I thought maybe you could help her."

"I can if she'll let me," Tommy said.

"Let's not give her a chance to ask," Emilie said. "We'll show up at her door and surprise her."

"Will she mind us coming this late?" Tommy wondered.

"She's going to be so happy to see you," Emilie said. "I promise you—she won't mind."

"If she's in Sevenna, I guess she hasn't received my letters," Tommy said. "I've been sending them to Black Rock. Do you know why she came here? She always hated the city."

"She came for work, like the rest of us," Emilie said.

"Mrs. Trueblood was really close to my mother." Tommy continued talking, mainly to fill the silence. "She went to work for

208

the Shores when my mother married into the family. She was with my mother when I was born and she was holding my mother's hand when she died."

"How did your mother die?" Emilie asked.

Tommy was surprised by her blunt question. Among the Zunft, it would have been considered rude to question someone about something that personal. Tommy wasn't sure what to say. He really didn't want to tell Emilie what had happened to his mother.

"It's a horrible story," Tommy said. "I shouldn't have brought it up."

Emilie stopped in the middle of the street. "But you did."

"It's not appropriate for me to talk about it with you," Tommy said.

"Please don't tell me that a cottager killed your mother," Emilie said.

Tommy was stunned. How had Emilie figured that out from the brief conversation? "He was a man who wasn't in his right mind. It wasn't political."

"But he was a cottager," Emilie persisted.

"Yes, he was," Tommy said. "He'd broken into the house at some point in the night and hidden behind the curtains. When my brother and I came into the room, he attacked us with a knife. He sliced me across my back—I still have the scar. My mother threw herself on him so he couldn't get at me again. He stabbed her ten times before the doorman overpowered him."

"I grew up near you," Emilie said. "How could I never have heard about this?"

Tommy shrugged. "It happened at our town house in Sevenna

when I was three. But she died on Aeren. She insisted on it. The doctors said she would bleed to death on the ferry, but she didn't. They carried her to the house, she asked for Mrs. Trueblood, and less than an hour later, my mother was gone."

"She died for you," Emilie said. "She wanted so badly for you to live that she was willing to die for you."

"I don't remember it," Tommy said. "And honestly, I don't remember her that well anymore, but Mrs. Trueblood always told me that Bern and I were the joys of her life. She loved us more than life itself."

"By the fields of Aeren, I am struck down," Emilie whispered.

Tommy glanced over at her. "I know that song," he said. *"King of Grief with golden crown / By the fields of Aeren . . ."*

"I am struck down," Emilie finished for him. "Do you know the rest of it?"

"I thought that was the end," Tommy said.

"The candle was lit / The fire dimmed but did not die / The world will never be the same," Emilie sang softly.

"You have a pretty voice," Tommy told her. Emilie stared at the ground and he couldn't tell if she was pleased with the compliment or not.

"Go on with your story," she said.

"Oh, there wasn't anything more to tell," Tommy told her. "Mrs. Trueblood didn't like my father, but my mother had asked her to raise us. That's why my mother wanted to make it back to Aeren alive. She didn't trust my father to ask Mrs. Trueblood to stay."

Low voices echoed down the street behind them, and Tommy glanced over his shoulder. A group of men were heading in their direction. They were keeping to the shadows along the opposite side of the street and were still a few blocks behind them. Tommy thought he counted five men but he couldn't see them clearly. Crime was rampant in the southern half of the city, and he wished he hadn't been so obvious about paying for the meal back in the pub.

Tommy realized how vulnerable they were. He was bigger than Emilie, but not by much. He wasn't going to be able to defend her from five men if they got attacked. He wouldn't even be able to defend himself. The men were gaining on them, but Emilie didn't seem to notice. They were on a deserted street with boarded-up storefronts and rubbish-filled gutters. Smokestacks rose into the sky above the decrepit buildings and there was a stench of rot in the air.

Tommy snuck another glance behind him. The men had stopped on the nearest corner under a darkened gaslight. Tommy was sure that the gaslight had been lit a moment ago, but it had either gone out or they had snuffed it. Either way, the entire street was now in shadows. The men on the street corner reminded Tommy of a wolf pack trying to decide whether they were hungry enough to run down their prey.

"Why do you keep looking over your shoulder?" Emilie asked.

"Haven't you noticed the men following us?" he said.

The men sprang forward as a group. They were running directly for Emilie and Tommy and their intentions were deadly clear. Emilie whirled around at the sound of their running feet.

"Oh, damn," Emilie muttered. "They *were* following us."

She grabbed his hand and sprinted around the next corner. They ducked into a narrow alley and she made a beeline toward a large, wooden dustbin. She dragged him behind the bin and pulled him down until they were hidden from sight. The bin had been pulled away from the wall at an angle, and there was a narrow gap facing the entrance to the alley. Tommy shifted slightly so he could watch the street. There were no gaslights, but by now his eyes had adjusted to the faint light of the moon. After a tense moment, a man in a flat cap and ragged coat ambled into the entranceway as if he had all the time in the world. He stopped and took a drag on his reet. The glow of the ember at the end illuminated his hard, age-worn face. The man walked a few paces into the alley, obviously searching for something. After an agonizing moment, he turned back to the street and disappeared from view.

"Should we go back?" Tommy whispered.

"Let's hide for a little bit," Emilie said. "And make sure they're really gone."

"Hide where?" he asked as they headed deeper into the darkness of the alley. He thought they were going to wait in the shadows, but there was a rustle and then the sound of a match being struck beside him as Emilie lit a small candle. In the tiny circle of light, he could now see that they had reached the end of the alley and were standing in front of a rusty metal door. She pulled a key from around her neck and unlocked it.

"You know where we are?" Tommy asked, confused and more frightened than he'd have liked to admit.

Instead of answering, she tugged on the heavy door and firelight shone unexpectedly through the narrow opening. She opened it wider to reveal a staircase leading down into a black void. A lantern burned at the top of the steps, but its light didn't reach all the way to the bottom, so Tommy wasn't sure how far down it went.

"What is this place?" Tommy asked.

"They're going to come back," Emilie warned. "Come inside, and we'll talk in there."

Tommy glanced over his shoulder at the alley. There was no sign of the men, but that didn't mean they weren't coming back. He stepped inside the narrow foyer at the top of the stairs. She yanked the door and it closed with a metallic clang. He heard a click as it latched automatically. They were locked inside.

"Do you know how much we hate your father?" Emilie said. "Do you know what kind of man he is?"

"What does this have to do with my father?" Tommy asked.

"I wanted to hate you, too," Emilie said. "I really thought I would. But Mrs. Trueblood didn't hate you. I've heard her talk about you and she wouldn't want anything to happen to you."

"Where is she?" Tommy asked.

"She isn't here," Emilie answered. "I want you to come down these steps with me and see the truth."

"What's down there?" Tommy asked.

"Nothing that will hurt you," she said. "Come and see for yourself."

"No offense, but no thanks," Tommy said.

"If I wanted to hurt you, I would have told the fellows at the pub that you were there," Emilie said.

"Yet you invited me there in the first place," Tommy said.

"There is something at the bottom of these steps that you should see," she said. "Not only as the son of Colston Shore, but as a human being who exists in the world."

Tommy felt a tug of curiosity. "We'll stay until those men are gone, and then we'll go see Mrs. Trueblood?"

"I lied to you about Mrs. Trueblood," Emilie said. "She's not in the city. But she would understand why I had to bring you here. She would understand why I'm doing this."

"Is there anyone else here?" Tommy asked.

"No, it's a historical record," Emilie said.

"What?" Tommy asked. He felt thoroughly confused, but not frightened anymore. The men outside were scarier than Emilie.

"If you want to know the truth about your father, you'll come with me," she said.

She took the burning torch from the wall and climbed carefully down the steep stairs. Tommy couldn't shake his growing curiosity and followed Emilie. When they reached the bottom, he was expecting a dank and miserable space, but instead the air was pleasant and smelled like flowers. Using her candle, Emilie lit a lantern near the door and the light flooded the sweet-smelling space.

Emilie moved around the small room, lighting several more lanterns, until it was as bright as day in that underground room. The walls were blanketed with hand-drawn portraits of men and women of all ages. Some of the portraits were painted with exquisite care. Others were scrawled by children on ratty paper. Some were perfect representations of the human face. Other pictures were more like scribbles with vaguely human features— angry marks gashed into paper. In the middle of the room, there was a large arrangement of violets and red tulips along with personal tokens—wooden beads and letters.

"What is this place?" Tommy asked.

"It used to be a root cellar," Emilie told him. "Now it's a shrine to the missing."

"Who are the missing?" Tommy said, and Emilie made a sweeping motion with her arm around the room.

"These people are," she said. "It started with the Ancestral Homes Act. No, actually, it started when your father took power. People are disappearing from the city. Our loved ones are gone without a trace. Where are they going? And why? Are they being deported to other islands? Maybe. Most don't have the proper identification, but then why don't we ever hear from them again?"

Tommy peered closely at the faces on the walls. A young woman with long dark hair smiled out at him from one of the paintings. The artist had painted her eyes and her dress the same cornflower blue. Whoever the artist was had known every curve of her face perfectly—this was someone who was loved. Near the door, there was a long, handwritten list of names. Tommy glanced at it, registering the first few names: *Aileen Teagan. Eleanor Carson. Jamie Lindsey. Meggie Stevens.*

"Those are their names, never to be forgotten," Emilie said. "Someday, there'll be a reckoning for every single one of them."

Tommy remembered the name Meg Stevens from that day at Mast Square when the soldiers attacked the demonstration. She'd been speaking from the prow of the ship.

"You should know who your father is and what he's doing," Emilie said. "The August 5 are going to die under his hand. He'll call it a fair trial, and then he'll kill them. Michael Henry is being blamed for the kidnapping of Hywel. I know that he isn't responsible for that, and he shouldn't die for it."

"How do you know he didn't do it?" Tommy asked. He didn't want to offend her, but he was curious how she knew such a thing.

Instead of answering, Emilie knelt and began adjusting her boot. Absurdly, Tommy felt embarrassed, like he was watching something private. So he turned around and faced the wall. He heard a rustling and a metallic clink. He had the sense that Emilie was approaching him, but when he turned around she was still crouched in the middle of the floor. But now she placed a hand on the shrine and rested her head against the edge in a defeated sort of way. Her shoulders were shaking as if she were crying silently.

He felt a rush of pity for Emilie despite her lies. Whatever manipulative game she had been playing with him was obviously over. He was disappointed about not seeing Mrs. Trueblood, and the sight of these missing people made him feel shaky and confused. But instead of sprinting back up the stairs and into the night, he knelt beside her and rested his hand on her shoulder to comfort her.

"I wish that the truth was as bright as the North Star," she whispered. "That no matter where in the world I was, all I had to do was look at the sky and know my way."

"It's like truth is determined by who can yell the loudest," Tommy said. "The people you're supposed to trust tell you the wrong thing."

"Who does that?" Emilie asked softly. Her forehead was still pressed against the rough wooden edge of the table.

"My father does," Tommy said. "All he talks about is honor. But what about these people? Where is the honor in this?"

"There is none," Emilie said. "His honor is a bloody lie."

"My brother says you can do whatever you want as long as you don't get caught," Tommy said.

"What do you say?" Emilie asked.

"I think honor is about what you do when nobody's watching," he said.

"And what about when everybody is watching?" she asked.

"It shouldn't change a thing," he said.

Emilie turned her head and studied him for a long moment. He was acutely aware of the burn marks on her throat. "Come on," she said. "I'll show you the way home."

22

VANISHED!

Tilo Locke, a beloved musician from Sevenna, is missing. He was last seen leaving the Plough and Sun in the early-morning hours of October 6 and failed to report to his factory job the next day. Locke was engaged to be married in December, and his family fears that he has been arrested. The Zunft denies that he's being held at the compound.

—*JFA Bulletin*, October 21

When they reached the Seventh Stone Bridge, Tamsin and Tommy parted company without a word. As Tamsin watched the slim boy cross the river, the knife felt heavy in her boot. The last hope for her father was walking back into the safety of North Sevenna. She waited until he was out of sight and then she, too, stepped onto the red-stone bridge. She moved carefully, as if she were afraid that the stones would crumble beneath her boots. At the midpoint, Tamsin stopped and listened for rover engines, but there was no sound of an approaching Zunft patrol.

Her head ached and she wished she could get out of the city. She wanted to be somewhere where the houses were far apart and the earth was unburdened by stonework. If she were on Aeren, she would seek solace in Wren Glade, the grave site where her family buried their dead. The glade was a natural clearing in the old-growth forest, and mossy cairns commemorated the lives of her kin. Every spring equinox, they would travel to Wren Glade to replace any rocks that had fallen and leave seed cookies for the birds who watched over the site. It was meant to be a day for the family to joyfully remember the lost.

Her father would need a cairn soon. She would have to stack heavy stones in memory of his life. She thought of the rubble left from the battle at the Grand Customs House, and it reminded her of a giant cairn. Since she couldn't go to Wren Glade, she would pay her respects at the last place Michael Henry had known freedom. Tamsin continued across the bridge, and when she reached the northern side of the Lyone River, she hurried to the harbor. Being out at night without an identification card was a foolish thing to do. If she got caught by the Zunft, she would join her father in the compound or have her face plastered on the wall in the shrine to the missing.

Tamsin felt reckless. As she ran through the sleeping city, she understood why Navid loved being a messenger. The wind whipped down the narrow streets, and the shops became a surreal blur in her watery eyes. Inspired by her young friend's preferred mode of travel, Tamsin decided to head to the rooftops. She found an alley near the Grand Customs House and searched for a way to climb up, away from the perils of the street and closer to the night sky.

She glimpsed a sturdy fire ladder in the shadows, and it made her smile. Navid would tell her she'd got off easy. As she scampered to the top of the three-story building, she remembered Tommy, and his mother's sacrifice. Michael Henry had done the opposite. He'd used Tamsin in search of his own glory and fame. Gavin had tried to tell her, but at the time, she hadn't been able to accept what he was saying.

At the top of the ladder, she hoisted herself onto the gravel roof of a tenement building across the alley from the customs house. In the months since she'd seen it, the Zunft had completely rebuilt the building. The scars of the battle were gone. There was even a new bell tower on top of the Grand Customs House, overlooking Sevenna Harbor. She stared across the expanse. Leaping from building to building was easy for Navid, but it seemed ridiculously far to Tamsin. *What do I have to lose?* she thought as she backed up a few paces and got a running start. She jumped as far as she could, but didn't make it cleanly onto the roof of the customs house. She slammed into the edge, her hands frantically grasping the edge of the stonework trim.

With her boots scrabbling against the stones, she hauled herself up. She was scraped and bruised, but felt an odd sense of accomplishment. She inspected the bell tower and rattled the glossy black door, which was secured with a padlock. There was a brass plaque that read: *In memory of the brave soldiers who lost their lives during the August Rising.* If the customs house was her father's tomb, then this was his epithet. Violence was his legacy to the world.

"I'm not high enough," Tamsin whispered to the bell tower. "I need to be closer to the stars."

The wooden bell tower was wider at its base, and became

narrower toward its peaked roof, which was painted cerulean blue. In the east, the sky was getting lighter as she scaled the outside of the twenty-foot tower. She was feeling confident until she tried to navigate onto the roof. Twice, she almost lost her grip on the planks, and the jolt of fear almost made her give up this dangerous pursuit. But on her third try, she ungracefully shimmied onto the top of the bell tower, which was barely big enough for her to sit cross-legged and catch her breath.

She was the highest thing in the city.

The sea stretched to her west. Although Aeren was too far away to see, she imagined her mother and her little sisters sleeping in the cottage near Miller's Road. She gazed north, where the Zunft Compound dominated the ridge overlooking the city. She couldn't see beyond the imposing walls, but she envisioned her father outside in the prison yard breathing the crisp early-morning air. Her eyes traced the winding Lyone River, which drew a line between the two halves of the city. North Sevenna had clean lines and sharp edges compared to the raggedy, haphazard buildings of South Sevenna.

"Am I a destroyer?" Tamsin asked the horizon, hugging her knees to her chest. "Do I want to tear all of this down, set fire to the world?"

The eastern sky turned crimson as the sun rose over the city. She could see crowds of people taking to the streets in South Sevenna as the cottagers prepared to make their way toward their jobs for the Zunft. From this height, the people seemed to move in unity, a mass exodus from the south to the north. As soon as they crossed the river, the crowd would be separated into individual parts. A cottager woman would go do a Zunftman's laundry.

Another would clear his table. Others would bake his bread and sew his suit.

What would the Zunft do if they woke up to dark houses with no one to do their work? What if the masses never came to light their fires, cook their breakfasts, or start their rovers? Tamsin stared out at the sea and said a prayer for her father, hoping the winds would whip her words across the waves to the green fields of Aeren. Then she laid down her knife and went to pick up a pen.

23

ILLEGAL TRIAL CONTINUES!

The mass trial against the August 5 is nearing its conclusion. The proceedings are closed to the public, but the *Zunft Chronicle* reported that the prosecution presented fourteen witnesses who testified that they saw the defendants exiting the Grand Customs House during the battle. The defending barrister, who was appointed by the state, presented no witnesses and finished his arguments in less than an hour. The evidence will now be judged by a panel of Zunftmen appointed by the chief administrator. The names of those on the panel have not been released. A verdict is expected within days.

—*JFA Bulletin*, October 28

Gavin tapped lightly on the Leahys' blue door, and Katherine Leahy opened it. She smiled brightly at him. "Come in!"

"Thank you," Gavin said, wiping his feet on the straw mat.

There was a light snow falling outside, and Gavin brushed the flakes off his cap.

"We're about to eat. Will you join us?"

It was late Sunday afternoon and the family would be sitting down to supper soon. Sunday night was usually the biggest meal of the week for cottagers, and often the only one where meat was served. The Leahys' row house smelled of stew and fresh bread. Gavin hadn't eaten anything that day and now he felt his hunger acutely.

"Thank you, but I can't," Gavin said politely, keeping his coat on. If he stayed for dinner, that would mean less for everyone else. "Navid stopped by the *Bulletin* and said that Mr. Leahy wanted to see me."

"Yes, thank you for coming," she said. "We'd love for you to stay. I already set another place for you."

It had been a week since Gavin had seen Tamsin at the Plough and Sun. Whatever she'd been planning to do with the young Mr. Shore hadn't happened, of that much he was certain. The world would have exploded if she'd kidnapped him, but there had been nothing in the news except the closed trial of the rebel leaders. Midweek, Gavin had stopped by the pub at the end of Tamsin's shift, but she was already gone. He didn't want to try to talk to her in front of other people at dinner. It would be better to catch her alone some other time.

"I need to get back to the *Bulletin* as soon as possible," Gavin said.

"I understand," Katherine said. "Any news about the verdict?"

"I don't know why they're delaying," Gavin said. "Maybe it's a show of legitimacy, but everyone knows what the final result is going to be."

Katherine nodded. It wasn't a question of whether or not the August 5 would be found guilty. The question was how long before they were shot.

"Brian's in the back by the woodshed," Mrs. Leahy told him. "Gavin, can I ask you a question?"

"Of course," Gavin said.

"Did something happen to Tamsin?"

"Why? Is something wrong?" Gavin asked worriedly.

"I think something bad happened last weekend," Katherine said. "At first I thought it was the stress of the trial, but now I'm not sure. She's working constantly. First at the pub, then at the Estoria, and she even comes home and works. She closes herself in that room. I can see the candle burning at all hours."

"Is she here?" Gavin asked. "I can speak to her."

"No, she's not," Katherine said. "I hoped she'd be here for dinner, but she said she had something else she needed to do."

"I'll talk to her when I can," Gavin promised.

"Good," Mrs. Leahy said. "I know she respects you."

Gavin wasn't so sure about that, but he thanked Katherine and found Brian in the backyard chopping up a log. It was snowing harder now. Even though Gavin was nearly eighteen years old, he still felt a childish excitement during a snowfall. He resisted the urge to bend down and scoop up a handful.

"How are you, sir?" Gavin asked. "Do you need any help?"

Brian took one more swing and left the ax buried deep in the wet wood. He reached into his coat pocket and pulled out a folded stack of papers.

"I'm not an educated man," Brian said. "But I know when I read something . . . exceptional. Tamsin wrote it. It's a treatise from Angry Em."

Gavin nodded. He'd asked Tamsin to write a treatise for the *JFA* weeks ago, but he hadn't been sure she would do it. Brian handed the bundle to Gavin. The pages were secured with a red ribbon. *Like a gift,* Gavin thought. *Or maybe a peace offering.*

"It's going to cause quite a stir, Gavin," Brian said. "She's definitely Michael Henry's daughter, but after all that's happened, and with what's about to happen, this could be dangerous."

"You mean the trial?" Gavin asked.

"Well, no, I mean the martyrdom of the August 5," Brian said.

"What makes you hesitate about the treatise?" Gavin asked. He wanted to understand what Brian was saying, but the man seemed to be skirting the point he was trying to make. Brian was like the patriarch of the district. He'd been involved with cottager politics before Gavin had even been born. The Leahys had run a soup kitchen out of their basement during the famine years and smuggled medicine for their fellow cottagers when the pox devastated the city nearly a decade ago. But like Gavin, he'd opted out of Michael Henry's Rising. He wasn't swayed by ballads and stories of glory on the battlefield. Gavin respected his opinion more than that of anyone else he knew.

"You've done amazing things with the *Bulletin*," Brian said. "You've started something meaningful. It's important work."

"Thank you. That means a lot coming from you," Gavin said sincerely.

"If you publish Angry Em's treatise, they won't ignore you anymore," Mr. Leahy warned. "The Zunft will come for you and they'll tear down everything you're trying to build."

"What did she write?" Gavin stared at the bundle of papers in his hand.

"She wrote the blueprint for a better world, Gavin," Mr. Leahy said. "Think carefully, son, before you send this into the world. Once this is free, there's no caging it again."

Gavin tucked the bundle inside his coat. "Thank you, sir," he said. "And thank you for watching out for Tamsin."

"When you make your decision, try to keep your feelings for her out of it," Brian said.

"Feelings for her?" Gavin asked.

"Ah, the blindness of youth," Mr. Leahy said, jerking his ax out of the log and swinging it through the air again.

At dawn on Monday morning, the snow turned to rain. It was a cold, harsh rain that pelted the city and turned the streets into muddy streams. At the Zunft Compound, the captain sent his men to retrieve the prisoners from their cells. The men had been in the compound since August, and the daily routine had always been the same. But now there were footsteps in the hall before the breakfast bell, and the men knew that the soldiers were coming for them.

Brandon Cook's cell door was opened first. He was gazing out his narrow window watching the rain pour down. He'd stood in that exact spot for many hours and knew the lines of the cityscape by heart. Off in the distance, there was a light blue house that stood alone on a hill. It didn't matter that he couldn't see it now through the mist and rain. He pretended his wife, Marie, lived in that light blue house. He imagined that she slept on a soft bed under the window. He'd thought about it so much that he now believed it to be true. When they led him out into the corridor and put a burlap sack over his head, he pictured Marie cozy and safe behind the light blue walls of that faraway house.

Hector Linn was as angry as he was the day of the Rising. He'd lost his parents and many other relations to a Zunft raid in Catille, and he was ready to rip the world apart with his bare hands. He fought the guards until they clubbed his head with a rifle, jammed the sack over his face, and dragged him down the corridor. Kevin Smythe didn't fight and neither did Jack Stevens. They were led into the corridor at the same time, and shared a glance before they, too, were blinded by the burlap placed over their eyes. In Jack's mind, he was already dead. Shot to death, instead of his son, Christopher, on the streets of Sevenna.

They came for Michael Henry last. He had heard Hector's shouts and the dull thud of the rifle butt against his friend's head. Michael had already decided it was futile to fight. They brought the men into the courtyard where the deep puddles were crusted with a thin layer of ice. The men kept tripping as they tried to walk blindly across the open ground led by men who didn't care if they fell. The soldiers brought out a wooden chair and set it near the east wall. Hector was still unconscious from the blow of the rifle. They tried to prop him up in the chair, but he toppled off and fell face-first into the mud. So they tied him to the chair and lined the other men in a row beside him.

The firing squad took its place. Each soldier had been issued a new gun to reduce the chance of a misfire. The captain gave the order silently. Each bullet found its mark, and the four standing men fell dead to the ground. Hector's head rolled back from the impact, and everything was still.

Gavin thought about Tamsin's treatise for the rest of the night. By Monday morning, he'd made his decision. Once he did, he wondered why he'd ever hesitated in the first place. By seven a.m., he arrived at the cellar that housed the *JFA Bulletin* and worked without pause through the morning to edit and type-set the words that Tamsin had written. His three-person staff arrived around lunchtime to prep the press. Theo, his artist, de-signed a simple line drawing of a rising sun for the cover. They kept their heads down, worked hard, and said little. Maybe it was Gavin's demeanor, but there seemed to be an understanding that something important was happening. When the prototype was finished, it was a twenty-four-page pamphlet called *The Right to Rule* by Angry Em.

At six p.m., Theo ran out to grab the *Zunft Chronicle*, and when he came back, his eyes were red. He laid the paper out on the workbench, and everyone gathered around to see the head-line: "Cottager Rebels Found Guilty, Executed at Dawn." A hor-rible silence followed.

"They didn't even let them see their families before they shot them," Theo said.

"Michael Henry is dead?" Shauna asked. She was one of Gavin's typesetters, and she had worked with Michael on the pre-vious paper. "The August 5 are dead."

Everyone looked at Gavin expectantly. For a moment, Gavin couldn't speak. At one time, Michael Henry had been like a father to him. Michael had hated Gavin after he wouldn't join the August Rising, and the two had never reconciled. Gavin wondered how Tamsin would hear about her father's death. He wanted to drop everything and find her before she heard the news from a Zunft newspaper, but he wasn't sure if she'd even want to see him.

"Let's get this work done," he said finally. "Believe me when I say that this will be a fitting tribute."

No one else had read *The Right to Rule* cover to cover, but they all trusted Gavin to do the right thing. Gavin asked Shauna to add a simple dedication to the title page: *In Memory of the August 5.* But otherwise, he let Tamsin's words stand as she had written them. A few hours later, Gavin sent his staff home when he knew he could handle the rest of the work himself. The press finished running at three a.m. An hour later, two hundred copies of *The Right to Rule* were ready to be bundled into crates. Soon, a horse and wagon rolled into the alley north of the basement offices, and Verner, an elderly man and one of Mr. Leahy's uncles, helped Gavin load the crates into the back. By the time they were done, it was five a.m. on Tuesday. It was less than twenty-four hours after Michael Henry had died at the hands of the Zunft. Gavin watched Verner's horses plod slowly down the muddy road and into the still-sleepy city. Despite the weight of what they carried, there was no urgency to their gait.

The *Bulletin*'s distribution system had been set up without Gavin's knowledge so that if he were interrogated by the Zunft, Gavin could never endanger the messenger boys or the shopkeepers who carried his illegal newspaper. He tried to imagine what would happen to Tamsin's treatise now, but his mind was too foggy. He hadn't slept since Saturday night, and then, only for a few hours. He no longer had any control over what happened, nor was he any use to anyone until he got some sleep.

I'm getting sick, Gavin realized. His body ached and he was starting to shiver but not from the cold. Gavin went back inside and cleaned up the presses. He took the southern route out of the warehouses and emerged four blocks away. By then, he was so unnaturally tired that he was afraid he wouldn't make it back to his rooftop shack. He didn't even take off his boots before he fell into bed. He dragged the quilt up over himself and faded into a deep sleep behind his blue door.

Meanwhile, in the streets of Sevenna, the words of Angry Em were spreading like wildfire.

24

The Right to Rule (excerpt)

In this story, a man is given power. He is not rewarded for any inherent goodness or innate skill. He is not a kind man. He was born into a world that favored him, but even that did not propel him to the pinnacle of control. This could be the story of how he got there—the lies he told and the people he harmed. But instead this is the story of what he did next.

When a man comes into power, his true nature reveals itself. And Colston Shore has revealed who he truly is, and we must stand up to him before it is too late.

I urge the immediate boycott of all Zunft businesses. Do not buy bread from those Zunftmen who have profited from Shore's war against us. Cottagers must turn to one another in this time. No matter what you make, sell only to cottagers. If you work for the Zunft in any capacity, you must stop immediately today.

Today is the Cessation. The cottagers will no longer serve their common master. Do not service their houses, their shops, their factories. Stay in your communities and take care of one another, the gardens, the health and well-being of your kin and neighbors.

We will bring Colston Shore to his knees, and we will do it through kindness to our fellows.

—Angry Em

Tommy awoke early to put the finishing touches on his math homework. He was finally getting his focus back after his strange night with Emilie in the cottager district. For days afterward, whenever he tried to do his work, his mind refused to cooperate. But finally, he flew through the arithmetic without getting distracted by thoughts of the red-haired cottager or the cellar with the portraits of the missing. His stomach growling, he ran down the steps, just in time to meet up with Kristin and Ellie as they were leaving for breakfast in the dining hall.

"Hello, ladies," he said, and they greeted him cheerfully. There had been no further incidents since Kristoph and Dennett called him a pansy boy in the dining hall. He wondered if Rannigan might target him during the lecture, but so far Rannigan hadn't paid any attention to him at all. The students avoided talking to him and went out of their way to avoid him in the corridors. He didn't really mind being an outcast because Ellie and Kristin were better friends than any of the lads had been anyway. Tommy still hadn't talked to Bern since the vandalism at the garden. He was mostly worried about what Bern might say to their father about him.

They were halfway across the Green with Kristin prattling about her mother when Ellie interrupted her.

"Something's wrong," Ellie said. Kristin frowned at Ellie's interruption.

"With my mother?" Kristin asked. "Well, I should say so. She takes everything I say out of context."

"What do you mean?" Tommy asked Ellie.

"The porter wasn't in his office," she said. "And the bells didn't ring this morning. Where's Bellkeeper Ben?"

Bellkeeper Ben was an elderly cottager who had worked for the Seminary since the dawn of time. He called all the boys John and when the girls had arrived, he called them all Missy. The bells rang on the hour, and the lads said that it took old Ben twenty minutes to climb up and down the bell-tower ladder every time. It was a running joke that by the time old Ben reached the bottom, he had to climb back up and do it again.

"There are no groundskeepers either," Tommy said.

They reached the dining hall where dozens of Zunft soldiers were gathered inside the doors, far more than usual for the morning meal. The soldiers stood at attention while the students began to file into the cold room. The kitchens were shuttered and dark. Most of the tables were bare, but someone had set out platters of last night's bread and hunks of cheese on a table near the back.

"Where's breakfast?" someone called.

The students muttered among themselves as it suddenly dawned on them that this was all there was to eat. The side door banged open and Headmaster Olberg stalked in with his black robes flapping behind him. His hair was uncombed and as he chatted with two of the senior professors, he surveyed the students with concern. The three men conversed while the students grew more impatient. Finally, Olberg climbed the platform, but he tripped on his loose robe and had to catch his balance on the top stair. Someone snickered, but the rest of the hall was silent with anticipation.

"Students, there has been a work stoppage among our cottager servants," Olberg said. "We are taking steps to make sure that their tasks are completed in a timely manner. But in the meantime, there will be no complaining. You will ignore any inconvenience and continue with your studies. Travel outside the Seminary is discouraged."

Ellie was standing next to Tommy and she whispered in his ear. "The cottagers didn't show up to work, and that's what he's warning us about? He's worried about people complaining?"

Dennett raised his hand. He was standing near the front by Olberg, who nodded at him. "What about breakfast?" Dennett asked. "I'm starving and this wouldn't keep the rats happy."

"Yes, well, you can leave the Seminary if you are hungry," Olberg agreed. "I don't expect this will continue long. Classes are going to be held on their regular schedules. Do not take the laziness of the cottagers as an opportunity to be lazy yourselves."

After a few slices of stale bread, Tommy headed to his lecture hall for math class. A group of his classmates congregated outside the entrance while a soldier struggled with a huge ring of iron keys. He tried one after another, but none of them opened the door. Tommy waited by himself off to the side. He wished Ellie was there. At least she would appreciate the irony that the Zunft couldn't even unlock a door without the aid of the cottagers.

Ultimately, the class was canceled because no one could figure out how to get inside. Tommy went back to his room and tried to read. But he kept staring out at the city, wondering what might be happening in the southern districts to keep the cottagers home. Around noon, he heard a tapping on his door. He hoped it was the porter telling him the status of the lunch meal, but it was Ellie and Kristin standing in the hallway.

"Any news?" he said.

"Yes," Kristin said excitedly.

"Can we come in?" Ellie asked.

"Uh, I guess," Tommy said.

"No porters. No rules," Ellie said as she marched inside. Someone was bound to report them, but Tommy would worry about that later.

"It's not just the Seminary," Kristin said. "We went up Dawson Street and it's deserted as a cemetery!"

"There are no cottagers anywhere," Ellie said. "Some of the Zunft shops are open, but no one is shopping. The city is the most deserted I've ever seen it, even on the Sunday night of a holiday weekend."

Tommy wondered what his father was going to do. He would be furious at the cottagers. Any defiance from his young children brought harsh punishment. How would he take it when half the city refused to do their appointed jobs?

"Did you get the *Chronicle* this week?" Tommy asked. "What's been going on in the news?"

"I haven't read one lately," Ellie said. "I've been busy with schoolwork."

Kristin hadn't seen it either, so they headed over to the Reading Room in the library, which was also unnaturally empty.

Usually, the soft armchairs of the Reading Room were filled with students.

"I'm starting to feel nervous about all of this," Kristin said. The volt-lamps glowed brightly on the polished stands beside the chairs, but there was no one there to use them. The librarians had hung the week's papers on wooden dowels in a glass case, and Tommy flipped through them. Monday's issue had the biggest headline: "Cottager Rebels Found Guilty, Executed at Dawn." Emilie had mentioned Michael Henry. Maybe the work stoppage had something to do with the executions. But Tuesday's lead article was something bland about the price of Aeren grain, not about the August Rising.

"What do you think?" Ellie asked.

"I don't know," Tommy said.

"Do you think you should talk to your father?" Ellie asked.

"Why?" Tommy wondered. It was a strange request from Ellie, who hated Chief Administrator Shore. And Tommy didn't like to seek his father out, especially in times like this. It wasn't like the man would have comforting words.

"We need to know what's going on," Ellie said.

"Let's give it some time and see if things go back to normal," Tommy said. "There's not going to be lunch, obviously. Do you want to go down to the harbor and see if we can find an open café?"

"It will be funny to watch a Zunftman try to serve his own customers," Kristin said.

But when they got to the waterfront, all the shops and cafés were shuttered. There were no workers, no crowds—only silent, empty docks. They strolled out to the end of the longest pier, where a lone wrought-iron bench faced the horizon. There was a bundle of papers on the bench, and Ellie picked it up and inspected the cover. It was a slightly damp pamphlet with a stylized drawing of a rising sun.

"*The Right to Rule*, by Angry Em?" Tommy read the cover aloud.

"It's put out by the *JFA Bulletin*," Ellie said. "I've read the bulletin before, and I recognize the symbol on the back. It says it was published on Tuesday."

The three of them squeezed together on the bench with Ellie seated in the middle. They took turns reading aloud from the treatise. When they finished, they sat staring out into the lonely sea and the flat gray horizon. "Today is the Cessation. The cottagers will no longer serve their common master."

"I guess we know where the stoppage came from," Tommy said.

"You mean the Cessation," Ellie corrected him.

"Is it strange to read about your father like that?" Ellie asked.

"I feel like a villain," Tommy said. "I wish I wasn't on the wrong side of this conflict."

"'When a man comes into power, his true nature reveals itself,'" Ellie recited from memory.

"Like Professor Rannigan," Kristin said. "He had his own little kingdom and used his power to bully Charlotte."

"I hope I'm never like that," Ellie said. "Do you think your father knows what a bastard he is?"

"I think he's justified it all in his mind," Tommy said. "I think he firmly believes he's doing this for the greater good."

"That's so scary," Ellie said. "There could be things that I do that are like that. What if I'm hurting people and can't even see it?"

Kristin patted her friend's arm. "I don't think so, Ellie," she said. "You think too much to be unconsciously cruel."

They sat in silence for a long while on the bench at the end of the pier and watched the rolling waves. It felt like they were alone in the middle of the ocean. Tommy felt a strange mixture of hope and fear. Maybe this would force his father to change— make him reveal what had happened to the missing cottagers. But there was a sense of dread, too. Like when he'd done something wrong as a child and knew his punishment was coming. He tried to tell himself that this was different. This wasn't one little boy hiding in his closet against the wrath of his father. This was thousands of people working together to send a message to Colston Shore.

"It feels like another world," Tommy said.

"Maybe it will be," Ellie replied. She took Tommy's hand with her left and Kristin's hand with her right, and the three of them held hands for a long time. While they sat there, Tommy felt safe and strong, as if they formed a bulwark against a coming storm.

25

SHORE PROMISES QUICK END TO COTTAGER WORK STOPPAGE

Chief Administrator Shore says the cottager work stoppage is an act of hostility against the Zunft government and people. He promises a quick and decisive resolution.
—*Zunft Chronicle*, November 1, Evening Edition

The demonstration was planned for Friday and it had the potential to be the largest protest in the history of Seahaven. By embracing the Cessation, thousands of cottagers were promising to join together and march north to Seminary Square. Tamsin had written about the need for such a march in *The Right to Rule*, but she had provided no details. Now, to make it happen, they had to decide the time and location. And they needed to do it soon, before cracks started occurring in the cottagers' resolve.

Tamsin wanted to find Gavin and get his opinion on the march. She tried to find him at the *Bulletin* offices, but he wasn't there. Then she got involved in a long discussion with Shauna, the typesetter, who was working on the announcement. Shauna needed a decision on when and where people were supposed to assemble. Tamsin knew she couldn't wait anymore if they wanted to get the news out in time.

"Eight a.m. at Shadow Bridge," Tamsin decided.

"Should we call it the Michael Henry March?" Shauna said.

"No," Tamsin said vehemently. "Five people were murdered this week. Call it the Martyrs' March."

"Sure, all right," Shauna said. "Tamsin, if you need anything—"

"Thank you," Tamsin said. She'd heard that same offer dozens of times in the past few days. The Leahys' row house was overflowing with food given by people who didn't have much to give. Tamsin appreciated people's concern for her and she knew they were grieving for Michael Henry, too. But she wished she could turn invisible for a few weeks. With the timing of *The Right to Rule* and the immediate Cessation, she hadn't had time to process what had happened to her father. They hadn't even held a wake yet. She'd sent her mother a message by courier, but had heard nothing back. Brian Leahy offered to pay for her ferry home, and Tamsin planned to accept—as soon as Friday's march was over.

Amidst all the hustle and planning, Gavin was the one person she wanted to talk to, but he was nowhere to be found. She tracked Navid down at the Ash Street Garden and asked him to see if he could find Gavin. After that, she headed to the pub, which was officially closed, but it was packed with people anyway. Tamsin had appointed a task force to set up a food depository and another to see about a citizens' militia, and both groups were meeting at the pub.

"Has there been any violence south of the river?" Tamsin asked Mr. Leahy, who was leading the militia task force.

"Nothing," Mr. Leahy said. "And the Cessation seems to be absolute. No one is going to their jobs. I have to say I'm shocked that it took effect this quickly."

Tamsin nodded in agreement. "It's the timing with the executions. I don't think anyone would have paid attention to Angry Em if not for that."

They walked to the back of the pub and sat in one of the alcoves where no one could overhear them.

"We're not going to be able to hold out for long, Tamsin," Mr. Leahy said. "There are already rumors of hoarding. Right now, there are enough supplies to go around and people are still willing to share, but . . ."

"I know," Tamsin said. "We don't have longer than a week before we'll start losing people."

"A week is optimistic, in my opinion," Mr. Leahy said.

"It depends on Friday's march," Tamsin said. "If people turn out—*thousands* of people—then the Zunft will have to listen to us."

Mr. Leahy nodded grimly. "You have my full support. Let me know what you want me to do."

"We need to get some kind of watch in the neighborhoods. The first news of violence among ourselves, and I think this dream comes to a very bitter end."

When she heard the door to the kitchen open, she slid out of the booth hoping to see Gavin, but it was Navid. The boy saw her worried face, frowned, and shook his head. There was still no sign of the young journalist.

"He's expected at the *Bulletin* tonight," Navid said. "Do you want me to stop by and talk to him then?"

"No, it's okay," Tamsin said, trying to hide her concern. "I'll take care of it."

"Did you check his house?" Mr. Leahy asked.

"I did," Navid replied. "He's not there."

"Well, don't worry. He'll show up," Mr. Leahy said, patting Tamsin's hand.

After Navid left, Mr. Leahy turned back to Tamsin and studied her somberly. "We have to talk about Michael's funeral arrangements."

"Not now," Tamsin said. "Have they even released the bodies?"

"You could include that in your list of grievances," Mr. Leahy said.

"Let's worry about the living now," Tamsin said. "I want every political prisoner released from that compound. I want to see all of our missing friends free tomorrow after we take the streets of Sevenna."

Because of the Cessation, Gavin had run out of paper to print the notices for Friday's big march. He spent the day in Verner's wagon, scouring the cottager districts for a supply of paper he could buy. Finally, after several hours and no success, Verner suggested they visit someone he knew on the coast, south of Sevenna. Gavin had heard of Mr. Ollav before. By reputation, he was more criminal than cottager or Zunft. Mr. Ollav was far too interested in Gavin's reasons for wanting so much paper, but after dodging his questions, Gavin paid the exorbitant price and headed back to the city with his precious supply.

By the time Verner dropped Gavin off in an alley near the *Bulletin* offices, it was early Thursday morning. Verner offered to help Gavin carry the heavy reams inside, but Gavin knew the old man was tired and sent him on his way. Struggling under the heavy load, Gavin carried two bundles down the stairs on his first trip. With his shoulder aching, he decided that one bundle at a time was more realistic. He was about to head back up to the alley when he noticed two notes on the workbench. The first was from Shauna: *The notice is ready to print, but we have no paper!* The second was Tamsin's handwriting: *Are you all right? Come and find me. Please.—T.H.*

Gavin checked his chronometer. He had enough time to get the notices printed and on the streets by the end of the workday. He really wanted to take a break, find Tamsin, and have a long talk, but there was too much work. His staff had prepped the press except for the paper. Gavin heaved one ream into place. As he turned the crank to feed the paper along the spools, he heard a noise outside in the corridor. Thinking that maybe Verner had followed him down, he opened the door—and saw a Zunft soldier. Gavin didn't have time to react before the soldier slammed him in the head with a truncheon. He fell backward, like a tree falls after a logger finishes his cut. After that, his mind was blank. He was unconscious before he hit the ground.

When Gavin woke up, he was still in the *Bulletin* offices, propped awkwardly against the wall near the entrance. His hands were tied behind his back, and his body felt bruised as if he had been tossed around. He wasn't sure how long he'd been out. Soldiers milled around the room and inspected crates and stacks of papers. Two of the officers seemed to be discussing the handwritten bulletin about the march. He tried to remember where he'd put Tamsin's note. Thankfully, she'd only jotted down her initials, and they wouldn't be able to guess her identity from that.

"Get the mallets," someone said, and Gavin felt an overwhelming sense of sadness. There would be no march now. No reunion with Tamsin. A soldier left to retrieve the sledgehammer. Another flipped the workbenches over. The soldier took his truncheon and smashed the glass on the compartments of metal letters for the press. Another lifted the rosewood case and hurled it across the room in Gavin's direction, who couldn't even raise his arms to defend himself. The case slammed against his shoulder and tore a gash. The metal letters scattered across the room. *The rosewood case held letters* A–G, Gavin thought. *Think how many words are lost to me without* A–G.

"You want him now?" a soldier asked an officer.

"No, they'll do that at the compound," the officer said. "Get him into the rover, and we'll finish up here."

The guard grabbed the ropes around Gavin's wrists and dragged him roughly into the corridor. His arms were twisted unnaturally as he struggled to find his feet. He made it upright, but the guard kicked his knee so it bent sideways. Gavin fell to the ground, the pain nearly making him sick to his stomach. Two guards each grabbed one of Gavin's arms and hauled him along like a sack of flour. Gavin felt the muscles in his shoulders tear with the pressure from the strange angle. Through the fog of pain and humiliation, he was vaguely aware of the soldier returning with a heavy sledgehammer. As they reached the alley, Gavin could hear the steady thud of the sledgehammer as they destroyed his printing press.

Gavin didn't lift his head when they threw him into the metal box mounted on the back of the rover, so he didn't see Navid on the rooftop, staring down in horror as the door slammed shut with a metallic clang.

Struggling to open his eyes, Gavin reached for his throbbing forehead. His fingertips brushed a cotton bandage that had been plastered over the wound. *Why beat a man only to patch him up? Why untie him only to throw him in jail?* Gavin wondered as he pushed himself up on his elbows and assessed his surroundings with blurry eyes. The door to the cell was partially open and Gavin could see indistinct figures moving around in the corridor outside. He sat up painfully and swung his feet to the floor. His spectacles were missing and his knee was so swollen he couldn't bend it.

He was in a windowless prison cell. But instead of being alone, a uniformed man sat next to his cot. Judging by the stripes on the man's uniform, this was a high-ranking officer. Expressionless, the two men considered each other. The Zunft officer was a tall man with a lean build who seemed familiar. He was middle-aged with gray hair. From his neatly trimmed beard to his golden cuff links, he exuded an air of prosperity. Suddenly, Gavin realized who was in the cell with him: Colston Shore. Gavin blinked his eyes, trying to get used to the world without his glasses.

Shore tossed Gavin's bent frames onto his lap. One of the lenses was cracked, but at least now he could see clearly. The chief administrator held up the handwritten notice about Friday's march that had been taken from the *Bulletin* offices. For all Gavin knew, Friday had come and gone.

"I'm told you are the publisher of the illegal press known as the *JFA Bulletin*," Shore said. "Is this true?"

Gavin said nothing. There wasn't much use denying it, considering he'd been found inside the press office.

"Either you are, or you aren't," Shore said impatiently. "If you don't admit to it, I will continue making arrests until I find the correct man."

"It's me," Gavin said.

"You are a rabble-rouser, Mr. Baine," Shore said. "A propagandist. You rile the common man over matters that don't concern him."

"How can our freedom not concern us?" Gavin asked quietly.

"Freedom?" the Zunftman scoffed. "You couldn't comprehend the word."

Zunftmen like Shore often used the argument that cottagers weren't intelligent enough for political thought. Gavin took a deep breath, but he felt strangely calm. He had little to gain by arguing with Colston Shore. He wasn't going to sway the man's opinions. He was now in the compound, the place where cottager rebels went to die.

"I read the treatise you published," Shore said. "*The Right to Rule*. It's the origin of this work stoppage, which threatens the health and safety of every man, woman, and child in this city."

Gavin thought about pointing out that the origin of the Cessation was as much the martyrdom of the rebel leaders as it was the treatise, but he stayed quiet. He was beginning to understand his purpose here and why Colston Shore himself was dealing with a lowly journalist.

"Who is Angry Em?" Shore said.

"Em doesn't exist," Gavin said.

"Who is Angry Em?" Shore repeated.

"Em doesn't exist," Gavin repeated. Shore's eyes narrowed.

"I don't like games," Shore said. "I don't like inane conversations."

"I wrote the treatise," Gavin said. "It's a pseudonym. I made her up."

"I didn't ask if Em was a woman," Shore said. "If it's a pseudonym, why does she have a gender? Who is she?"

"I am. I wrote *The Right to Rule*." Gavin tried to reassure himself that he hadn't given anything away. Shore was trying to rattle him.

"Do you have children?" Shore asked.

Gavin took that as a threat and stayed quiet.

"I have children," Shore said. "And I want them to live the life they deserve."

And what about the lives of our children? Gavin wondered to himself. But Colston Shore was incapable of seeing the world in any other way but his own. Gavin didn't want to waste any more of his words on a man who wouldn't listen.

Shore stood up and opened the door wider. "Guard," he called into the corridor.

A large man with short brown hair appeared in the doorway. Except for his uniform, he looked like an ordinary man, neither particularly cruel nor particularly kind. He could be a husband, a father, or one of the men who shot the August 5 dead. Gavin had the absurd thought that it would be easier to recognize evil men if they had some visible sign, like horns, or fangs like a snake.

"Mr. Baine is not cooperating," Shore told the guard.

The guard grabbed Gavin's shirt with one hand and dragged him off the cot. Gavin couldn't support his weight on his hurt leg, so he stood on one leg awkwardly, still in the clutches of the guard.

"Who is the woman?" Shore asked. "Is she family? A close friend? Why are you protecting her?"

"I am Angry Em," Gavin said.

Shore nodded at the guard, who casually backhanded Gavin across the face like he was swatting a fly.

"I *am* Angry Em," Gavin repeated, louder this time.

"Officer Sanneral," Shore called.

A smallish officer with a tidy beard on a pointy chin came into the room. "Yes, sir?"

"We're having some trouble with the prisoner," Shore said. "He's a liar. He needs some help in learning to tell the truth. Officer Sanneral, would you please assist Mr. Baine in our quest for the truth?"

With that, the chief administrator left Gavin in the hands of the other men. Even before the next strike hit him, Gavin willed himself to forget Tamsin, to forget her face, her laugh, to forget dancing with her in the pub. From this moment on, he could never let himself speak her name again. As the blows rained down, he kept repeating the same phrase to himself again and again: *I will prove to you I'm not a coward, Tamsin. I will prove it to you.*

26

COTTAGER GANG
LEADERS ARRESTED

In their ongoing effort to curb the work stoppage, soldiers have raided the headquarters of a notorious cottager gang in the basement of an abandoned glassworks factory near Seventh Stone Bridge. Stolen property was recovered and several criminals were arrested, including Gavin Baine and Verner Leigh.

—*Zunft Chronicle*, November 3

A soldier delivered a note to Tommy's door at Seminary. Colston Shore was hosting another dinner party on Friday, and his son's presence was required. No excuses would be tolerated. Tommy was surprised because the Cessation was still going strong. Streets were deserted, shops closed, and soldiers patrolled the streets like they were at war. While Seminary had brought in workers from Catille to keep the school functioning, the city was far from normal. Still, Tommy decided it was easier to comply than risk his father's ire at a time like this.

Tommy hadn't spoken to Bern, so he didn't bother to stop by his brother's room in Sachsen Hall before he set out for his father's town house on Friday. As he stepped outside Dawson Street Gate, a hooded figure came out of the alley and moved toward him. There were still beggars in the northern district despite the Cessation, so he avoided eye contact. The person intercepted him on the corner near Abel's Toys and held up a cap, as if for a donation. Tommy dug in his pocket for a coin, but then the beggar said his name: "Tommy."

Tommy peered at the person's face. It wasn't a beggar at all. It was Emilie. The dark hood covered her red hair, and her face was gaunt and tired. She stared at him with bleary, bloodshot eyes.

"Hey," he said in surprise. "What's wrong?"

"Pretend you don't know me," she whispered. He glanced around quickly, but there was no one near them on the street.

"Are you waiting for me?" he asked.

"Your father arrested my friend yesterday," Emilie said. "He's in the compound and they're going to kill him, like they did my fath—I mean, like they did Michael Henry. I need to find out what's happening to him. Please, can you help me?"

"Oh, Emilie, I don't know what I can do," Tommy said. "If I ask, it will mean trouble for everyone."

Emilie's eyes brimmed with tears. "I know. It was so stupid to come."

"I want to help," Tommy told her. "But even if I asked him, he wouldn't tell me anything, and he'd want more information about you."

"I know you can't *ask* him," Emilie cried. "But is there any other way to find out? My friend's name is Gavin Baine. Is there anyone else you can trust?"

Tommy realized how desperate she must feel to have waited for him here in the heart of a Zunft district on the off chance that he could help her.

"I'll try," Tommy said. "But please don't get your hopes up."

"Leave a note for me in the mail slot of Ash Street Garden," she said. "Address it to Emilie and give me a time to meet you. I'll be at the north end of the garden at the appointed time."

"All right," he said. Suddenly, she shook the cap aggressively in front of Tommy's face.

"Coin!" she said loudly.

"Hello, crazy cottager," said Bern, who appeared at Tommy's elbow. "Why don't you go play in front of a wagon?"

Emilie glared at him. Her hostility toward him was evident, and it made Bern cross.

"I said, go away," Bern told her. Tommy could feel the tension between them escalating dangerously.

"Let's go, Bern," Tommy said, dropping a coin into the cap.

Bern made a sudden lunge toward Emilie, pretending like he was going to hit her. She flinched and took a step backward. Tommy wanted to kill his brother for being such a bully.

"Cut it out," Tommy insisted. Bern made the stupid gesture one more time, only this time, Emilie didn't flinch. Emilie spun on her heel and walked away.

"Maybe you should get a job," Bern called to her back.

"Leave her alone," Tommy said.

"You never learn, do you," Bern said with disgust. "You're still taking the wrong side."

The boys took separate routes to Colston's house, but they arrived at nearly the same time. Instead of a butler, a soldier opened the door. When the twins stepped into the foyer, Tommy counted five guards stationed along the corridor and standing watch at the front windows. Bern and Tommy made their way into the sitting room, where a handful of Zunftmen and their wives stood near a refreshment table. It was a much smaller number than at the festive gathering earlier in the autumn. Tommy recognized his father's old friends and political allies, but he didn't see any of the new Carvers who had joined Colston after the August Rising. The mood in the room was tense, and conversation seemed strained.

"What's going on?" Tommy whispered to Bern. "Why did Father insist on hosting people tonight? And where is he?"

"After avoiding me for weeks, now we're talking?" Bern said.

"I thought you weren't talking to me," Tommy said.

"You're the recluse, not me," Bern said.

"I've been busy with schoolwork," Tommy explained.

"Whatever you say, Tommy," Bern said.

Kristin entered the room with her father, but when Tommy waved at her, she shot him a warning glance. He got the message—she wanted him to pretend not to remember her. Tommy felt disappointed. Talking with Kristin would have made the night bearable. He spent the next hour watching men play billiards and wondering why his father hadn't yet made an appearance at his own party. The bell rang in the kitchen, and as the guests filed toward the dining room, Kristin maneuvered her way beside him.

"Miss Sommerfield would like to see you tomorrow at noon," Kristin whispered. "You're to meet her on the bench. She said you'd know what that means."

Tommy nodded. The "bench" was where they'd sat in Sebastian's Circle on the day that Charlotte had been taken to the hospital.

"What's wrong?" Tommy asked as quietly as he could.

Kristin shrugged and tossed her blond curls. "I'm so excited about dinner!" she said in her stupid-girl voice that she used to make Tommy and Ellie laugh. She was warning him it wasn't safe to talk anymore. Tommy turned away from her, but he felt irritated and unsettled by everything that was happening that evening. And he hadn't even seen his father yet.

As the guests were taking their assigned seats, Colston strode into the room and took his seat at the head of the table.

"My apologies, everyone," he said. "I'm sorry to keep you waiting. There was a crucial matter I had to attend to."

The guests were murmuring to one another and arranging napkins on their laps when a loud noise startled everyone. It was a sound like thunder, but the sky had been cloudless all day. One of the wives gasped dramatically and clutched her husband's elbow. Colston raised his hands as if he were about to speak, but a loud explosion in the distance jolted the floor. In the middle of the long table, a goblet teetered and then tipped over. Everyone stared as red wine seeped into the white tablecloth. A few of the guests started toward the windows, but Colston said sharply: "There's no need for that. Please, sit down."

Outside, another explosion boomed in the distance, and people glanced at one another nervously. Tommy was sitting two seats away from his father, and from his vantage point, he could see the southern horizon outside the open balcony door. There was an unnatural red glow above the skyline. The southern district was ablaze.

"Welcome, friends," Colston said with an air of satisfaction. "We are witnessing the end of an era. Tonight, the cottagers will learn their place in Zunft society. They will no longer feel entitled to use violence to destroy our way of life. Tonight, our traditions will be upheld. Our glory finally restored."

Across the table, Kristin's eyes were huge. She reminded Tommy of a frightened animal. Her father laid a protective hand on her back. Even Colston's longtime political allies seemed perplexed. Apparently, none of them knew what was happening to the city any more than Tommy did.

"They will see that my reach extends into every rat hole in this city," Colston said. "After tonight, the Cessation will be over, and its leaders will understand—without a doubt—that such gestures are futile. Tomorrow, we will wake up and our lives and livelihoods will be returned to normal. You have my word."

Another loud explosion rocked the room. This one was only a few blocks away. A breeze blew through the open balcony, bringing in the scent of burning wood and something metallic. Everything seemed surreal and frightening. His father seemed unnaturally calm, which was adding to Tommy's fear. How far would his father go to make people heel to him?

"With the exception of the leaders, the cottagers will be

forgiven," Colston said. "I will welcome them back to decent society with open arms."

There was an awkward silence, and then Karl Anderson began applauding. One by one, the other guests joined in. But even the sound of clapping did nothing to drown out the violence outside. Still, Colston seemed pleased, especially when Anderson raised his glass and said: "Heritage, honor, good health!"

Colston raised his own glass, smiled magnanimously, and motioned to the guards to bring the food in. As dinner progressed, Tommy marveled at the inane attempts at conversation while something terrible was going on outside. People avoided political talk entirely and the conversation flitted around ordinary things, like the weather and the flavor of the wine.

"The food is delicious," Mrs. Johnston said. It was the third time someone had said it. They'd already been informed that the chef from the officer barracks had been brought in to cook for them.

"Yes, the fish was caught fresh off Norde this morning," Colston told them. They already knew that the pears had come in from Catille and the cheese from Aeren. They'd discussed how the menu favored Catille cuisine as opposed to the Aeren tradition. They talked about Norde culinary traditions versus those of Sevenna. They kept talking and saying nothing until Tommy felt like screaming. While waiting for the dessert to be brought in, Tommy excused himself from the table, but instead of going to the washroom, he ducked into Colston's library. Behind him, he heard Mrs. Johnston extolling the virtues of the lemon crème pie.

The volt-lamps were off in Colston's library and the only light came from the glow of the fireplace. Tommy didn't know what he hoped to find, but he'd promised Emilie that he would try. He slipped behind Colston's massive mahogany desk and flipped through the stack of papers sitting on the corner. Most of it seemed innocuous, but he noticed the name of the pub the *Plough and Sun* on a handwritten list. Tommy peered more closely and realized that it was a long list of businesses: *Abel's Toys. The Rising Sun Café. Alfred's Fine Imports. Piper Leaf Market.* Tommy didn't recognize all of them, but he knew a few, like Abel's Toys, which he'd passed on Dawson Street on his way up to his father's house.

He heard quick footsteps in the corridor outside. He dropped the papers and scooted away from Colston's desk just as Bern came through the door. Tommy gazed into the fireplace and tried to act natural.

"What are you doing?" Bern demanded.

"I wanted to listen to the sound of explosions in private," Tommy told him.

"Seriously, Tommy," Bern said. "What is going on? You were talking to the cottager on Dawson Street for a couple of minutes before I came over. Are you in some kind of trouble?"

"She was a raving lunatic," Tommy explained. "And now I wanted a few moments to myself. The world is falling apart outside and everyone is acting like nothing is happening. Can't you understand that?"

"The world isn't falling apart, Tommy. It's being restored."

"Apparently, you and I have different definitions of that word," Tommy said.

"Oh, come on," Bern said in frustration. "What was Father supposed to do? Let them get away with it?"

"I don't care about politics," Tommy lied. "I'm tired of this party."

"Well, dessert is being served, and then we'll get out of here."

After devouring the pie as fast as possible, the other guests made their excuses and fled in their rovers. Tommy heard Colston tell Bern to wait in the foyer so a driver could take them back to the Seminary, but Tommy wasn't about to wait. He crept down to the cellar and let himself out the door. He waited until there were no guards in sight and then he threw himself over the fence into the neighbor's yard. He cut through several lawns and a park to avoid the route he would usually take to the Seminary. As he hurried through the deserted streets of the northern district, he expected to see the aftermath of something awful—people in distress, rubble, burning buildings—but there was nothing amiss among the town houses of the Zunft's elite.

It wasn't until he reached Dawson Street that he witnessed what his father had done in response to the Cessation. At the end of the street, directly across from the high Seminary wall, a sea of broken glass sparkled in the moonlight. The windows of Abel's Toys had been smashed and the insides gutted by flames. He splashed through puddles of ashy water in front of the ruined shop. The toy store had been one of the names on the list he'd seen in his father's library. He suddenly realized he'd seen a list of targets to be destroyed that night. But why destroy a toy store? Tommy tried to remember how many names had been on that list. Thirty? Fifty?

When he was back inside his room in Tauber Hall with the door locked, he stared out the window at the fires flickering on the horizon. What would the world be like tomorrow? Across the river, the Plough and Sun was either under attack or burned to the ground. Somewhere, Emilie was harboring the vain hope that Tommy might be able to do something to help. But he had nothing to offer her or anyone else.

27

OFFICERS RAID ILLEGAL
COTTAGER BUSINESS

Zunft soldiers raided Green Timbers, a grocery in South
Sevenna that has been linked to illegal cottager activities.
"There are many more of these establishments," said
an officer from the Zunft army. "They are like a cancer
eating away at the economic health of Seahaven."
—*Zunft Chronicle*, November 3, Evening Edition

Bern Shore had rekindled Tamsin's rage. She had so many trou-
bles on her mind, but all she could think about was his smug
face. It was no wonder that Mrs. Trueblood had hated him so
much. Tamsin wished she had punched Bern and broken those
pearly white teeth. She stalked the streets for a while, but eventually she grew weary of being furious and headed toward the
Plough and Sun, where hopefully someone had news of Gavin.
When she reached the other side of Shadow Bridge, she heard

boots pounding toward her. She whirled around, ready to fight, but it was only Navid.

"Not that way," he said desperately. "Come *this* way."

"What are you doing?" she asked.

"I've been waiting and waiting for you," Navid said. The boy was visibly upset. "Mama said to wait by this bridge because you would most likely use it. I waited forever, and I was certain you wouldn't come. But you came!"

Confused by his babbling, Tamsin let Navid lead her into an alley and out of sight. It was getting dark, and she couldn't imagine the Leahys telling their son to wait by Shadow Bridge for her. Sure, she used it often, but there were a number of other routes she might have taken. They had no idea what direction she would be coming from.

"Slow down," Tamsin said, and laid her hands on Navid's shoulders. He was a tough boy, and he was doing his best to seem that way now, but his lip was curled like he was trying not to cry. "I don't understand."

"Papa told me that I had to watch for you," he said. "He said if I didn't see you by the time I heard the eight o'clock bell, I was supposed to find a hiding place on the rooftops and spend the night."

"Navid, what is going on?" Tamsin asked.

"The Zunft soldiers crossed the Seventh Stone and Hanged Bridges," he said. "And they have checkpoints at the corner of Connell and Ash."

"How many?" Tamsin asked.

"I don't know," the boy said helplessly.

"Let's go to the pub," Tamsin said. "Let's see what's happening."

"No, Papa told me to find you and *not* let you go to the pub," Navid insisted. "He made me promise. He said that you're in charge of me now. You have to keep me safe."

"You're not fooling me," she said, trying to sound lighthearted. "No one needs to keep you safe. You're the one helping me."

Navid gave her a shaky grin. "Either way, Papa said we had to stick together. And we can't go to the pub."

"All right, we won't go by the street," Tamsin agreed. "But what about we take the roofs? I'm sure you know the way."

Navid thought about this seriously. "Yes, and there aren't any big gaps between here and there. But you have to stay down and follow me."

"I promise," Tamsin said. She watched Navid as he quickly scampered up the drainpipe like a squirrel climbing up a tree. Tamsin was strong, but she wasn't sure she could manage the same feat. Then she noticed ridges in the bricks that she could use like a ladder, but it still took her twice as long to reach the top. She was climbing over the railing and onto the roof when a loud explosion jarred them. The impact knocked Tamsin and Navid off their feet and onto the rough shingles. Had the explosion happened a moment earlier, Tamsin would have fallen down to the cobblestones. Tamsin started to pick herself up, but Navid tugged her back down.

"You're too tall," he said. "The soldiers might see you from the ground."

Hunched uncomfortably, they crawled across the roofs of three row houses that abutted one another before Navid stopped and pointed at the far corner. The roof had a decorative wooden railing and a small section had broken away.

"You can see the pub through that gap," he said. "But keep your head below the railing."

"I'll check it out, and then we'll go somewhere safe," she said. "You stay here, all right?"

She thought he would disagree with this, but he didn't. He nodded and chewed on his dirty fingernail. Tamsin crept forward and peered through the ruined railing. Across the street, the Plough and Sun was engulfed in flames. Fire shot out of the open door and through the shattered windows. Guards with chatterguns forced people to kneel in the middle of the street. From where she was, Tamsin couldn't see their faces clearly, but one of them had muscular shoulders and a lean stature that reminded her of Brian Leahy. There were no women to be seen, so she didn't know where Katherine might be. She pushed herself back from the edge and crawled to where Navid was waiting.

"What did you see?" Navid asked.

"It's on fire, but they got everyone out," Tamsin said.

"Are they trying to put it out?" Navid asked.

"Yes," she lied. "Let's go find somewhere to hide, like your papa wanted. You know where the shrine is? Can we get there on the roofs?"

Navid nodded. "We can get all the way there. I've done it before."

"All right, I'll follow you," she said. "We'll go as slow as we need to. We'll be like shadows, and no one will ever know we're here."

Having a plan seemed to cheer Navid up, and the two of them climbed across the rooftops until their hands were raw and bleeding. Explosions rocked the night and sparks rained down, and it took half the night to make it to the dead-end alley. They spent the rest of the night huddled together in the cellar deep underground behind a locked door while the faces of the missing watched over them. Finally, they fell asleep as the sun made its way into the sky, but its rays went unseen by the exhausted pair.

It was late afternoon when they finally made their way up the stairs. Tamsin pushed the door open a crack, almost expecting to see soldiers waiting for them. There was no one in sight, not even when they reached the street.

"It's like we're the last people in the world," Navid said, glancing up and down the deserted street.

She took Navid's hand. She wanted to tell him that everything was going to be fine, but she didn't know if that was true. They didn't have to go far before they saw wreckage. A building on the corner had been reduced to rubble. It had been a produce market, one of the bookless shops operated by cottagers but owned by a cottager sympathizer. Tamsin tried to recall the name, Green Timbers, or something like that. They turned the corner and the next street was worse. One entire side had caught fire, and all the row houses were reduced to ash.

"Where should we go?" Navid asked, still gripping her hand.

"Let me think for a second," Tamsin said. She knew that wandering around in the open wasn't very clever, but she couldn't go back and hide in the shrine without more information. She was the author of *The Right to Rule*, and Shore had attacked the cottagers because of the Cessation. With every footstep through the ash and rubble, Tamsin's guilt grew heavier. She had been a destroyer after all.

"Do you think my parents are alive?" Navid asked. "Can we see if they're at our house?"

"The soldiers might be there," she said. "We can't go to the pub either."

She suspected that the pub had been destroyed by the fire, but she didn't want to tell Navid that. Tamsin thought desperately about where they should go. Her father was dead, and Gavin was in the hands of the Zunft. Back on Aeren, her mother and sisters would stand by her, but they were as yet unaware of what had happened. Maybe she should take Navid back to Aeren, but there was no way to afford the ferry.

"Ash Street Garden," Navid suggested. "Let's go talk to Nova."

Tamsin nodded in agreement—maybe the Zunft had left the garden alone. On Ash Street, one store had been burned, but most of the street was undamaged. Rover engines rumbled to life in the distance. Navid glanced at Tamsin fearfully and they rushed through the open gate of the garden. Except for the broken greenhouses, which had been destroyed the previous month, the garden was unaffected by the previous night's violence. But there was no one inside the walls, and Tamsin wondered if every cottager in the city had been killed or arrested. Then something moved inside one of the ruined greenhouses. Tamsin and Navid crept cautiously toward it. There was a flash of gray, and then Nova appeared. She was backing through the doorway and trying to tug an unbroken pane of glass out the door.

"Nova!" Navid called.

Nova spun around, and when she saw Navid, joy bloomed on her aged face. She fell to her knees and wrapped her arms around the boy.

"Your mother is searching for you," she said after a long hug. "She's staying at the Millers' house. Do you know where that is?"

"Sure," Navid said. "It's the third house from the corner of River and Front Streets."

"Go straight there," Nova said. "Your mother will be frantic by now."

Navid nodded. "Bye, Tamsin. I'm going to see Mama."

After Tamsin watched him run toward the gate, she turned back to Nova. "Is it safe for him to go?"

"The Cessation is over," Nova said. "I guess you haven't seen the damage, but it's over."

"Katherine Leahy is safe?" Tamsin asked. "Who else? Who did we lose?"

Nova shrugged helplessly. "I don't know. There were a lot of arrests. Brian Leahy, for one."

"Did the soldiers leave?" Tamsin asked. "Did they go back to North Sevenna?"

"After they burned our businesses to the ground," Nova said.

Tamsin sank down on her heels and stared up at the gardener. "What do I do now, Nova? Tell me what I should do."

Nova gazed down at her sadly. "Help me put this glass in. Help me make the plants grow. That's what I'm going to do. That's all I know how to do."

28

RETURN TO NORMALCY

"The work stoppage is over, and our city is returning to normal," said Chief Administrator Shore.

—*Zunft Chronicle*, November 4

When Tommy awoke, it was a beautiful day outside his window. For a moment, he forgot that the world had turned upside down, but then he remembered the sea of sparkling glass in front of the burned-out toy store and the glow of the fires that had burned long into the night. Quickly, he rolled over and checked his chronometer. He was supposed to meet Ellie at noon, and it was now past eleven. It was much later than he usually slept, and he had missed the morning meal, if there had been one. As Tommy dressed and scrubbed his face, his heart was beating with nervousness. It seemed like the sun shouldn't be shining today. Like even the sky should show some indication that something had changed.

On his way through the Seminary grounds to the gate, he

reminded himself that he didn't know what had happened, not for certain. Maybe every place on that list *hadn't* been destroyed. Maybe his father's ominous pronouncements were only rhetoric and not facts. On Dawson Street, he passed cottager laborers cleaning up glass in front of the boarded-up shop. For the first time in days, there were shoppers along the street. It was a lighter crowd than typical for a Saturday morning, at least before the Cessation, but everything seemed so normal.

When he got to Sebastian's Circle, Ellie was perched on the edge of the bench. She shivered in the shadow of the old oak tree. The hood of her green wool coat was pulled up, and she was smartly dressed in black leather gloves and a scarf, but she was clearly miserable. The bench across the path was in a beam of sunlight, and he found it endearing that she was so particular about waiting for him in the correct location.

"Hey," he said. "Are you all right?"

"I hate the world," she said miserably. "I hate my place in it."

He sat down beside her, unsure of what to say.

"Do you know how many explosions there were?" she asked. "They're calling it the Night of a Hundred Fires. Abel's Toys was the only business hit on Dawson Street, but I heard the porters talking and they said the cottager districts were decimated."

"I guess it ended the Cessation," he said.

Ellie nodded. "It's horrible that your father gets to win this way. Oh, and Kristin and I are expelled."

"Wait, what?" Tommy asked.

"It happened yesterday," Ellie said. "That's why I wanted to meet you up here. But it seems so unimportant compared to what happened last night."

"It *is* important!" Tommy said. "What's going to happen?"

"I'm all packed," Ellie said. "After we're done here, I'm taking the ferry to Norde. I'm going to stay with Kristin's family. With Hywel missing, I don't have anywhere else to go."

"Oh, Ellie, I'm so sorry," Tommy said. "I wish there was something I could do."

She scooted closer to him and grabbed both his hands with her gloved fingers. "I only have a few minutes, but I need to tell you something."

"All right," he said. He was feeling a little choked up. Ellie was smart, tough, and courageous. And now he had no idea if he was ever going to see her again.

"I didn't really trust you," Ellie said, struggling with her words. "Not for a long time. You were the son of the chief administrator."

"Do you trust me now?" he asked.

"Yes, and I should have said something earlier," she said. "I should have told you."

"Told me what?"

"I was with Hywel the night before he disappeared," Ellie said. "Since I became his ward, I handled his paperwork and calendar. I spent a lot of time in his office. Honestly, I probably knew his business better than he did. He was an extremely disorganized man. Anyway, we were planning on going to Norde for the summer holiday, but that night, he got a message from your father."

"From my father? What night was this?"

"Two nights before the August Rising," Ellie said. "I don't know what your father said to get him to go all the way to Aeren, but he immediately changed his plans and left for Shore Manor."

"Wait, he went to Aeren the day before the Rising?" Tommy asked.

"Toulson Hywel wasn't in Sevenna City when he was kidnapped. He wasn't on Norde. He was with Colston Shore at your manor on Aeren."

Tommy stared at her. "What does that mean? He was kidnapped by cottagers on Aeren?"

"I don't know," Ellie said. "You were there that day, right? You never saw him?"

"No, I didn't," Tommy said. As soon as the words were out of his mouth, he remembered the carriage in front of the manor house when he and Bern had set out for Giant's Ridge. The Zunft symbol had been removed, and he'd found that strange at the time. He'd seen two figures standing near the window of his father's library. Could it have been Colston and Hywel? There was no way to tell.

Tears filled Ellie's eyes and she wiped them on her sleeve. "I'll miss you, Tommy," she said. "If things ever get better, come and visit me on Norde. Or send word to Kristin's family, and I'll come back for a visit. We'll meet here and freeze together on this bench."

Tommy put his arm around Ellie's shoulders and hugged her. "Don't worry, we'll see each other again," he said, wondering if it was a promise he could keep.

Back at Tauber Hall, he opened the door to his suite and had an unpleasant shock when he realized that someone was already there. Bern sat in his chair with his feet up on Tommy's desk, pretending to read a book.

"Get your feet off my desk," Tommy said. He couldn't believe that he'd forgotten to lock his door. "And turn the book right-side up."

Bern grinned sheepishly at the cover and then tossed the book onto the desk.

"Hey, little brother," Bern said. "Where have you been?"

"I went for a walk," Tommy replied.

"You shouldn't have left the dinner party without an escort," Bern informed him. "Father was furious. He had a rover waiting to take us home."

"Well, I made it fine," Tommy said.

"The cottagers went back to work today," Bern said. "Everything is going back to normal."

"And is all forgiven, just like Father said?" Tommy asked.

"They should be happy they get to come back at all," Bern said.

Tommy didn't want to talk about politics with Bern. He wanted his brother to go away so he could think about Ellie leaving and how he felt about it. Her news about Hywel seemed especially strange. She had acted like it was a major revelation, but he wasn't sure what it meant. Maybe the investigators should search for Hywel on Aeren, but there hadn't been any new demands for a few weeks—at least not that the *Zunft Chronicle* had reported. Hywel was probably dead by now.

"Are you listening to me?" Bern asked impatiently. "We need to get going."

"Where?" Tommy hadn't been listening.

"To the headmaster's office," Bern said. "They're meeting with everyone."

"Why?" Tommy asked, following Bern out into the corridor. He locked the door. When they were halfway down the corridor, he went back to double-check that he'd locked it.

"You're so annoying, Tommy," Bern said, when Tommy caught up with him. So Tommy went back a third time and checked the door again.

They took the path around the Green, which was crowded with lads enjoying the unexpected sunshine. Many were playing Litball, their jackets strewn on benches despite the chilly temperature. A few boys greeted Bern, inviting him to come and join the game.

"I'll be there later," Bern called.

"What's this meeting for again?" Tommy asked.

"It's a check-in after all the drama," Bern said. "Father arranged it, I'm sure."

They reached the new administration building, which was one of the most modern buildings in all of Sevenna. While most of the structures on campus had been built a century ago, this building was less than a year old. It seemed out of place to Tommy, like a shiny silver coin mixed in with a handful of old money. Bern yanked the front door open harder than necessary. He paused inside the threshold and glared back at Tommy.

"You've handled everything wrong," Bern said. "You were so easygoing as a child. We used to get along so well, and you've changed."

"We got along because I did what you said," Tommy pointed out. "You can't expect me to do that forever."

"Do you remember playing toy soldiers?" Bern asked. "You were the blue soldiers, and I had the red ones. What did you call them? The Annihilators?"

"That was your army," Tommy said. "Mine were the Falcons. And I only played blue because you took the red. They were nicer by far."

Tommy had an unexpected memory of their mother standing near the stained-glass window that she had installed in the playroom when they were little. In the afternoon, a kaleidoscope of light flowed through the colored glass, casting mottled blocks of color on the floor. That had been the boys' battlefield—a tapestry of light on a lazy summer afternoon. Bern would get angry, and Tommy would let him have his way, and they'd go back to their innocent games.

"Sitting with the girls," Bern said. "Making yourself an outcast with the lads. It should have been so easy for you. We are the sons of Colston Shore! When you do the wrong things, it makes my life harder."

"This has nothing to do with you," Tommy said.

"We're brothers. Twins! Everything that you do reflects on me and on Father. And you're embarrassing yourself. So you deserve everything that happens to you."

Tommy scowled at his brother. "Same to you, Bern," he said inadequately.

It was a stupid retort because Bern lived a golden life. At any rate, nothing bad ever seemed to happen to him. Bern opened the door wider and let Tommy go ahead of him into the foyer. They climbed the stairs and entered the gaudy waiting room. Golden couches faced each other across a mahogany table. Gilded molding accented the room and official state portraits hung on the walls. Even the wallpaper had a thread of gold running through it. No wonder Rannigan was so keen to have an office here, Tommy thought.

A soldier waited near Olberg's office, and Bern half-saluted him when they entered the lobby.

"Mr. Shore," the soldier said to Bern. "You can send your brother in now."

"Is the guard a friend of yours?" Tommy asked. He suddenly felt uneasy.

"The headmaster isn't meeting with other students," Bern said. "He's only meeting with you."

"You lied to me?" Tommy asked. "Why would he want to see me?"

"Well, Father heard about you snooping in his office last night—" Bern began.

"I wasn't snooping!" Tommy interrupted. "I can't believe you ratted me out."

"It wasn't my fault," Bern protested. "Father kept asking questions, and I couldn't lie to him."

"You just lied to me," Tommy said. He thought about ducking out the door, but the soldier seemed to read his mind and moved closer to him.

"Headmaster Olberg is waiting for you," the guard said.

"This will make you a better Zunftson," Bern said. "And a better brother."

"How is your Honor Index, Bern?" Tommy asked. "You're a liar and a vandal. I think you're on the negative side of zero."

"At least I'm not the one spending time with the enemy," Bern said, turning away from his brother.

"You are. You just can't see it," Tommy told him. But Bern was already out the door. Tommy imagined him bursting through the front door as the lads called him over to join their game in the sunshine. The guard jerked his head toward the headmaster's office, and Tommy followed him inside. Compared to the garish waiting room, Olberg's office was unexpectedly plain. The heavy drapes pulled across the window made the room feel claustrophobic. A volt-lamp glowed on the desk, which was cluttered with books and papers. Dozens of official portraits hung on the walls and the painted faces of the Zunftmen seemed to gaze down on Tommy in judgment.

"Please, sit down," Olberg said. He nodded at the soldier. "Shut the door behind you."

Thomas took the chair directly across from the headmaster. His heart was beating fast, making him dizzy and disoriented.

"I assume you've heard about the end of the Cessation," Olberg said. "Welcome news, indeed."

"Yes, sir," Tommy said. There was an awkward silence as Olberg waited for Tommy to say something more. There were dark circles under the headmaster's eyes and he shifted uncomfortably in his chair.

"Yes, well, I suppose you're wondering why you're here," Olberg said. "I received an order from the chief administrator, and I am compelled to act upon it. In the past, Seminary had autonomy from the Zunft and the actions of the Chamber, but with its dissolution, well, now it's a different world."

"My father sent you an order?" Tommy said. "What does that have to do with me?"

Olberg sighed. "It's about you, Thomas. Your father says you are guilty of actions unbecoming of a Seminary student. You are to be expelled immediately."

His father had cast him out and he hadn't even bothered to tell Tommy himself. Tommy felt like a stray dog who had been kicked away from the door.

"What actions?" Tommy asked in a quavery voice.

"I have no idea," Olberg said. "As far as I can tell, you've been a fine student, so this must be a personal matter. If I had authority to protest the matter, I would. But I don't, so here we are."

"What am I supposed to do?" Tommy asked. His cheeks flushed and shame overwhelmed him. He tried to reassure himself that his father was wrong, not him. But suddenly his future seemed like a scary black void.

"A guard is waiting outside to take you to the ferry," Olberg told him. "You are to return to your family's estate on Aeren. At least that's what it says in the message."

Tommy stared at Olberg. "And do what?"

"I don't know, Thomas," Olberg said with genuine sympathy in his voice.

"I'm not guilty of anything," Tommy said. "I haven't done anything wrong."

"Like I said, I can't choose to ignore this," Olberg said. "I have no recourse or appeal since the Chamber no longer exists."

Tommy blinked quickly, but tears pooled in his eyes. Horrified that Olberg might notice, he turned away slightly in his chair. He wanted to run away and lose himself in the city, but there was a guard in the hall and one waiting for him downstairs.

"Take a minute, Thomas," Olberg said quietly. "Get your wits about you. It's a lot to deal with."

Tommy's eyes darted along the portraits on the wall in front of him. There were few splashes of bright color among the mainly dark masculine hues depicting the former headmasters and professors of this renowned institution—where he was no longer welcome. A daub of purple caught his eye and he turned toward it. The painting showed a tall, thin man with prominent cheekbones above a red beard. In the painting, he was wearing a bowler hat and a shiny purple vest. He looked oddly familiar . . . particularly the purple vest. Not many Zunftmen would be seen in such a thing.

"Headmaster, who is that?" he asked, pointing to the man in the painting.

"Oh, that's Toulson Hywel. It was painted a few weeks before he was kidnapped. I don't suppose there's much chance he's alive now."

If the man in the purple vest was Toulson Hywel, then the former chief administrator had been on Miller's Road the day of the August Rising. Tommy had seen him near the entrance to the Harrow Trailhead. According to Ellie, Hywel had been visiting Tommy's father that very same day. Hywel had been in Colston's forest with two guards, but why?

"I'm ready to go," Tommy said loudly. "Now."

"Go where?" Olberg asked, obviously surprised at Tommy's change of demeanor.

"Now, to Aeren. You said there's a guard who will take me to the ferry?"

"Yes, that's right," Olberg said. "Your father said to tell you that your things will be shipped to you presently."

Tommy didn't care about his books and papers. He wanted to return to Aeren, climb up the ridge to Miller's Road, and figure out what secrets were lurking in the forest. The guard led him out of the administration building and toward the main entrance. As they were passing Tauber Hall, the main door opened and Ellie walked outside. She was laden with heavy tote bags, the last of her possessions that she was going to take to Norde. It suddenly occurred to Tommy that Ellie was heading to the port, too, and he had an idea. He broke away from the guard and ran over to her.

"Hey!" the guard protested.

"Tommy!" Ellie said in surprise. She was even more surprised when he threw his arms around her and put his lips close to her ear.

"I've been expelled, too," he whispered. "Take the ferry to Aeren instead of Norde. Hire a coach to take you to Shore Manor a few miles north along the coast. I'll meet you there tomorrow morning. Do you have money? Can you do that?"

"Yes," Ellie said. "I can, and I will. But why, Tommy?"

"I think I know where to find Hywel," Tommy said.

29

IT WAS EARLY THE NEXT MORNING
when the hired driver dropped Tommy and a single suitcase at
the desolate Shore Manor. As the carriage rolled away, he stood
on the dead grass in front of the bleak house, too exhausted to
be angry. He remembered walking with Bern past this very
spot on the day of the fire in Port Kenney. He felt sadness for
Bern because he knew his brother would never change—he
would never be able to see what life was truly like for the cottagers. But he also mourned the people he'd seen in the shrine
and even the August 5, who had lashed out when they felt they
had no other option. Back in Sevenna, the buildings destroyed
in the Night of a Hundred Fires were probably still smoldering
while Colston celebrated his destructive triumph over the cottagers. Tommy picked up his suitcase and tried to squelch his
growing sense of despair.

When the carriage was out of sight, he began to search for
Ellie. His escort had shadowed him during the ferry ride back
to Aeren, so he hadn't had a chance to look for her on the boat.

Throngs of people disembarked at Black Rock, and she was nowhere to be seen. She could have easily blended in with the crowd—or maybe she hadn't come at all. Tommy headed toward the back entrance. Olberg had told Tommy that the groundskeeper would leave the door inside the kitchen garden unlocked for him. With the sound of the crashing waves echoing against the façade of the manor house, he ducked inside the garden gate.

When he entered, he expected to find a dark, cold house. Instead, there was Ellie, curled up in a rocking chair in front of the blazing fire.

"Ellie!" he said happily. "You made it."

"I was on the same ferry as you," she said. "But you were still with the guard. Did he come with you? What is going on?"

"My father expelled me for inappropriate behavior," Tommy explained. "Basically, my brother betrayed me, and my father thinks I'm a lousy Zunftson."

"Better to be a lousy Zunftson than a dutiful one," Ellie said. "What did you mean about Hywel?"

"After you told me that Hywel was here on the day of the Rising, I remembered something," Tommy said. "There were two people in my father's library when Bern and I were leaving for a hike on the ridge. And then after the Rising, there was a man up in the forest. It was Hywel."

"How could you have forgotten that?" Ellie asked.

"At the time, I didn't know it was Hywel," Tommy said. "I had no idea what he looked like. It wasn't until I recognized his portrait in Olberg's office yesterday that I put it together. He was a tall, thin man wearing a purple silk vest."

"Oh, that's him, for sure," Ellie said. "He always wore colored vests to annoy the conservative Zunftmen. But what was he doing in the forest? Did you talk to him?"

"No, he was with two soldiers," Tommy said. "I thought they were trying to find me after the explosion in Port Kenney. But now I wonder if they were *taking* him somewhere. He wasn't with them by choice at all."

"Your father kidnapped him," Ellie said with resignation. "That's what I've been afraid of. He took him and blamed the cottagers."

"Maybe," Tommy said. "We don't know for sure."

"Do you think they killed him?" Ellie said. "His body is rotting somewhere out there?"

It was such a grisly thought that Tommy didn't want to answer. "I remember exactly where I saw him, at the entrance to Harrow Trailhead. I want to go up there, but maybe you should stay here."

"No way," Ellie said firmly. "I'm coming, too."

"We might not find anything," Tommy said. "There's a lot of forest up there."

"We have to try," Ellie said.

They paused only long enough to stuff water jugs and volt-cell lanterns into a backpack. Then they headed outside. He led Ellie along the gravel road away from the manor. The trees had lost their autumn glory and their branches were bare. They hurried toward the ridge, which loomed like an imposing black wall against the morning sky. Both of them felt a sense of urgency that didn't make sense—wherever Hywel was, he'd been there for months. Tommy thought Ellie might have trouble hiking in her long dress, but she tied the skirt in a knot at knee level and climbed as quickly as he did.

"I keep seeing houses through the trees," Ellie said when they were about halfway up the ridge. "Who lives here?"

"There's a cottager community," Tommy said. "I'm not sure how many people exactly. We were pretty isolated from them."

"Maybe we should visit them," Ellie said. "Someone might have seen Hywel."

"Sure, we can try," Tommy said. "Our former housekeeper, Mrs. Trueblood, probably lives along this ridge. She had kin all along here. I'd like to try to find her."

"Do you think she knows something?" Ellie asked.

"No, she was in the manor on the morning of the Rising," Tommy said.

"Then she might have seen Hywel in the manor herself," Ellie said.

"But we already know he was there, right?" Tommy said. "That doesn't get us anywhere. It's why he was up on this ridge that's the question."

By the time they reached Miller's Road on top of the ridge, it was nearly midday. They didn't have to go far to get to the Harrow Trailhead and the exact spot where Tommy had seen the rover and Hywel walk into the woods. They searched the road and the bushes along the trailhead.

"Maybe this is stupid," Ellie said. "It's not like the answer will be written in the dirt or carved in a tree."

"They were headed down Harrow Trail," Tommy said. "We could follow the path."

"How did Hywel seem at the time?" Ellie asked. "Was he upset?"

"He was in front of the soldiers, but they didn't have their weapons out," Tommy told her. "I assumed he was leading the search for the rebels. At the time, there was no indication that they were forcing him to go into the woods."

"It doesn't make any sense," Ellie said. "He goes to see your father, and then willingly takes a stroll into the woods with some soldiers?"

As they stared into the twilight world under the dense trees, Tommy realized he smelled peat smoke. They retraced their steps along the road until they could see black smoke rising above the trees to the north of them.

"Do you see that?" Tommy said. "I think that's the cottage where I left the injured girl, Emilie."

"How do you know her name?" Ellie asked.

"I ran into her in Sevenna," Tommy said. "She was working at a cabaret that my brother dragged me to."

"So she was all right?" Ellie asked. "That must have been a relief."

"I'm glad she recovered," Tommy said. "She was kind of a strange girl, though."

"You didn't like her?" Ellie said.

"It wasn't that," Tommy said. "She was really intense. She was interrogating me rather than having a conversation."

"Well, you are the son of the chief administrator," Ellie pointed out.

Tommy didn't want to tell Ellie about the shrine—not at that moment anyway. And he didn't want to tell her how unsafe he'd felt that night. Or that Emilie had lied about Mrs. Trueblood. It was better to focus on their search for Hywel.

"Maybe I'll change my name," Tommy said. "My father's probably going to disown me now."

"We can be orphans together," Ellie said. Her brow was furrowed and she glanced nervously up and down the road.

"What's wrong?" Tommy asked.

Ellie gazed into the darkness under the trees. "I'm getting the creeps thinking about Hywel's corpse up here. What do you think we should do?"

"Take the trail and see what's there," he said. "I know it seems futile—"

"But let's do it anyway," Ellie said.

They walked quietly down the trail, scanning the trees. The branches rustled in the brisk wind, and the weak sunlight provided barely enough visibility to avoid the roots and rocks along the path. Mounds of dead leaves and small hillocks of earth dotted the forest—each one could be a grave. They padded along in the dim light for about half a mile without speaking.

"What's that?" Ellie said, grabbing his arm and pointing off to the left of the trail. Through a gap in the trees, he could see the edge of a roof.

"Maybe another cottage?" he said.

"Let's go talk to whoever lives there," she said. "We're not going to find anything like this."

They left the trail and headed toward the structure, but it turned out to be a deserted, ramshackle cottage. Half the roof had caved in and the shutters were hanging from their hinges. They picked their way through fallen timbers and rubbish to the other side of the structure. The door was missing.

"Do you want to go inside?" Tommy asked.

"It would be easier to hide a body in there than dig a hole," Ellie said frankly.

They peered inside the ruined cottage. The roof over that half of the house was still intact, and it was too dark to see very clearly. Ellie slid off her pack and dug out a volt-cell lantern. She flicked it on and shone the beam of light across the threshold. Something metallic glinted in the far corner behind some old boards. Carefully, they crossed the room to see what might have been left by the previous occupants.

The glint came from the corner of a crate partially covered by a tarp. While Ellie held the lantern, Tommy tugged off the tarp. Underneath, there was a stack of metal shipping crates emblazoned with the Zunft symbol.

"Smugglers?" Tommy asked.

"Or the Zunft has been here recently," Ellie said.

"Maybe someone took these from Port Kenney after the Rising," Tommy said.

"What is this?" Ellie asked. She crouched down and held the lantern closer to the floor. There were boot prints in the dust. Near the wall, someone had discarded the butts of their cigars and reets.

"Someone must have been here a long time for such a large pile to accumulate," Ellie said.

"Did Hywel smoke reets?" Tommy asked.

"No, he hated the smell of them," Ellie said. "And why would he stay in here against his will? There's not even a door."

"Can I see the lantern?" Tommy asked.

Tommy crept along the edge of the room with Ellie close behind him. He carried the lantern into the darkest part of the room where a section of the floor had been swept clean of dust and other debris. Near the wall, there was a notch cut into the floor. They crouched down and set the lantern next to the wall. Inside the notch, there was a shiny padlock attached to a metal hook. Now that they were looking closely at the floor, they could see the edges of a trapdoor.

"There must be a cellar beneath us," Ellie said.

"And someone doesn't want us down there," Tommy said. "There was an old shovel outside. I'll use it to smash the lock."

Tommy handed Ellie the lantern and rushed back outside. He scanned the woods for signs of life, but nothing moved except the trees blowing in the wind. If this was a smugglers' shack, they weren't using it now. He grabbed the rusty shovel that lay on the ground near the door. When he came back inside, Ellie looked scared.

"I thought I heard something down there," she said.

"Maybe rats?" Tommy said.

"Or my vivid imagination," Ellie said.

Ellie stepped back as he slammed the shovel against the padlock until the metal hook broke off. Then he reached down and yanked up the trapdoor. The cellar below was utterly dark. The air wafting up smelled rotten. Neither of them moved for a long moment, unsure of what to do next. Ellie crouched near the edge and held the lantern over the hole. Now they could see an old wooden ladder leading down into the cellar. Tommy heard a faint noise from below. A rustle, a scratch, and then another rustle.

"Please help me," said a voice from the darkness.

The feeble plea made Tommy jump, and Ellie was so startled that she nearly fell into the hole. Tommy grabbed her elbow to steady her, and the jarring motion on her arm made her drop the lantern into the cellar. Remarkably, it landed on soft dirt and didn't shatter. The light flickered for a moment and then regained its strength. The words had been muffled but unmistakable. Someone was down there in that unforgiving darkness, and he was begging for help.

"I'll go see," Tommy said. He swung himself onto the ladder and climbed down quickly. The air was stifling, and Tommy had to stoop because of the low ceiling, which was matted with cobwebs. His eyes darted around the cellar and he found it hard to breathe inside the enclosed space. Seeing no one, he had to fight the urge to scurry up the ladder, when he heard a groan. A ragged figure hunched in the shadowy corner behind the ladder. It was a tall man with long red hair and a scraggly beard.

"There's someone here," he warned Ellie, who had reached the bottom rung of the ladder.

Ellie picked the lantern up from where it had fallen and shone it on the man. "Hywel!" she cried. "It's him, Tommy! It's Hywel."

The former chief administrator was dangerously thin and his skin was chalky beneath his ratty hair. His eyes seemed out of focus, and when he talked, it was like he didn't know they were there.

"Amy? Is that you?" Hywel whispered.

"Does he mean Ellie?" Tommy asked.

"Amy was his wife," Ellie said. "He's confused about where he is."

"Come on, Mr. Hywel," Tommy said. "Let's get you out of here."

"Amy? Where did you put my violin?"

"Who did this to you?" Ellie asked.

"The Zunft!" Hywel exclaimed.

"The Zunft kept you prisoner?" Tommy asked.

"Shore," Hywel whispered. "The man with two faces . . ."

"Did he say Shore?" Ellie asked. "Are you talking about Colston Shore?"

"He can't have survived for months without someone feeding him," Ellie said.

"He hasn't been eating much," Tommy said. The man was a sack of bones.

"Still, he couldn't have survived here alone," Ellie insisted.

Hywel muttered insensibly under his breath while Ellie and Tommy tried to maneuver him toward the ladder. Tommy's mind was racing. Hywel had been missing since August. It was now November. Someone must have been watching over him—they might be coming back at any moment. Tommy and Ellie had to get Hywel away from here immediately. But where should they go?

"Amy! The dogs are pawing at the windows!" Hywel ranted.

As Tommy helped Hywel onto the ladder, he thought about his father back in Sevenna, claiming victory over the cottagers now that the Cessation was over. If Colston really was responsible, then how could he justify this? How could he talk about honor and then imprison and nearly starve to death an innocent man?

Hywel was too weak to climb the ladder, and Tommy had to lift him while Ellie dragged him up from above. Once they got to the top of the ladder, Hywel collapsed on the floor of the ruined cottage. His breath sounded raspy.

"Let's get him some water," Tommy said, rummaging in the backpack for a jug.

Ellie held the jug to Hywel's lips, but he sputtered and called for his dead wife.

"Should we take him to your manor?" Ellie asked. "I'm not sure he'll make it that far."

"We need to get him away from here," Tommy said. "We'll figure something out on the way."

Tommy stood on one side and helped Hywel stand, while Ellie stood on the other. Each of them put an arm around the man's back, and they managed to shuffle down to the trail. Finally, after what seemed like hours, they reached Miller's Road. The wind whipped through the trees, and Hywel was shivering uncontrollably. By now, they were practically dragging him and Hywel's eyes kept rolling back in his head.

"I'm not sure he can go any farther," Ellie said. "Or me. My spine feels like it's about to snap."

They dragged Hywel off the road and found a sheltered place at the base of a tree. Tommy covered the man with his coat and left the knapsack with Ellie.

"If you hear a rover, don't let the driver see you," Tommy said. "My father has the only rovers around here."

"I'll stay here no matter what," she said to him. "Don't forget where I am."

Tommy ran through the trees, oblivious to the branches scratching him through his shirtsleeves. He burst into the yard of the cottager's house—the same one where he had left Emilie—and banged on the door. An older man with a gray beard opened the door a crack. He looked puzzled at the unexpected intrusion.

"Can I help you?" he asked politely.

"Please, I need to find Mrs. Trueblood," Tommy pleaded. "*Greta* Trueblood. Please, can you help me?"

Hywel stirred on the cot near the blazing fireplace in Anna Henry's cottage. Anna and Greta Trueblood exchanged worried glances while Ellie checked to see if he had woken up, but he was only mumbling in his sleep.

"Will he be all right, Mrs. Henry?" Ellie asked.

"With rest and food he should recover," Mrs. Henry said. "But it'll take some time for him to regain his strength."

Ellie sat back down at the table while Mrs. Trueblood poured her another cup of black tea. Mrs. Henry's young daughters were asleep in the back room, so they spoke in low tones. Outside, another Aeren storm lashed the ridge, but as Tommy sat near Mrs. Trueblood in the cozy warmth of the fire, he felt a strange sense of contentment. He wished he never had to go to Sevenna again, but then his father would win, and Tommy would never forgive himself.

"Are you sisters?" Tommy asked the two women sitting at the table. Anna looked to be in her midthirties, while Greta was older, with graying hair and smile lines.

"My whole life, she's been telling me what to do," Mrs. Henry said.

"What would you have done without a sister like me?" Mrs. Trueblood replied.

"I'd have been very, very lost," Mrs. Henry said. There was a profound sadness in the woman's eyes. When Tommy had heard that her surname was Henry, he'd wondered if there was a family connection to the Michael Henry who had been executed for his role in the August Rising. Michael Henry had been from Aeren, but it could also be a very common name.

"You're lucky that you went to Mr. Fields's house," Mrs. Trueblood said. "He knew that I moved in with Anna after I left Shore Manor. Not many people along Miller's Road would have been able to find me."

The man who had responded to Tommy's desperate knocking did indeed know Greta Trueblood, and he'd been happy to help Tommy find her. He'd followed Tommy through the forest to retrieve Ellie and Hywel, who was now unconscious under the oak tree. Mr. Fields had driven the three of them in his wagon to a cottage a mile up Miller's Road, where Tommy had been ecstatic to see Mrs. Trueblood again.

"Thank you for taking us in tonight," Ellie said to Mrs. Henry.

"You can stay here for a few days if you want," Mrs. Henry said. "It's probably best if he doesn't move around too much at first."

"Thank you," Tommy said. "But we don't want to be a burden."

"What's your plan?" Mrs. Henry asked. "Until we find out what happened, taking him back to Shore Manor isn't a good idea."

"What do you want to do, Tommy?" Mrs. Trueblood asked.

"If Father is responsible, then he has to be held accountable," Tommy said. "He can't get away with the lies anymore."

"Your father is the law," Mrs. Henry said bitterly. "He can do whatever he wants."

"I'm not so sure," Tommy said. "Two days ago, he held a

gathering in Sevenna at his town house, and very few people attended. Maybe his support is waning."

"Dissolving the Chamber can't have made the other Zunft-men happy," Ellie said.

"But he controls the army, so it doesn't matter what they think," Mrs. Henry said.

"What if we reveal the truth about Hywel?" Mrs. Trueblood asked. "Publish another treatise and tell the world that Shore kidnapped him and blamed us."

"But what about the prisoners?" Mrs. Henry asked. "How long will they live if the truth comes out? Besides, Shore will spin it as a cottager lie."

"I think we should contact the cottager leaders in Sevenna," Tommy said. "There's a girl I know in Sevenna. She says she's a relation of yours, Mrs. Trueblood. I think she might be able to help us."

"A relation of mine?" Mrs. Trueblood asked. "What's her name?"

"Emilie Johns, although I'm not sure that's her real name."

"Why do you say that?" asked Mrs. Trueblood.

"I'm not sure," Tommy said. "It's only a hunch."

"How do you know her?" Mrs. Henry asked.

"She showed me a shrine with pictures of people who have disappeared since my father has been in power," Tommy said. "Then a few days ago, she asked for my help in finding her friend Gavin Baine. That's the last time I saw her."

"I told you, Anna," Mrs. Trueblood said. "He's not in league with his father. If Tamsin told him about Gavin, then she must trust him."

"Who's Tamsin?" Ellie asked.

"Tamsin is my daughter," Mrs. Henry said. "And the daughter of Michael Henry."

There was a moment of silence, and then Tommy spoke. "We're sorry for your loss, Mrs. Henry."

Mrs. Henry gave Tommy a sad smile. "Greta has told me stories about you since you were a little boy," she said. "You have a good heart. If Tamsin trusted you enough to ask about Gavin, then I trust you as well. And if you mean to hold your father accountable for his crimes, then I will help in any way I can."

"I told her I'd try," Tommy said. "I went through my father's papers, but I got caught. That's why I got expelled from Seminary."

"Wait, I don't understand what's going on," Ellie said. "Tamsin and Emilie are the same person?"

"She took a fake name to protect us," Mrs. Henry explained. "Tamsin was the architect of the Cessation. She wrote *The Right to Rule*."

"Angry Em!" Tommy said. "I had no idea. I thought maybe she could get us in touch with the people behind the Cessation, but she was the one I needed to talk to."

Near the fire, Hywel stirred and propped himself up on his elbows. "Amy?" he called loudly.

Ellie went over and sat on the edge of the cot. "It's Ellie," she said. "It's your ward."

"Ellie?" he asked. "Where are we?"

"At a friend's house," Ellie said.

"What friends?" Hywel asked. "And damn it all, I feel like I've been crushed by wild horses."

Mrs. Trueblood stood up abruptly, and Mrs. Henry followed

her lead. The women obviously wanted to give Ellie and Hywel privacy, which seemed silly to Tommy. He didn't want Mrs. Henry to feel like she'd been chased out of her own sitting room.

"I'm going to put some soup on," Mrs. Trueblood said. "Come on, Tommy."

Mrs. Trueblood gave him a no-nonsense look that he remembered well from childhood, so he followed the sisters into the tiny kitchen at the back of the cottage. A pot of soup was already bubbling away on the woodstove. The kitchen was not really big enough for the three of them, but they stood huddled around the iron pot like witches making a brew. They could hear Ellie and Hywel talking in low voices in the other room. After about twenty minutes, Ellie came and joined them.

"He's asleep again," she said.

"Did he tell you who did this to him?" he asked.

"Your father," she said grimly. "It was Colston Shore."

"How did he end up on Miller's Road?" Tommy asked.

"Your father sent him a message that a rebellion was imminent," Ellie said. "Shore said that he had arranged a meeting with the rebel leaders, but they would only talk to Hywel. That's how your father got him to come to Aeren. Hywel thought he was headed to that meeting when you saw him along Miller's Road. He was with the Zunft soldiers, but had no idea that they meant to harm him. He thought they were taking him to a rendezvous point."

"So that's why he was so calm," Tommy said. "He didn't know it was all a lie."

"Once they were in the woods, Hywel was ambushed and someone knocked him unconscious," Ellie said. "When he woke up, he was in the cellar. For weeks, they made him think that he'd been kidnapped by cottagers. Apparently, Shore was trying to pull off an elaborate ruse so Hywel wouldn't know he had been taken by Shore and his guards."

"Why would he do that?" Mrs. Trueblood asked.

"He thinks that Shore was going to 'rescue' him from the cottagers and be a hero," Ellie said. "If that's true, then Shore wasn't planning on killing him, at least not at first. He wanted him out of the way so he could take power, and use the kidnapping as an excuse to persecute the cottagers."

"So what happened?" Tommy asked. "Hywel obviously discovered the truth."

"He said that the guards got lazy, and he could hear them talking through the floorboards," Ellie said. "Then something changed, and the guards came less and less frequently. A few days ago, the guards disappeared and never came back. Perhaps they meant him to starve to death? He had a jug of water that kept him going, but he wouldn't have lasted much longer."

"Did he drink anything while you were talking to him?" Mrs. Trueblood asked.

"I gave him some of that root tea," Ellie said. "He drank the entire cup."

"Well, he won't be awake for a while," Mrs. Henry said. "What do we do now?"

"Do you think he'll help us if we ask?" Tommy asked Ellie.

"Yes, I do," Ellie replied. "I think he'd do anything to make things right. When he heard about what happened to Michael Henry . . . He never wanted anything like that to happen."

"I'm afraid if Hywel confronts Father directly, he'll be arrested and we'll gain nothing." Tommy said.

"He's too feeble to make a show of strength," Mrs. Trueblood said. "I doubt he could even manage a flight of stairs at this point."

"So what do you suggest?" Mrs. Henry asked.

"Can you get the three of us to Sevenna City?" Tommy asked. "I need to see Emilie—I mean, Tamsin. We need to find a way to reveal to the world what my father has done."

30

"DO YOU WANT ME TO GO IN WITH you?" Ellie asked.

"No, I need you to back me up out here," Tommy said, brushing aside the leafy branches to get a better look at the house on the other side of the hedge. They were crouched outside Colston's town house in Sevenna. It was still dark, and most of the houses along the street were dark. But the volt-lamps had flickered on inside the library. Colston was awake, and Tommy needed to enter the house while his father was still reading at his desk.

"How am I supposed to do that?" Ellie asked crossly.

As if in answer to her question, Tommy searched the ground at the base of the shrub. His fingers picked through the brown leaves while Ellie stared at him in confusion. Since they had left Aeren with Hywel in tow, they'd endured a whirlwind of night-time boat rides, hiding in basements, and endless conversation with Tamsin and her network of people. There were heated discussions, particularly among Tamsin, Tommy, and Ellie over the future of the cottagers, Colston, and Hywel. Since Hywel was often too weak to speak for himself, Ellie had been a stubborn advocate for him. But Ellie was also a realist, and she knew that lives would be lost unless they came to an arrangement. Finally, both she and Hywel agreed to Tamsin's proposal.

Tommy had to admire Tamsin. She was gambling with the situation, but she was so confident about how her plan would play out that she swayed everyone with her conviction. Tommy had his doubts, but he kept them to himself. He *wanted* her to be right, he *wanted* his father to fall, he *wanted* the world to change. And that was enough to convince him to confront Colston. For Tommy, this meeting with his father was the crucial moment. If he failed, then Tamsin's plan would crumble. With his fingers in the dirt, Tommy finally found what he was looking for. He plucked a palm-size rock from under the hedge and showed it to Ellie.

"Tamsin arranged for the bodyguard to be detained in South Sevenna so Father's alone in the house," Tommy said. "But if there's a problem, you need to go back and tell Tamsin and the others."

"But how am I going to know if there's a problem?" Ellie asked.

"I'll throw this through the window," Tommy said. "If you see the glass smash, there's a problem."

"Usually people throw rocks from the outside," Ellie said.

"Well, it's my best idea," Tommy said.

"A rock is your best idea." Ellie sighed. "I think we're in trouble."

"It'll work," Tommy assured her. "Really, it will."

She cuffed him gently on the arm and nodded toward the house. "Well, do it then."

Keeping his head lower than the windows, Tommy ran for the cellar door at the back of the house. The hinges of the door were well oiled and didn't make a sound as he slipped inside. He climbed the stone steps to the cold kitchen and padded quietly down the corridor to his father's library, where the door was open a crack. Clutching the rock in his hand, Tommy hesitated and peered through the opening. His father sat behind his desk, writing in a thick ledger. When Tommy was a child, he had imagined Colston's Honor Index was kept in such a ledger, and it had given him a sense of security that all the evils of the world could be tabulated and controlled. It was time to let go of such childish notions. His father couldn't see his own transgressions. Even his worst sins were filtered through a veil of self-righteousness. In Colston Shore's mind, his honor was pure and untarnished.

When Tommy pushed the door open, Colston glanced up in surprise. It was unusual to see Colston in a moment of vulnerability. With his unblinking eyes and pursed lips, he reminded Tommy of an owl, which made him less intimidating. But his father's face darkened when he recognized his son standing in the doorway.

"What are you doing here?" Colston asked angrily. "I was told you went to Aeren."

"I did," Tommy said. "But now I'm back."

"You're not enrolling in Seminary again," Colston said. "Bern told me what you've been doing. You've consorted with the enemy and alienated yourself from your peers. You've made your choices and now you have to face the consequences."

"What have I been doing that's so wrong?" Tommy asked.

"Why did you come back?" Colston asked, ignoring his

question. "You are to return home immediately. You may not return to Sevenna until I give you my permission."

"You're so confident in your power," Tommy said. "It amazes me. You expect the world to bow to your wishes."

"I am trying to keep chaos at bay," Colston said. "If the cottagers got their wish, society would disintegrate and violence would destroy us."

"You don't know that," Tommy said.

"Don't I?" Colston said. "Do you remember what they did to your mother?"

Tommy's heart lurched. "That was one man. Not an entire group of people. He wasn't representing an agenda. He was deranged."

"Who told you that?" Colston said. "Your cottager nanny? She has poisoned your mind against your own people. I respected Rose's dying wish, but it has cost me my son."

"Mrs. Trueblood hasn't poisoned me against you," Tommy said. "I have my own mind. Now that I've witnessed the things you do, I'm horrified."

Tommy had never seen his father so angry. His hands were clenched on the desk and his shoulders rigid with fury.

"I am the last thing standing against the destruction of Seahaven. Everything I do, I do to protect you and Bernard."

"You commit crimes in the name—" Tommy began.

"What crimes have I committed?" Colston interrupted, rising to his feet and practically shouting.

"I know what you did to Hywel," Tommy said.

The silence was powerful. Colston stared at his son, unable to keep the surprise off his face.

"What did you say?" he asked.

"I found Hywel in the cellar off Miller's Road," Tommy said. "I know it was you all along. Were you going to let him starve to death? And it's not just Hywel, of course. It's what you've done to the cottagers. How many are missing? How many have you executed? Are you keeping them locked up in the compound? Are they even still alive?"

"I had nothing to do with Hywel's kidnapping," Colston said. "If he was taken on Aeren, that's news to me."

"Except he was with your guards that day on Miller's Road," Tommy said. "I saw it myself."

Colston's hand shot out to open a desk drawer, but before he could open it, Tommy tossed the rock into the air and quickly caught it. His father paused, squinting at the object in Tommy's hand. When he had his father's attention, he threw the rock into the air again.

"What is that?" Colston asked.

"An ordinary rock," Tommy said. "But it has a lot of significance. Don't move again, or I'll show you what it means."

"I won't play games with you," Colston said icily. Tommy wondered what was in that drawer. A handgun? A knife? A letter opener?

"If you don't sit down and keep your hands on the desk, I throw this rock through your stupid beveled window," Tommy said. "And that is the signal for the men waiting outside to come in and drag you out. They *hate* you. So if you don't want to be tied to the back of a wagon and dragged through the streets of Sevenna, then I'd suggest you sit down."

Colston stood completely still. Then he sank into his chair

with an air of defeat. Tommy was shocked. He could feel the shift of power in the room and it made him dizzy.

"What do you want, Thomas?" Colston said.

"I have a proposition," Tommy said.

Colston clasped his hands on top of the desk. "Fine, what is your proposition?"

"We'll make a trade," Tommy said. "You'll bring every political prisoner from the compound to Seminary Square at dawn tomorrow."

"You want the prisoners?" Colston asked. He obviously hadn't been anticipating that request.

"I have a list of the cottagers that I expect to see tomorrow," Tommy said, pulling a folded square of paper from his pocket and tossing it onto Colston's desk. Tamsin had copied the names from the list at the shrine, and added one more at the top: Gavin Baine. "Once we have the prisoners, we will give you Hywel. Every person on this list should be accounted for, or I will go public with Hywel and you can face the consequences."

"How do I know you really have him?" Colston asked.

"He said to tell you: 'Next time you can find a different negotiator for your secret meeting with the cottager rebels.'"

Colston smiled grimly. That was the last thing that Colston and Hywel had discussed alone in the library back in August, and something only the two of them would know about.

"You're giving Hywel to me, to do whatever I want with him?" Colston said. "Did he agree to this?"

"It's the only way to save the innocent lives of the prisoners in the compound," Tommy said. "If we went public with the information without the trade, we couldn't guarantee the safety of the prisoners."

"I'll still remain in power, Thomas," Colston said. "Getting the prisoners back will ultimately change nothing."

"It will change something for the families of the missing," Tommy said.

"Don't you care what happens to Hywel?" Colston asked. "You can't imagine that I'll permit him to have a fulfilling retirement."

"Sometimes sacrifices must be made for the greater good," Tommy said.

"I know, Thomas. Why do you think I've done the things I've done?"

"It's not the same," Tommy said.

"It is," Colston said. "And if you understood that, you might have made a decent Zunftman after all."

31

THAT NIGHT, THE CITY WAS BUSIER THAN
usual. South of the river, Navid was running. By the light of a full
moon, he dashed up alleyways, across rooftops, and past the
wreckage from the Night of a Hundred Fires. Never once did he
feel sleepy. Before he'd set out, Tamsin had given him a scrap of
paper with a place and a time. His job was to show certain
people the information on the paper. There seemed to be an
endless number of cottagers to visit, but Navid didn't mind,
even though his legs started to get sore. He had an important
job and he liked feeling useful. Something big was coming,
and that made him shiver with excitement. So he ran from
house to house until dawn and he whispered a secret that was
becoming less and less one with every step he took.

North of the city in the Zunft Compound, the guards were
counting. They were busy unlocking cells, making marks on lists,
and bringing the cottager prisoners into the walled courtyard.
Rovers idled in a line outside the gates, and each pulled a trailer
with a metal passenger compartment mounted on it. Although

the prisoners weren't allowed to talk to one another, the sight of the rovers gave them hope that this dawn didn't mean the firing squad. Mr. Leahy and Gavin acknowledged each other across the muddy courtyard, but they kneeled quietly and waited to see what the new day might bring.

In a borrowed kitchen near the burned-out husk of the Plough and Sun, Tamsin was planning. A teakettle whistled again and again as she and her mother and Greta Trueblood kept tossing yet another log onto the fire. Every few minutes, someone would knock on the back door and one of them would answer it. They would offer their visitors a cup of tea and thank them for coming out in the middle of this cold night. Tamsin would take a deep breath and begin talking: "He has lost the support of his people," she would say. "These are his final days."

On the south side of the river, Tommy was watching. He and Ellie sat on the cold stone floor of a warehouse, guarding a door. On the other side of that door, Hywel slept, still weak from his months in captivity. Ellie was the worst guard Tommy had ever seen. She had fallen asleep beside him with her head leaning against his shoulder. Tommy kept glancing at his chronometer every few minutes, and the night seemed to drag on forever.

But dawn came as it always does, and Navid appeared at five a.m. as scheduled. Tommy greeted him, and Navid gave him a shy smile. Tommy gently shook Ellie awake and helped her to her feet. Tommy stretched and yawned. His legs felt prickly from hours of sitting on the floor.

"You'll accompany Hywel?" Tommy asked.

"As long as I can," Ellie responded. "He was much better last night. He knows what's happening."

"And no arguments?" Tommy asked.

"He hasn't changed his mind," Ellie said.

"Well, that's something," Tommy said. "Tamsin and her people will be here any minute. Are you ready?"

"I'll get Hywel up as soon as you go," Ellie said. "How do you feel?"

"I'll tell you when it's over," he said.

"That's right, you will," she said. She reached up, pulled off the red ribbon that held her braid, and shoved it unceremoniously at him. "I'll see you soon."

He tucked the ribbon in his pocket, embraced her quickly, and then followed Navid down the corridor. The plan called for Navid to lead Tommy to Seminary Square using the underground coal tunnels so Colston's guards wouldn't see them coming. Hopefully, his father would keep his word and meet him with the prisoners. And if Colston Shore didn't keep his word, Tamsin had contingency plans.

With a lantern held high, Navid led Tommy through winding tunnels that ran under the streets of Sevenna. Tommy felt like a rat sneaking under the soldiers who were waiting to snatch him before he ever reached Seminary Square. As they crept through the darkness, a memory of Mrs. Trueblood swept over him. It was a few years after his mother died, and he was in the kitchen at the manor house on a cold winter's day. Tommy was crying because Father had taken Bern with him to Sevenna for a week and left Tommy on Aeren. Mrs. Trueblood had sat down with him on the floor in front of the blazing fire and gently held his hands. He still remembered what she had said to him, as if it had happened the day before and not a decade earlier: *Your mother was the strongest woman I knew. She could bear the weight of the world and still have room to love you. You are her son—in face, in mind, and in spirit. Your father has given you nothing but his name.*

When they reached an iron door marked thirty-one, Navid stopped. "At the top of the stairs, you'll come out behind a row of coal bins in Long Alley. Stay behind them. It's a tight squeeze, but you can make it to the square without being seen by the soldiers."

Tommy thanked the boy for his help. When Navid had disappeared back down the tunnel, Tommy pushed the heavy door open. When he emerged from the tunnel, the alley was deserted. As Navid had promised, there was a narrow gap between the wall and the stinking bins. It wasn't far to the square, and he kept an eye out for soldiers as he shuffled along. But only the ravens perched along the rooftops watched him approach. When he reached the end of Long Alley, he took a deep breath and strolled into the square, the so-called crown jewel of the Zunft.

Colston Shore waited on the slick cobblestones in the shadow of the towering statue of the Vigilant Zunftman. He was flanked by two guards, but neither appeared to be armed. Seeing his father gave him a sick feeling. There would be no reconciliation with Colston—or Bern—after his actions today. By standing here, he was letting his family be lost to him, and he would be barred from his home on Aeren. But he reminded himself that so many things had already been lost. The front gate of the Seminary was closed and locked, and his father had taken away his education. Maybe in another time and place, he'd walk into the walled campus again. In his perfect world, people like Tamsin and Navid would be welcome to learn alongside him.

"Where's Hywel?" Colston asked when Tommy drew near.

"Nearby," Tommy said. "Where are the prisoners?"

"I'll signal and the rovers will drive them here." Colston waved toward the buildings behind him. The perimeter of the square was lined with government buildings, and Tommy could see several rovers parked in the alley beside the Records Hall. He couldn't see anyone behind the darkened windows, but that didn't mean Colston hadn't stationed guards inside.

"That's not how it's going to work," Tommy said. "Get the prisoners out of the rovers and have them walk into the square. When I can see them, I'll have Hywel brought to you."

Colston motioned to one of the guards, who disappeared into the alley. After a few moments, Tommy could hear the squeal of metal doors being opened. He could see a woman in a prison uniform climbing down from the back of the rover. Tommy tried to guess his father's plan. He would let the prisoners out, but as soon as they brought out Hywel, guards would emerge from their hiding places and swarm onto the square. They would take Hywel into custody and force the prisoners back into the rovers. Tommy had no way to know for sure, but that was how he imagined his father would handle the situation.

"Have the prisoners come forward," Tommy said. Colston motioned again, and the men and women began to file into the square. Their hands were still bound with cords.

"Now, show me Hywel," his father said.

Tommy pulled Ellie's red ribbon from his pocket and waved it. "He's here," he said.

Colston scanned the square. "Where?"

Tommy pointed up to the rooftop behind him. Hywel

appeared at the edge of the roof with Tamsin holding on to his arm.

"Right there," Tommy said. "But out of reach. In a moment, I'm going to get a signal about whether you've kept your word and brought all the prisoners."

By now, scores of disheveled cottagers had entered the square. Above him, Tamsin waved a red handkerchief, the sign that all the prisoners were accounted for.

"I've had enough!" Colston said in irritation. "There are guards in the alley and in the Records Hall. They're about to converge on that roof and take Hywel. You are outnumbered."

"You're wrong," Tommy said. A whistle sounded above, and in response, cottagers stepped into view on every rooftop along Seminary Square. Dozens of people had hidden themselves throughout the night, and now they revealed themselves as a phalanx of silent witnesses beyond the reach of Colston's guards. Before Colston could respond, a chorus of voices rang through the streets. Protesters chanted together as they moved up from Shadow Bridge and into the northern district. Navid had shown the scrap of paper to dozens of people, and he'd asked each one to tell two more. The message had traveled more quickly than expected, and thousands of cottagers had answered the call.

The panic was evident on Colston's face. Here was a man who cultivated control, and it was crumbling before his eyes. A flood of people was spilling into the square. The guards began backing toward the alley where the rovers were parked without waiting for Colston to give them orders. As they deserted their posts, Tommy was filled with hope that Tamsin's plan would work. She had believed that the army wasn't loyal to the chief administrator anymore, but that was the terrifying gamble they were taking with this plan. Success hinged on the idea that Colston had become so unpopular that he had to bribe the soldiers to protect him. The men in uniform weren't there out of patriotic fervor, they were there for a handful of coins. Now vastly outnumbered, would they murder people for Colston, a man they didn't believe in?

"You can't kill them all," Tommy said to Colston as throngs of people engulfed the prisoners and began untying their hands.

"Fire!" Colston yelled. "Shoot them!"

But the people began chanting and they drowned out his words. It took a second for Tommy to realize what was being repeated over and over. *"I am Angry Em. I am Angry Em."*

The crowd surrounded Colston's guards and moved them toward the line of rovers, like a river carries driftwood down toward the sea. None of the soldiers lifted their guns. Instead, they let themselves be escorted to the rovers and sped away as the crowd parted for them. Tamsin had been right. Colston's leadership had crumbled, and his guards weren't willing to fight the tide of change. Colston Shore was left alone in the square, surrounded by his former prisoners.

As the sound of the rover engines disappeared in the distance, Hywel stepped to the edge of the roof to address the crowd.

"Colston Shore kidnapped me and he blamed you!" he said, his voice ringing across the square. "He used his lies to further his power and that must end—today!"

The crowd erupted into cheers. Hywel waited until the joyful noise died down and then he spoke again.

"Colston Shore will be arrested and imprisoned. He will face trial. He tried to stop the progress that we had made toward equal rights. We can't continue as two separate groups. We must find a way to be one people."

The people cheered again and the sound reverberated off the buildings and rang through the streets of the city.

"But it's not my day to speak. This is a new day, and *your* leaders are the ones to thank for this."

Hywel stepped backward, away from the edge, leaving Tamsin in the forefront to address the crowd.

"Tamsin!" Gavin yelled, waving frantically from the midst of the crowd. "Speech!"

When Tamsin saw that he was safe, the relief brought tears to her eyes. She covered her mouth with her hands for a brief moment. A song from her childhood played through her mind. She remembered her father singing it to his daughters at night in front of the fire. His strong, clear voice had made her heart soar. *The candle was lit / The fire dimmed but did not die / The world will never be the same.* She whispered goodbye to her father. Then she opened her arms wide to embrace her people, and she began to speak.